A HOUSE
OF WOMEN
H. E. Bates

A House of Women is the story of
Rosie Perkins, a barmaid, rich in living
and good humour, She marries a farmer
whose skinflint family is steeped in the
tradition of its own prosperity. All
Bates' craftsmanship, sympathy and skill
are deployed in the telling of their story.
He achieves a picture of a woman and an
age deeply moving in tragic reality and
ultimate triumph.

A HOUSE
OF WOMEN

by
H. E. BATES

SEVERN
SH
HOUSE

This edition published 1988 in the U.S.A. and Great Britain by
SEVERN HOUSE PUBLISHERS LTD of
40–42 William IV Street, London WC2N 4DF.
First published in Great Britain 1936 by Jonathan Cape Ltd.
This original U.S.A. publication 1988 by Severn House Inc.

British Library Cataloguing in Publication Data
Bates, H. E. (Herbert Ernest), *1905–1974*
A house of women
I. Title
823′.912 [F]
ISBN 0–7278–1644–6

Printed and bound in Great Britain

CONTENTS

Book One

THE ANGEL   11

Book Two

THE FARM   81

Book Three

FRANKIE   113

Book Four

A HOUSE OF WOMEN   159

Book Five

CHANGE AND DECAY   203

A HOUSE OF WOMEN

BOOK ONE

THE ANGEL

CHAPTER 1

I

THE Alf Jefferys were turning their hay in the sunless heat of a June afternoon, the first rows of the first crop, the whole family stretched out like a line of dark and white washing across the river-meadow. The five rakes skimmed the sun-whitened rows and fluffed them up and over, the undried hay a cloudy green and moistly fragrant. Once touched, the hay never moved, the wisps motionless where they fell the heads of dog-daisy and buttercup and clover as still as though woven in a pattern of white and gold and pink among the pale green lace of grass. There had been no sun or wind all day. The dark serge skirts of the three women never moved except under the motion of their thick legs. The two sons were like images in corduroy and white, their faces shaped in wax, the sun-darkened skin moist with sweat. The damp heat filtered down through a thickness of cloud that was never broken, and beyond the last hay-rows the river flowed slowly past like a stream of lead between stiff spears of summer reed that moved only with the little somnolent turns and eddies of water.

And in the field only the Jefferys moved. They walked with precision, bringing their rakes up and over without variation of pace or gesture, never speaking, looking up only when a row was finished and it was time to begin another. They looked up then with automatic eyes, fixedly, for just so long and no longer, looking at the field or the sky or each other with pale eyes, almost expression-

11

lessly. They behaved as though, having begun a task, it would be some sort of sin not to go on doing it without speech or rest until it was finished. They worked quite fast, flicking the hay with desperation in a race against the sky.

"Tom," the mother broke out once, "I count I felt a spot, seem'ly!"

"Ah?"

The family stopped, like a machine. The rakes were held in suspense, Ella and Maudie holding out fat hands, upturned to the sky, the thick sausage fingers slightly curved from the curve of the rake. The old woman stood immobile, watching Tom, the eldest son. Tom was staring at Frankie, and Frankie at the sky. Resting on the hay-rakes, watching, they looked even more squat and dwarfed than when in motion, their heads sunken and graceless on their broad shoulders like lumps of ponderous clay. And as they stood there, in heavy suspense, waiting for the rain, their large grey eyes never flickered. They brimmed over with a kind of resentment at something, the light in them as thick and sleepy as the June air.

And nothing happened. The air was breathless and rainless, the scent of new hay and dog-roses and the forests of meadowsweet creaming the unmown dykes at the field's end seemed sweeter and thicker than ever, and there were no sounds except the repetitive calls of odd yellow-hammers and the clack of a hay-cutter somewhere beyond the Jefferys' land.

"What's goin' a-be, Tom?" the mother said. "What d'ye think?"

The family turned to Tom. He was the thickest of all, a young bullock, with the fixed bullock stare straight before him. His nose was very straight and rather fine, his thick

12

yellowish hair sun-bleached almost white above the forehead. He was the eldest son and, now that his father was
dead, he had become the oracle too.

"Ain't rainin' now," he said.

It was a pronouncement. Hearing it, they stood in
meditation, still pondering and watching and feeling
for the fall of the rain. Nobody contradicted what Tom
had said, but Maudie said :

"I never felt nothing."

"I did, I felt it," the mother said. "I know I felt it."

"Flies," Frankie said.

He was the youngest, twenty. His eyes were blue and
fresh, with liveliness in them. But no one laughed. With
the hay-crop half turned and the air full of thunder and
the sky threatening rain it was no time for laughter. Even
Frankie himself did not laugh. He rubbed his left hand
backwards and forwards across his upper lip, feeling the
young moustache. It was growing nicely : the fine short
hairs prickly as the new thorns on a young raspberry
cane. Tom had a good strong moustache, light brown,
thickening. And looking from the sky to Tom, Frankie
could see Tom caressing his moustache too, and a little
sudden flicker of jealousy went through him. It was a
family emotion. He was jealous of Tom's moustache just
as the family, altogether, were jealous of Gus Warren's
binder and the twenty acres of barley Will Middleton had
up in the field next to the road, and when there were
neither binders nor crops of barley nor anything else
beyond their own world for them to envy, they were
jealous of and among themselves, Frankie jealous of
Tom's moustache, the girls jealous of each other, the
mother jealous of each of them in turn against the other.
But in the hay-field, listening and waiting together for

the thunder and the rain and wondering if they could scratch over the last rows before the sky broke, they were united in a common fear against catastrophe. They met the shadow of disaster before it came, feeling the rain dropping thick and warm in their minds before it dropped on their hands. The air was more than ever strangely still. The clouds seemed to press down and concentrate on the low meadow with its too-rich grass and the sleepy river and the drowsy boundaries of meadowsweet. And at last as though by mechanical impulses they began working again, now more feverishly, flicking up the rich pads of hay with almost desperate rapidity, the soft sounds of their rakes and their progress only thickening the thundery silence.

"If we can git this done," Tom said, "and it holds off and we can git carried, I don't know as we shan't ha' two crops off o' this meadow yit."

"Two crops !"

To the Jefferys it was like a promise of reward. Two crops ! – something to boast about, something nobody else could do. Two crops off one meadow.

"When did we get two crops last?" Frankie said.

"Seven year ago," the mother said. "I remember that. 1898 – that were the year. Two good crops. It come hot about hay-making and then it broke directly and we had wet till August time –" she was babbling on in a sudden fervour of reminiscence, raking and panting and talking and whipping the grey hair out of her grey eyes in a constant fever of activity, "– and then come September we had it hot again and we –"

"Ah, mother, git on," Tom said. "Git on, do. You'll want that breath."

And the woman went quiet at once, in meek obedience,

14

unresentfully, and the whole family worked in silence again, transforming the face of the field as they went, the long white rows breaking like waves into pale green curves of foam.

And when, nearly an hour later, they were walking up the cart-lane towards the farmhouse, the two sons leading, the mother straggling behind, all with hay-rakes shouldered, the rain had still not come. And though they could look back and see the hay fleeced up to the last spare rakefuls, more meadowsweet than grass, by the hedgesides, they were still afraid and still not satisfied. Skimming swallows were constantly crossing and re-crossing the lane, almost brushing the pink wild roses on the hedgetops, and the mother, hobbling behind in old skin-tight button boots cracked by work and her swollen feet, kept saying over and over again that it was a bad sign.

"I like to see 'em high," she prattled. "That's what your Dad used to say, and it's right. If they're high it's all right. I don't like it if they git low. Look at that one, see. Wonder as it didn't knock itself against the ground. I don't – there's another. See it? Frankie, Tom – you see them swallows? You remember what your Dad used to say?"

The girls too walked in high boots too tight for them, the cracks whitened with hay-dust, a settling of hay-seed in the fissures made by the ill-tied tops, the larger and more feathery seeds fixed like darts of barley in their black skirts and stockings. The black meant that they were still in mourning; that more than a month had still to go before they ceased paying funereal respects to their father, Alf Jeffery, who had died from pleurisy and complications in the early year, leaving the farm to his widow in trust for Tom, and two hundred each to the four children. It seemed a fair arrangement, but to Maudie and

Ella, older by nearly ten years than their elder brother, it seemed a wicked arrangement, and they lived in a state of restless jealousy. "What chance for us when our Tom gits married? Our Dad never thought of that. What chance do we stan'?" Unmarried, they were figures carved out of springless and virgin wood as hard as bone, the creaks made by their tight earth-dry boots like the creakings of complaining wood.

The cart-track went in a diagonal line across the slope between fields of rising corn and beans, and as the slope increased the two girls lagged farther and farther behind the brothers and the mother farther and farther behind the girls, until finally the mother's prattling about the rain and the thunder and the swallows was too low for anyone but herself to hear, and she had to raise her voice to a squawk, and then repeat herself, before her sons could hear at all.

"Tom, Frankie, you know what time it is?"

"Eh? What's she say?"

Ella and Maudie took it up :

"She wants to know what time it is?"

Tom looked at his watch through the celluloid dust-case as he walked along.

"Quarter arter five !"

"What?" Deaf at the best of times, the mother stood still in the cart-track to listen. "What time? What's he say?"

And the girls took it up again :

"Quarter past five. Quarter past," they shouted.

"Eh?"

And then, after another fifty yards, another stop and another shout. This time :

"Tom ! You seeing Elsie to-night? Tom !"

And again Tom could not hear and again his sisters relayed it, tittering now, singing the words in a half-teasing sing-song :

"Tom ! To-om ! Is it courting night?"

"Yeh ! What about it?"

"Mum wants to know."

"What's she want?"

"What do you want? Mum !"

"Eh?" The mother stood in the track, sixty or seventy yards back, her face screwed up, not hearing. What? Eh?"

"What do you want?"

"I got – Oh ! my Lord, you hear that?" Standing still, she caught what was for her the first far off murmur of thunder, a murmur that only she herself heard, as though it were some muttering of her own mind. "Did you hear that? Tom ! Thunder."

"What's she want?" Tom called.

"She says it thunders."

"Thunder? Been thundering all afternoon !"

"She ain't been jis' right since Dad died," Maudie said to Ella. "Her hearing don't –"

"Tell Tom I got a pot o' gooseberry for him to take –"

But the distance between the mother and the two girls was increasing every moment and this time they caught nothing of the prattling at all but the word gooseberry, which set them tittering again with dark hints of meaning which only they understood.

And finally when they reached the farm-yard they were still tittering, and the mother, too far behind now even to shout, was still prattling half to herself of thunder and rain and gooseberries and swallows, turning at intervals to look at the sky beyond the other valley-slope or at the

17

hay-field plainly visible now beyond the greener fields of summer corn. By the time she had reached the farm-yard her sons had disappeared and the two girls were hanging their rakes from long strict habit on the beams in the open cart-shed flanking the yard on the north side.

The house itself stood at the extreme opposite end of the farm-yard, cut off by a stone wall from the muck-heaps and barns and hen-houses and the orchard where many generations of colts and calves had worn the trunks of apple and plum and pear to the smoothness of saddle-leather by the rubbing of their soft necks. The house too, like the barns and the wall, was stone built, the roof beams here and there knuckled up under the earth-coloured tiles like the ribs of a starved horse, the stones themselves freckled with lichen-patterns of green and buttercup. A line of horse chestnuts between the house and the road kept the afternoon sun from the walls and dripped heavily on the roof from the flagging leaves during and after rain. Frankie and Tom and sometimes the two girls kept the garden on the west side of the house in decent order, carefully training the wall cherry trees and the odd apricot, weeding among the old clumps of pæony and lily and growing good potatoes in the middle plot. Away from the river, on the slope, the air was less rich and heavy, but still rich and heavy enough with the close odours of cows and cow-barns and straw and dung and earth to be a sleepy drug on the senses, the richness of it sweetened and made richer by the fragrance of hay as though every one of the farm's two hundred and ten acres were grass. Jefferys of careful and pinching habits of life and dealing had breathed the same smell for nearly a hundred years, the rich smell of rich land well-farmed and well-mucked. And though they had listened in chapel

18

to sermons on change and decay and had believed every word of them, change and decay had no meaning for them and never touched them. They took care never to make a change unless it was a good change, a change showing some profit for them or a change putting them a notch higher in possession or prestige than a neighbour; and decay was not decay at all but a mere translation from one form to another, from straw to muck, apples to pig-food, trees to firewood, fire to ashes. The house itself they felt could never change and never decay. Magpie Hall seemed as permanent as the sky and much less changeable, as fixed a part of the farm as the river itself was part of the valley. Standing high on the valley-side, visible from all points across and along a stretch of land that was without woods, it was a landmark that no one could ever miss.

The thundery light under the chestnut trees seemed to be thickening as the Jefferys' mother shut the yard-gate and hung up her rake in the cart-hovel and crossed to the house. The young calves were standing motionless under the fruit-trees, soft-eyed, sensing the thunder but too languid to stir. Hens of all colours, brown and reddish and black and white and even freckled, moved as though on drugged feet across the calf-worn grass. The woman moved on drugged feet too, tired out. Then as she approached the wall she saw where a hen had laid an egg in a patch of nettles at the foot of a cherry tree. And stooping, she parted the nettles and picked up the egg. It was cool against her sweat-hot hands, and she carried it gently into the house, sucking the stung parts of her hands as she went.

Tom was in the kitchen, shirt off, washing, and she said as she came in :

"Tom, here's egg. You take and have it for Elsie. She'll like that."

"Put it on my cap," Tom said. "Else I s'll forgit it."

"I'll git that pot o' gooseberry too."

And later, as Tom crossed the yard, dressed up in black, his hair watered, Ella and Maudie watched him from the farm living-room and Ella said :

"She give him egg too."

"Ought to know better, taking it, taking eggs and things every time."

Tom crossed the yard and went in under the gloom of the still chestnut trees and began to walk along the road in the thundery light.

"Rain afore he gits far," Maudie said, in hope.

And standing like figures of wood, they watched him go.

I I

Whenever the brass-barred doors of The Angel in Orlingford flapped open and shut and people hurried in out of the thunder rain, Tom Jeffery, waiting under the archway for his girl, could see inside the bar the red coat of a soldier. He was a tall man and his tunic, very tight as he leaned on the bar, made it seem as though he were wearing corsets. Tom had dull almost colourless eyes that became almost sightless as they stared into space, so that whenever the bar door opened his eyes seemed to be fixed in lost fascination on the soldier.

The soldier was drinking whisky. It was the first thing Tom noticed as he went into the bar. Then as he waited for his half-pint he noticed the soldier had a thin tight-skinned face, a sun-yellow colour, with bright blue but sun-tired eyes. Then when his beer was drawn and standing on the bar he noticed something else. He could see the reason for the soldier's preoccupation. A pink and silver Indian shawl was spread across the bar like a tablecloth, with the silver tassels hanging over the edge, and the soldier kept smoothing it over and over with brown hands as he showed it off to the barmaid. It was a fine shawl. Tom put his hand on the handle of his beer-mug and stared at the shawl, letting his hand rest.

"Lovely, aint it?" the soldier said.

Tom kept his eyes on the shawl and his hand on the beer-mug and didn't say anything. And suddenly the soldier raised his voice:

"Here – you! Don't you reckon to speak when you're spoke to? Huh?"

"Me?" Tom said.

"Yeh! – you."

"H'm."

"Said it's a nice shawl ain't it and you never said nothing."

"I never knowed you were speaking to me."

"Never knowed – what th' 'ell? Some o' you chaps want a dose o' soldiery. Nice rain, ain't it?"

"H'm."

"Where this shawl came from it rains like that, on'y harder, for six weeks on end. On'y harder."

"Welcome," Tom said.

The soldier finished his whisky and slid the glass across the bar.

"Give us another, Rosie."

And while waiting for the barmaid to draw the whisky the soldier kept smoothing the shawl softly with his brown hands, over and over, as though he were caressing

a woman. But Tom was no longer watching either him or
the shawl. In the wall-mirror behind the wine and whisky
bottles at the back of the bar he could see the reflection
of the barmaid's face. It seemed to be looking straight at
him. He looked straight back. And for what seemed a long
time he stood there with his hand on his beer-mug and his
eyes fixed on her reflection. She drew the whisky slowly.
He saw, without looking at them directly, her hands on
the glass and the bottle. She wore three rings. Her hands
were very long, with pinkish slender fingers that were
absolutely steady. She seemed to be holding the bottle
and the glass for so long and with such steadiness deliberately, just so that she could watch him. Her face
had exactly the same steadiness. It was a full face,
strong, full-coloured. She had brown rather frizzy hair
pushed back from her ears so that he could see her
white drop ear-rings. Her eyes were dark brown and
rather large. They were the only things about her that
moved.

Then she came and put the whisky on the bar. And
when she held out her hand for the soldier's money she
rested it on the shawl, palm upwards, and Tom looked
at it, and the pink of her skin against the lightest pink of
the shawl and the shine of the gold rings against the silver
threads held him in fascination. The soldier, half-drunk,
fumbled for his money, first in his tunic, then in his
trousers, his cap cocked back and showing his sweat-
pressed hair.

"All bloody thumbs and pockets," he kept muttering.
"Bloody thumbs and bloody pockets –"

"Language," the barmaid said.

She smiled without moving her lips and Tom, the rain
and his girl forgotten, half-smiled back, and they stood

like that, smiling in secret, until the soldier found his money.

He put half a crown on the bar and said, "Keep a change, Rosie."

She took up the half-crown and went at once to the end of the bar and opened the cash-drawer and as she stooped to get the soldier's change Tom could see the sudden fall of her breasts, too heavy and rich to support themselves, pushing hard against the shining black of her high dress until he could see the clear lemon-shape of the ripe nipples.

"Rosie's my Donah," the soldier said.

A moment later Rosie came along the bar chinking the soldier's change in her hand. She spread the money on the shawl without a word. The soldier stared, his mouth open a little. "Keep a change, Rosie."

"No," Rosie said.

The soldier took the shawl by the corners and began to fold it over the money, saying all the time, "Here, Rosie, I want y' t' 'ave the shawl and the money an' all. Go on, Rosie. Go on, me old duck. Rosie. Here, Rosie, half a mo. Don't go away. I want y' t' 'ave the shawl, Rosie. Rosie, don't go away.'

"I'm here."

"It's your shawl, Rosie."

"Drink your whisky."

"Go on, Rosie. I brought it all the way from Allahabad for y'. Don't be snotty."

"I didn't quite catch what you said?" She was looking at him quite quietly, quite still.

"I said I brought it all the way from Allahabad for y'."

"Not that. The other."

"What? I —"

"Don't you snotty me !"

The flash of her anger left her quite white at first, then crimson, her blood up. Tom could see her breasts quickly rising and falling with anger. The soldier began to profess great sorrow, leaning over the bar, lugubriously folding up the shawl into a crumpled mass of pink and silver and trying at the same time to thrust it into her hands. The girl stood very still except for the rise and fall of her breasts. The stillness, lost on the soldier, fascinated Tom. It was volcanic. He took a quick drink of his beer and the motion of his arm seemed to break the tension between Rosie and the soldier. The soldier began to say something, but in another moment a man was calling for a quart from the other end of the bar and Rosie walked away as though the soldier and Tom had ceased to exist for her.

"Rosie's my Donah," the soldier said to Tom.

"Ah?"

"Do what I like with her. Turn her round me finger. Do what . . ."

The soldier rambled on, fumbling all the time with the shawl, but Tom did not speak. The quart seemed to take a long time. When it was ready Rosie had over-filled the mug, so that little suds of foam and a splash of beer were spilled on the bar. And finally when Rosie had taken the money she came along the bar to fetch the glass-cloth.

The soldier waited for her, the shawl crumpled up in his hands.

"Go on, Rosie. I want y' t' 'ave the shawl. Go on, Rosie."

Rosie paused, picked up the cloth from the counter, came back and passed again.

"Rosie! Here. Don't be'n hurry, Rosie. I want y', Rosie."

Tom took another drink of his beer and wiped his moustache with the back of his hand.

"Can't you see she don't want it?" he said.

"Eh? What? What's that do wi' you? Eh? You mind your own bloody business ! See?"

"Language !" Rosie said from the end of the bar. "Language."

"She don't want it," Tom said.

"Who're th' 'ell you talking to, eh? Who –"

"Keep your hair on."

The soldier began to thrust his chest out. "Rosie's my Donah, I tell y'. Rosie's my Donah."

"Who said so?"

Tom stood wiping his moustache.

"Christ, I'll wipe y' moustache off y' face for you !" the soldier shouted.

The whole bar came to life as the soldier lashed out wildly with his left hand, men standing up, the barman rushing out from behind the bar with his sleeves rolled up, Rosie leaning across the bar and banging her fist against the soldier's arm, the soldier manoeuvring like a heavy battleship, in clumsy menacing side to side motions of his arms and shoulders.

"Outside if you want to fight !" the barman said. "Get out. Outside."

"I don' wanna fight," Tom said.

"Frit," the soldier said. "Frit."

"Fred, Fred," Rosie kept saying. "Listen to me, Fred."

"Frit," the soldier kept saying. "He's frit."

"Who is?" Tom said. "Who is?"

"Offer him out, soldier."

"I offered him," the soldier said. "He's frit. I offered him once. Frit."

"Fred, listen Fred. I'll have the shawl if you'll shut up, Fred. I don't want nobody to get hurt over me. Fred! Listen to me, Fred. Fred!"

Engaged in savage manoeuvres, the soldier seemed not to hear. The bar was in an uproar, men shouting, drowning the sound of the rain still hissing down outside. Suddenly the soldier lurched up against Tom, his tunic half-buttoned, his cap far back on his head, and Tom struck out, catching the soldier in the ribs, forcing him back against the bar, his own blood wild now too.

The uproar was furious. The barman shouted "Outside! outside," seized Tom and the soldier by their collars, forced them through the bar doors with a single motion of ejection that sent them staggering together in the archway outside. The soldier made a wide circle, swinging his arms as he went. Coming round he hit Tom with mad fury in the chest. Tom stood still. He could not breathe. His heart seemed dead. It was an extraordinary sensation of paralysis. It seemed to rise in his throat. He tried to say something. A great force and pressure of pain on his heart kept him dumb. He put up his hands in a wild manoeuvre of defence. The soldier hit him again. The blow smashed across his ear, deafening him temporarily and then magnifying the uproar of all the voices of the men crowding round and through the flap-doors of the bar.

"Christ, lammas him!" they were shouting. "Lowk him, lam him! Blimey, you ain't stannin' that. Lammas him, lowk him."

"I'll lowk him," the soldier said.

Tom staggered about in the archway like a bewildered bullock, his legs sick. When he lashed at the soldier, it seemed always as if the soldier hovered and pranced at a great distance, maddeningly unassailable. Once the

soldier forced him back and back until he staggered out
into the still hissing rain. The sensation of the rain on his
bare head and face awoke in turn the anger at the thought
of his hay lying rain-smashed in the meadow, and he came
back at the soldier with the sudden motion of a boomer-
ang, his arms windmilling frenziedly, until by the sheer
force of fury he struck the soldier full across the throat.

He heard the soldier choke, saw him stagger wildly
back, then more wildly forward again. Then the soldier
hit him twice, madly, in furious succession. They were
blows that were like the double reports of a shot gun held
just under his face. Tom fell as though shot against the
pub-wall. He was conscious enough to feel the gooseberry
jam running from his pocket and down his leg in a slow
ooze like a thickness of cold blood. He could hear the
crowd too, laughing about the jam and bawling for the
soldier to hit him again. He got up. The soldier was a red
ghost. The crowd bawled wildly. "Lammas him, finish
him." The sound of the hissing rain and the jabbling
voices and his own breath half deafened him. He tore
forward, shouting:

"This ain't th' only night! By God, this ain't the only
night – Wait, let him wait. By God, you wait."

"Wait?" the soldier said. "Wait. You'll wait three bloody
year. I'm off back to-morrow. I'm –"

The rest of the soldier's voice was drowned for Tom
in the tumult of the crowd yelling for the soldier to hit
him again. And before Tom could move or speak again
the soldier did hit him again, and for the last time.

CHAPTER II

I

Rosie Perkins, up at five, dressing at the bedroom window, looked beyond the river flowing past the pub-yard and across the hay-meadows extending beyond the river as far as she could see. The little summer mists still hanging in the low places like wisps of hay themselves were the same cloud-colour as the water. She was so dizzy with sleep that the river, flowing heavily after the storm, seemed as she looked at it to surge gently up and down like a sea, little back-washing waves slapping the mud of the tow path bank on one side and the stones of the pub wall on the other. A sight of hay was out, drenched, more than she had ever seen, and the feeling of thunder was still everywhere. The air in the room drugged her. In the valley the first rooks were flapping over to the east like birds half in a swoon. Picking up her corsets, she stood with them in her hands for a moment before slamming them down on the bed again. Damned if she would! Either she was filling out or the stays had shrunk in the wash or something. Whatever it was, she was ribbed all over. Needn't wonder folks fainted. All day in the bar yesterday it had been like hell. She swirled her black dress over her head and thrust up her head and arms and tugged the dress down over her shoulders and chest, her brown hair brushed, her breasts splendid under the thin stuff. If they didn't like it they must lump it, and if they couldn't lump it they must do the other. She pulled down the dress over her hips, straightening it and smoothing it

28

with her flat hands, her blood working with her thoughts, her sleepiness dissolving. If it got much hotter she'd go into the bar and serve in her underskirt and see what that would do. She combed her hair once or twice with her fingers and then frizzed it with the brush, leaning forward to look in the window mirror, her breasts free and heavy, her hair light as wool. Couldn't make them any sillier, the wet fools, always fighting over her. Look at that jabey last night, the soldier an' all, both of them. Suddenly, too impatient to think of it any longer, she turned and went downstairs with her shoes in her hand.

Downstairs the pub, with all its windows closed, was faint with the stale beer and tobacco smells of the night before, the beer-rings still wet on the bar where she had been too tired to wipe them off. She opened the windows of the bar first, hooking them right back on the yard side and half way on the street side, pulling on her shoes as she leaned on one sill and buttoning them at another. The street was quiet and dull; no sun yet; nobody about. The barman slept out and wouldn't be in until half-past six and her father wouldn't be up till eight, if she was lucky. What day was it? Saturday – any races? The bar looked dim, with its dowdy varnish and the piano keys like yellow teeth, the scarlet geraniums at the windows the only scraps of colour. And as always in the mornings she half-hated it, the familiar dreariness of the morning stretching out before her : last night's glasses to be washed, the bar to be scrubbed, the brasses polished, breakfast to be got, the bar to be opened up, and finally a stack-up before she got her father out of bed. That was the worst of a little pub like The Angel : all work and no play. In big pubs, hotel publics, the boots did this and the barman something else and the barmaids could keep up appearances a bit. Whereas in The Angel, with its one big front saloon and the private down the other end of the passage and only the barman and herself really doing anything, it was a bright look out, no mistake. Up at five and lucky if she was in bed by twelve again. Wonder she kept anything like a figure at all. She was proud of her figure: her straight soft neck, easy shoulders, strong round arms, splendid bust. And careful how she carried it too. Even in the morning, with her down-at-heel shoes on and the weight of sleep and the thundery air still drugging her, she walked about the bar and from the bar to the kitchen with easy steps, very erect, but languidly, as though it were something offhand and as though she really didn't care.

She did care. Still more, she had to care. Back in the kitchen, with its little square glass peep-hole looking through the door to the bar, she raked out the fire and laid the paper and sticks afresh on the dead ashes. If she didn't care, who would? Not her father, pretty certain, not his lordship. Who kept the pub going? She put the match to the paper, and the flames sparkled up much as her thoughts shot up, in little leaps, with half angry brightness. Well, who kept it going? Who stopped in bed till he was dragged out and then slommacked about the bar all morning in his canvas shoes if there were no races on and bunked off in the ten train if there were, and then spent his evenings in the private bar with his private cronies, having the horses over again and too silly half the time to know what whisky was being drunk?

Impatient again, she opened the kitchen window, the fire drawing a little better, the flames running higher. By now it was ten past five: time for a cup of tea before she started. If she didn't get it now she mightn't get it at all.

She filled the kettle with water from the tap in the wash-house behind the sink, scotching it on the fire-edge, gently. Back in the wash-house she swilled her arms and face and neck with running water, looking at her nails intently, nicking the rings of dirt off one nail with the point of another, washing her ears with her wet fingers. Nice to feel her ears, without her ear rings on, and to sit in the kitchen and dry herself, slowly. Cool for once, nice and easy without her corsets. Always the last chance on a Saturday. By the way, were there any races? She tried to think as she finished drying herself, but she could not remember.

She sat drying herself a little longer, waiting for the kettle, her eyes on the fire, her last chance for a minute's peace. She knew only too well how long the day could be : the extra midday rush for market, the bar open all afternoon and all evening, the night hot enough to stifle anybody. Everybody expecting she had forty pairs of hands, everybody wanting beer at once, everybody shouting for a tune on the piano and nobody but Rosie to do it and lucky if she got the barman's brother for an hour or two to help in the wash-house. It spread before her with the dreariness of long familiarity.

The kettle ready and the tea made, she sat down at the kitchen table with her cup, resting both elbows on the scrubbed deal, the cup held in both hands, the tea-smell rising into her face. About her and above her the pub was very quiet : no sound from his lordship, only the clock ticking. Why wasn't it always like this? It was a nice little pub really, neat and snug. She took great pride in it, liking it in her heart. But whether she was unlucky or whether it was just that there was no peace for the wicked, she didn't know, but somehow the pub enslaved her and had done now for years, ever since the death of her mother. And there were times when she felt that there was no escape. Her life was bound up with beer and glasses and the eternal drawing of beer and washing of glasses : no half days, no evenings, no Sundays off, always the pub, an unchanged and it sometimes seemed an unchangeable life of beer and men.

The beer did not trouble her; she liked a glass herself. She drew a pint every morning about eleven, drank it standing behind the bar with a mite of bread and cheese in her fingers. She had another glass at night, for supper, but no more. It never troubled her; she wouldn't mind if she never touched it. But men were different; enough to make a saint swear. The fight last night was nothing : always somebody fighting, scarcely ever a night, and never a Saturday night for as long as she could remember, when some fool didn't call Rosie his donah and some other fool didn't try to stop him. She was sick of it, but there it was, what could she do? She knew what they were after, and sometimes, well, you couldn't always ride the high horse. No use keeping yourself in a glass case for ever. She was twenty-five, and that was bad enough, without being an angel on top of it. With the tea held just under her mouth, the steam rising up into her face, she stared into the fire, caught up in an unconscious spell of meditation.

Here, Rosie, come on, come on. Time's time. She drank the last of her tea in a gulp and set down the cup, half-impatient with herself. Never get the bar swept out afore bull's noon at this rate. Come on, up's a daisy.

She got to her feet with an effort, her big limbs languid as she went into the wash-house for the broom and from the wash-house to the bar. Leaning on the broom, she unbolted the bar doors, swinging them back. The sun was coming up, a yellow wedge of light cutting across the passage-way, a strong hot light already. She rested the broom on the bar while she moved the chairs and tables aside and kicked the spitoons against the window bench. Then, sleeves rolled up, she began to sweep out the bar with strong strokes, tobacco ash rising, beer-slops smearing the floor-boards a dirty mahogany and here and there running into little dust balls, the dark specks soaring like smoke in the shafts of sunlight now coming in at the windows. Upside down, the bar looked more tawdry than ever, the red plush of the benches mangy, the piano bloomed over with dust you could write your name in, beer-slops everywhere, the varnish dowdy, the quicksilver worn off the backs of the bar-mirrors so that the glass was foxed, the ceiling scorched in smoky patches by the gas-light. And Rosie conscious of it, swept quickly, a nip of viciousness in the motions of her bare arms, not resting until she had heaped the dust together and had brushed it in one movement into the passage outside.

The passage was filthy too; odds and ends, papers, a bottle, dog-turds. She began to sweep it as she had done the bar, strongly, with impatient strokes that hurled the rubbish over the flagstones. She brought it finally into a heap, the dust from both inside and out, in readiness for gathering up. That finished, she saw something else lying in the passage corner : a cap. She picked it up : a very good light check cap. She dusted it on her knee, flicking it, holding it by the peak. Better keep it – somebody would ask for it when he sobered up and remembered.

Turning, half-leaning on the broom, she threw the cap like a quoit through the bar door. The cap sailed over the tables, striking the bar and sliding across the smooth top to hit a half glass of stout still standing there. The glass

reeled and scuttled like a ninepin, the stout swilling over‐
long before the glass itself smashed down behind the bar
with a crash that echoed all over the pub.

Watching the glass reel and tumble at last, she felt her
heart stand still as the crash came. Blimey, another glass.
Saturday an' all. Her lucky day.

I I

THE sound of the smashing glass woke Rosie's father,
Turk Perkins. Startled, he lay awake after the fashion of a
potentate, on his back, mouth open, his big belly heaving
slightly, his eyes swimming in the waters of sleep. What
was that? Rosie? The sunlight was yellowing the window-
blind and as he watched it, wondering what time it could
be, his eyes sinking and drowning in the flood of sleepiness, he heard the distant tinkle of glass as Rosie swept up
the broken tumbler in the bar. Another glass! He puffed
out his beet-coloured cheeks, giving a sort of half-belch of
disgust, the wind released before he could check it.
Pardon. Manners! What was the good – his eyes sank and
drowned again, pulling his thoughts down and down into
the depths of sleep – what the hell was the good of him
trying to keep the place going properly, trying to make it
pay, if Rosie didn't do her share? Always breaking something. He closed his eyes, his mind suffocated under the
weight of sleep, his thoughts for a moment blackened out.
And he lay like that for what seemed to him a long time,
drowned in a great depth, the tinkle of the broken beer-
glass sounding like the tinkle of water on the surface, far
above him.

Suddenly he woke again, his eyes bleary. What day was

it? Saturday, Moses, must be some races. He lay thinking, potentate fashion again, his hands now behind the back of his head, his eyes glancing from his trousers, hanging on the bottom bed-rail, to his coat, hanging on the door peg. Blimey Charley, the trousers were getting shiny in the behind and no mistake. He took a long look at the coat. It was a sort of frock coat with black braid buttons sewn vertically down in front and horizontally across the back, where the tails began. The coat wasn't very sparklers neither. He must get Rosie to give it a wet and a press again. Couldn't expect him to go about in a coat like that. Still, barrel and a bung, it had been a damn good coat. Come out of an odd lot from Lord St. John's when Rosie was a little mite, and that hadn't been five minutes. He couldn't remember where the trousers had come from – but Moses in the bulrushes, they were gettin' thin. Shine on 'em like a pint pot. It hurt him to see 'em. Shiny breeches – he hadn't come down to that. Never do. It was a damn good thing the coat had tails on it. His eyes rested on the coat again and his mind dreamed off into admiration of. it, remembrance of how long he had had it and of the luck it had brought him, of the day when – wasn't that the day? – the day when, wearing this same coat, he had all his money on –

"Dad !" Rosie called. "Going up hill for seven !"

"Jis' gettin' me trousers on," he called. "Jis' gettin' me trousers on."

Cut off in their course of remembrance, his thoughts were scattered like a crowd of sparrows. He drowsed and belched and sighed until they gathered again. And then, half-turning over towards the wall, he remembered something else.

The fight last night – who was that fighting? Not Fred,

the other. He tried to recollect where he had seen his face before, but the effort overpowered him. Better ask Rosie.

"Rosie!"

No answer. He lay listening, not hearing Rosie at all. Missing again. Always missing. Always missing when he wanted her. Licker what she did with herself. Always dolling up or something. Licker.

"Rosie!"

He heard the splash of water in the pub-yard below, and then, after an interval, Rosie's voice from the passage, calling up:

"You want me?"

"Ah. What about that fight, last night?"

"Well, what about it?"

Just like Rosie, always a back answer.

"Nothing," he said. "I only wondered who the bloke was, not Fred, the other."

"I don't know, and I don't care."

He lay silent, at a loss for an answer, and then Rosie called again:

"Are you getting up? You're pretty quiet about it if you are."

"Jis gittin' me trousers on," he called, "jis gettin' me —"

He went off into a new slumbrous meditation, staring at the enlarging patches of sunlight on the window-blinds. Starch an' hair oil, how was it they all got worked up over Rosie? Every week, almost every night, he would be fetched out of the back room on account of a fight of which Rosie was the cause. Time it stopped. Time Rosie decided who was who and got married. Standing there behind the bar and having all the bar fighting over you one time or another was all apple pie as far as it went, but it didn't get him far. It didn't solve the everlasting problem of how to get through the day without overtiring himself. He so easily got overtired. A stroke or two too much and he was pipped, done for. It didn't get him a new pair of trousers either. It was time Rosie got married to some hard-working chap who didn't mind a little elbow grease, so that Turk himself could take the rest he had needed so badly and for so long.

"You heard what I said!" Rosie called. "It's going uphill for seven."

"All right, Rosie, all right," he called like a shot. "Quick as I can."

"Breakfast's on and I shan't keep it."

"I'm out, I'm out. Jis' running the comb through me hair now."

A pause, and then: "That's funny. Your comb's down here on the shelf."

He lay very quiet. No fooling Rosie. He could catch, now, the odour of bacon being fried. No fooling Rosie. Why didn't she bring him a mite o' something up in bed and save all that trouble?

And after another period of deliberation, blinking and belching and lolling out his tongue, he at last upraised himself on his elbows. He remained like that for more than a minute, at rest. Careful did it, mustn't over-exert himself. Then as he half-sat there he looked at his trousers again. Blimey Charley, they were thin. They looked even worse now, in the stronger light. Anything like a sudden bit of exertion and they'd be done. He must look out and not exert himself.

He speculated for a moment. If Rosie were anything of a girl she'd do something about –

"Rosie!" he called. "Can't you ask one o' your best

blokes if he's got a pair o' breeches he's done with? Mine are as thin as a bit o' paper."

"Eh? What's that?" Rosie called. "You mind your business and get up. And another thing –"

Turk lay back on the pillows, apprehensive.

"The next time I hear you betting with anybody on the size of my stays, I'll smash you. You're betting mad."

That'd done it. That'd done it. He was done for now.

"I heard you!" she called up. "Haven't you got any manners or respect or sense or anything?"

He lay quiet. He was done. No chance of the breeches now. He was done.

"And don't grouse at me if your bacon fat's cold. I told you until I'm sick of telling you."

"All right, Rosie, all right," he called, subdued. "I'm jis' gettin' me trousers on, jis' gettin' me trousers –"

One of her snotty days. Be better if he got out of the way and stayed out. And remembering suddenly again that it must be Melton races and that he could catch the ten train without exerting himself a bit, he pushed back the coverlet and swung his ponderous hairy legs out of bed.

III

By eleven o'clock, with its brasses polished, chairs and benches dusted, glasses in sparkling upside-down rows on the shelves below the wines, the bar was transformed. Leaning behind the bar, arms no longer bare, her pearl ear-rings on and her hair done up in a sort of half pineapple dome, Rosie herself was transformed too, her outward appearance matching the pub's. Her dress was pink, a crushed-strawberry shade, with light patterns of red, the sleeves slightly puffed. Scratching her hair with the tip of her little finger, she turned to look at the clock. Not more than half a dozen people in the bar and it wanted five minutes yet. Better draw her beer and have her lunch while she got the chance. The first rush came about eleven on market days.

A minute later she stood with the beer on the counter before her, the froth settling as she ate her first mouthful of bread and cheese. Now and then the bar doors flapped, and watching them, she could swallow hard at her cheese, and wipe the beer off her mouth, swiftly, with the back of her hand. Couldn't be too careful. Never knew, in a pub, who might drop in on you next.

"Morning, Rosie, how's Rosie?"

"Rotten."

"Oh ! don't say that."

"Threepence change, thank you."

"Late night?"

"Early morning. Banging about since five."

"Hot day."

There were remarks that needed no answer. Rosie rubbed the nails of one hand on the palm of the other and stared through the windows, beyond the geraniums, to the hot street outside. Talk for talking's sake, some would.

She buried her lips in the beer-froth. The doors flapped. Hurriedly she wiped her lips with the back of her hand and thought for a moment that the rush had begun. Men poured into the bar in a sudden crowd, the doors flapping like shuttles. She saw a dozen elbows leaning on the bar, looked into half a dozen faces and in the space of a minute or two drew half a dozen orders, listening and answering mechanically, skimming the froth swiftly, wiping up the bartop, her ear-rings quivering and dancing.

"Keep cool, Rosie?"

"Been cooler."

She answered tersely, saving her breath, her face good-humoured.

"Give us another, Rosie. Dad about?"

"Want to see him?"

"Well –"

"Come in about eight tonight, and you might be lucky if you're lucky."

She moved along the bar, taking money, pulling at the beer-engines, giving change, acting and speaking with one part of herself, thinking with the other. Bitter, don't forget your change, thank you, whisky, the water's in the jug, two stouts and a mild, I'm very well thank you, considering.

Talk the hind leg off a donkey. She drew the last beer, giving the change with one hand and taking up her own beer, almost simultaneously, with the other, bending down a moment later to pick up her bread and cheese from the shelf under the counter.

"Ain't seen a cap about, I suppose?"

She straightened up, mouth full of cheese, swallowing.

"What sort of cap?"

She spoke with serenity, almost impersonally.

"A check cap," Tom Jeffery said.

She reached under the bar, running her hand along the shelf. All the time she could feel him watching her. He was still watching her when she laid the cap on the bar.

"Anything like that?" she said.

"That's it."

The cap lay on the bar between them. She waited, saying nothing. The big fathead, why didn't he take it?

40

Why didn't he take it and be done and let her get on with her beer?

Still staring at her, he spoke. "Glad you found it. It's a new cap."

"I've a good mind to say it'll cost you threepence."

"How's that?"

"Somebody got throwing it about and broke a glass with it."

"I never broke it. I –"

"I didn't say you did. I said somebody. It's over and done with, anyway." She pushed the cap across the counter, the silky lining sliding on the smooth wood. "You'd better take care of it before it walks away again."

He stood mute, not taking the cap, but simply staring at her. The bar doors flapped, shut, open, knocking back against a crowd of shoulders.

She picked up her cloth, wiping the bar in a quick circle, pursing her lips to speak.

"Are you ordering anything?"

"Who? Me?" He looked surprised. "Ah ! Half mild."

"Half?"

She put an accent of distinction on the word, her lips in a half-smile, ironical.

"All right. Pint," he said.

She drew the pint before he could speak again, skimming the froth and wiping the bar in time to face fresh customers.

"Well, Rosie, how y' blowing?"

"Threepence change. Well, might be worse."

"Right day for a boat. How about it, Rosie?"

"When?" She was smiling, her head back.

"S'afternoon."

"*All* afternoon?"

41

"If you like, Rosie. If you –"

"Screw your head on straight. There's only one boat for Rosie, today, and she's in it."

She took orders, served them and gave change mechanically. Wiping the bar, looking up to catch the eyes of customers, she could catch momentary flashes of the street outside, the sunlight white and scorching already on the stone walls opposite, the sky still and brilliant beyond. Inside, the bar was thick already with fumes of beer and smoke, the air breathless. A boat out – nice for some folks. Blimey.

"Any boats left for the afternoon, Rosie?"

"Better see the barman. He's round the back. No, wait a minute. What time did you want it? I'll call him."

"Half-past two."

"Joe!" She leaned on the lintel of the passage door, calling into the back recesses. "Any boats for half-past two? Eh?"

She came back to the bar.

"Only punts."

"Give us a punt then."

"Punt for Mr. Thompson at half-past two," she called.

The bar reeled with figures, men pushing in and out, the doors everlastingly shutting, the faces crowding at the bar as though she were an animal behind a cage. Half-past eleven – another twelve hours, the heat of the afternoon and evening to be survived, the night too far off yet and too much of a good thing even to think of. And his lordship by this time half way to the races. Two bitters, thank you. Threepence change. Enough to make a saint swear, enough to –

She was caught up in a whirlwind of fury against her

father, the pub, the customers, the heat and even herself, clenching the handles of the beer-engines fiercely, scarcely speaking, the first rush of the market on her, the bar a tumult of voices deafening her, the heat weighing her down.

No use, couldn't manage. Must call Joe.

She leaned back on the door-lintel, flattening her voice, pressing the anger out of it by a great effort.

"Joe ! I can do with you as soon as you're ready."

She served on, in the vortex of a turmoil, no longer even thinking, scarcely even looking, serving only by ear, the clamour of voices sending her almost frantic.

Finally the barman came, a little dark fellow, wiping hands on apron, his stiff hair quiffed up.

And suddenly, as soon as he arrived, the turmoil ironically lessened, the faces drifting away from the bar, the voices loud but no longer clamouring, the pause giving her time for a sip of beer and a mouthful of cheese and a wipe-over for the bar.

"Take a boat out with me?"

She looked up slowly, surprised, mechanically wiping the beer off her mouth with the back of one hand.

"You talking to me?"

"Ah."

"Well, talk sense then."

Tom Jeffrey's eyes were fixed on her in a stare of dumb persistence. Wiping beer and crumbs off the bar, had no effect on him. The stare went on unbroken, transfixing her.

"I only asked you."

"You heard me tell that gentleman there was no boats left?"

"Yes, but –"

"Very well then."

Stare, go on. Who was he, anyhow? Face seemed familiar. Go on, stare.

"Could git a punt, couldn't we?"

Rosie leaned forward on the bar, resting on her flattened hands, looking straight into her face, her voice tired.

"Didn't you hear me say I was behind this bar all day?"

"Tomorrow, then. Sunday."

"Sunday the same."

Suddenly she saw his face change, the flesh colouring darker, the eyes lighting up in a flash.

"Out with the soldier, eh?"

"What soldier?"

Instantly she remembered.

"Look here," she flashed. "There might be a battalion, but that wouldn't make no difference to what I said. See?"

"All right, all right. I only asked."

"You asked and you got your answer and now you know."

She wiped the counter with the bar-cloth in a sudden swish of finality.

"Don't you never git no time off?" Tom said.

"Does that concern you?"

"Yes."

"Does it?" she said. "How nice."

He had not time to answer before the bar doors flapped and men poured in, and she was caught up again in the rush and clamour of voices questioning and answering. Two stouts, a bitter, thank you, change, no I'm not drinking anything, thank you all the same. She drew beer, took change, spoke and wiped the bar automatically, not thinking.

All the time she could see Tom Jeffrey, standing behind

the bar-loungers, his beer half-finished, watching her. Her
eyes flicked over him, derisive, never resting. And when
the rush had passed again, leaving her high and dry like
something thrown up on a tide, he was still standing
there, with the same bull-stare of fixed attention.

In a minute he came up to the bar, his glass empty.
She felt tired. All right as long as she kept going, but
when she stood still –

"I'll have another," he said.

She drew the beer slowly, with tired indifference, looking out of the window as she set the glass on the bar.

"You have summat," he said.

"No."

"Ah, go on."

"You heard what I said."

At the other end of the bar someone was jingling a
coin on the counter, spinning and catching it. The barman had disappeared. She walked along the bar, served
a whisky, collected half a dozen glasses on her fingers,
put them under the bar for Joe to wash, and then returned, wiping the beer-froth from both the bar and her
fingers with the screwed-up cloth. She felt a little like the
cloth herself, damp and screwed up, her clothes already
too tight, her body damp with sweat. For a moment she
stood still, inert but not resting, her body heavy, her
arms hanging at her sides as though weighted. Motionless,
she looked at the clock and saw that it was past twelve
already. Well, that was a blessing anyway. Another hour
and Joe could take charge while she had a mouthful of
dinner in the kitchen – a bit of cut ham or a fried
sausage or two if she was lucky. The morning lay behind
her like a dream, the hours a whole day in themselves.
The afternoon and the evening were like the promise

of another, and her mind drooped at the thought of it.

Then, as she took her eyes away from the clock, she saw Tom Jeffrey still watching her, the stare unlessened, as though he were transfixed in a mood of perpetual adoration for her. And seeing her look at last, she came forward, leaning elbows on the bar.

"I came down a-purpose to ask you to come out wi' me."

"I can't help that."

"Don't you wanna come?"

"Oh! Cheese it. Didn't I tell you once I s'll be here all day, worse luck?"

"You'll change your mind."

"I should only like the chance."

She walked up to the other end of the bar, her head up, her ear-rings quivering slightly, without another look at him or another word.

"I s'll be about if you do," she heard him say.

And long afterwards, looking up, she would see him still standing there.

IV

By nine o'clock in the evening the bar had changed again, and Rosie with it. The evening was dusky early. The barman had lighted the gas, and the light was greenish white on the faces of the customers, the roar of its burning a fly-murmur against the jabber of voices. The bar doors were hooked back and customers overflowed into the archway outside, men elbowing in and out, swaggering, hats back. The barman and his brother, their faces gleaming with beer-coloured sweat, shirts undone in the heat, worked behind the counter like men doing a theatrical act, juggling with glasses, skimming froth, sleighting change across the wet bar. Men crowded to the bar, shouldering, as though to watch a dog-fight, and the barman, looking up, saw an everlasting regiment of leaning elbows.

All day, behind the bar, Rosie had been like a wire, tightened up, the hours twisting her still more tightly. Half an hour off for a bit of dinner, five minutes for a cup of tea, no more until in the evening, when the barman's brother arrived and she had twenty minutes to change her dress and wash herself and sit on the bed in her underskirt, and manicure her nails. Five minutes peace, peace and quietness and rest.

She half lay on the bed in her room, her unsupported breasts drooping heavily, her whole body sagging, the wire of her strength cut. Sick of the beer-smells and the heat, tired of seeing faces and answering questions, sick of everything, she lay and trimmed her nails, skinning out the dirt-rims, pressing the quicks softly back, showing the pink half-moons, admiring them. She had soft small hands that were out of keeping with the rest of her body, and she kept them nicely. That was a thing she'd always noticed : after your face they looked at your hands, and then after that, when they thought you weren't looking, they looked at your bust.

She knew. She knew, if anything, a bit too well. Long ago she'd had a lesson about that. Lying back in bed, resting the bun of her hair against the iron railing, she looked with tired eyes at the blaze of the late afternoon sky. July tomorrow, half the summer gone. Half the summer gone and not a free half day or even an evening, not even a boat on the river.

A boat out! Hardly time to turn round, let alone a boat out. This summer, for some reason, the bar seemed

47

more crowded than ever. The rush of prosperity after the war, perhaps; something, anyway, seemed to have sent everybody gadding about, enjoying themselves, everybody on the free and easy.

All except herself. And suddenly she was consumed with the old impatience, almost anger, against the pub, her father, the day in and day out life, herself. A boat out! Blimey, for two brass tacks she'd go down into the bar straight away and tell that chap in the check cap she'd come.

The anger rushed over her in a hot wave, the new sweat pricking her skin. After it, she lay quieter, relieved. She could hear the boats on the river below, the cool summer water sounds, people laughing. She remembered the man in the bar, holding his check cap, staring at her with the intent bullock-stare of fascination. Her nails finished, she lay full length on the bed, her white arms thrown back and resting on the cool iron of the bed-rail, thinking of the man and the boat, turning the idea of it over and over in her mind.

She got up off the bed at last, slowly, her limbs impotent after their rest. No. Start it for one and she could start it for the lot. She walked over to the bedroom window in her bare feet, stood on the cool oil-cloth and looked out of the window at the river below. The summer sounds came up to her more clearly. She could see straw hats, girls in white frocks, the boat-varnish golden in the sun. She could smell the water, the hot afternoon, the scent of hay. It all come up to her in rich and sleepy waves.

Footsteps ran half way upstairs a moment later and stopped, and she heard Joe's voice :

"Rosie !"

"What say?"

"All right, Joe. Coming."

She heard him begin to move downstairs and then called him back :

"Joe. What time is it?"

"Nearly seven."

"Is Turk back?"

"Ain't seen him."

She sat on the bed again and began to draw on her stockings. He wouldn't be ! She smoothed the black silk with her hands, slowly, straightening the clocks. Dressing herself, putting on first her stays and then another dress, she came gradually to life, the light red dress filled to tightness by her strong hips and breasts, the slackness of her body vanishing as she held herself straight and buttoned the dress and smoothed the stuff and ran the comb through her hair. Dressed, she felt better, and looking into the mirror she felt that she looked nice. The light red suited her and she felt the wire of her strength tighten up again. In five minutes she was ready to go downstairs and as she opened the bedroom door she felt alive for the first time that day, her ill-temper dropping away. The bright dress was a pleasure to feel and see. The prospect of the hours in the bar no longer terrified her. There was a change in her blood, and as she stood on the landing she could smell the beery smell of the bar coming warmly up to her, and half-consciously she liked it. Funny how she woke up when it was time to go to bed.

Down in the bar they welcomed her.

"Good old Rosie, thought you'd done a bunk. Give us a tune, Rosie, go on."

"Let me git here."

The bar was in a clamour, the men bantering.

" 'Song at Twilight', Rosie. Go on."

"You'll get twilight."

"Anything, Rosie, go on, long as it's a tune, anything."

She sat down at the piano, flouncing her dress over the stool, her foot on the loud pedal.

"Here, have summat to drink, Rosie. Go on. Have a port."

"I'll try anything once."

"Betcha life. Good old Rosie."

A moment later she began to rattle with great energy on the notes of the pub piano, her fingers thumping strenuously on the yellow keys, her foot hard on the loud pedal, the faded pink silk behind the fretwork front quivering with the same trembling motions as her earrings and arms and breasts, the tune gathering its force and life as suddenly as she gathered her own. Whenever she played "Ta-ra-ra!" the bar answered it with a "Boom-de-ay!" of thunder, the song working up until the answering shouts of "Boom-de-ay" drowned the noise of the piano itself. The glass of port that someone had set down on the open piano-top quivered until the wine tilted and spilt in little waves down the glass-neck and on the piano, but Rosie played on with great gusto, not noticing it, her hands and her right foot coming down simultaneously, her body swaying forward and back and then from side to side, with new energy.

She played the song through twice and then stopped. Resting, with the glass of port in her hands, she revolved on the piano-stool and looked at the bar, her eyes travelling over the faces.

Blimey, what a jam. Glory alleluia. Like a Feast Sunday. Faces, white in the gaslight, revealed and hid each

other in a moving crowd. The bar doors rattled back on
their hooks under an endless pressure of many shoulders.
Everybody coming in, nobody going out. People coming
in she didn't know. The hot white faces reeled and revolved, surged and receded. Voices were raised, calling
her.

"What cheer, Rosie? How do, Rosie, me old duck!
All dressed up, Rosie, that it? All right, all right, never
meant nothing, all in good part, no harm Rosie. Straight.
Goin' give us another tune, eh? Go on, Rosie."

"Tune!" Voices clamoured, hands clapped, and men
whistled on their fingers. "Keep it alive, Rosie. Sing
summat. Rosie's goin' sing summat, ain't y' Rosie?"

Rosie patted her hair into place, her head high. "Give
us a chance."

"Give y' two chances, Rosie, if y' like!"

Her tongue flashed out, the bar roared, and a moment
later she swung round on the piano-stool reaching out for
her port glass, her foot ready on the loud pedal as she
drank.

Turning, she suddenly caught sight of Tom Jeffery. He
was sitting in the far corner of the bar, on a bench, staring
at her. Surprised, she drank quickly, wiping her mouth
on the back of her hand.

A moment later she set down her port glass on the
piano and began to thump the keys again, Tom's steady
bullock stare photographed on her mind. She'd had some
funniosities running after her in her time, but never anybody who done nothing but sit in the corner and stare at
her all day. Blimey! She played the piano with one part
of her mind and thought with another. There were some
shoots about, no mistake. She played strenuously, raising
her hands, banging the keys in full-blooded conflict, the

chords full of muscle. Her tiredness had long ago dropped finally away. She could feel the wine working in her blood and singing a little in her head. She did some fancy bits, crossing her hands. They loved it fancy. She kept the loud pedal hard down. The pressure of her foot and the opening of the volume seemed to release her own locked-up feelings, and she felt suddenly alive, alight, not caring. Blimey, it was Saturday night, wasn't it? What the pipe! Who cared? Somebody took away her empty wine glass and filled it and brought it back again. She took it off the piano with her left hand and went on playing with her right, drinking the wine quickly, spilling a trickle down her chin and throat. A minute later she finished the tune, playing it out with a run of fancy bits and singing with the bar as she played, the wine still wet and red on her lips, her forehead golden with little sparkling beads of sweat.

She had no sooner finished playing than Joe came, wiping his hands on his apron, then resting them on his knees in order to bend and whisper.

"Turk's back. He wants you."

"When did *he* creep in?"

"Come on the nine train.

"Cuss it."

"Better look out. He's half-soused and a bit more."

She swivelled half-angrily on the stool and began to bang out another tune. Let him wait! Who'd he think she was? What'd he take her for? She went on playing with great gusto, working the loud pedal like a treadle-machine, the bar roaring:

> *"I know she likes me,*
> *Because she says so!*

At the end of the tune Joe came to whisper again :

"Better go, Rosie. He's shoutin' the ceilin' down."

She got up and with fury in her movements walked through the bar, not speaking, and through the counter-flap and then through the bar door into the passage beyond. It was cooler in the passage beyond, the liquor smell thinner, but she hardly noticed it. She walked rapidly down the passage, her head up, and opened the door at the end of it without knocking.

Inside, she stopped, holding the door open with one hand.

"Well?" she said.

At the round veneer-walnut table her father, his bowler hat tilted back on his head, his coat off, his collar undone, sat playing a hand of cards with three cronies. The pack was new and the cards, backs alone showing, made blue fans in the gaslight.

She stood still, waiting, holding in her temper, speaking suddenly.

"Well, do you want me?"

Turk spoke without looking at her.

"Ah, mop the table and bring us another glass and another bottle."

Her fury rushed up.

"You talking to me?"

"Ah. Look slippy."

"Then talk to yourself !"

Turk was on his feet, his chair knocked back.

"Wha'd you say? Wha'd you say?"

"You know damn well what I said."

"Fetch me that whisky."

"By God, I'll fetch you something you won't forget in a hurry !"

"What? What, what?" he bawled.

"Keep your hair on."

Unsteady on his feet, Turk staggered about for a moment, making efforts as though to come towards her, shouting:

"All you gotta do is play that damn piano, and then when I ask you . . ."

What he had to say was never finished. Rosie, striding across the room in fury, half-pushed, half-knocked him back in his chair, his big body shaking the table with a shock that sent the card-tricks slithering and the whisky swilling up and over the glass sides. Then as he opened his mouth to bawl a protest she snatched the cards from his hands and threw them in his face, she herself shouting this time:

"Any more big talk like that from you and I clear out, see? I clear out, and for good."

"Clear out!" He struggled helplessly to rise, his big face swollen, his cheeks and neck purple colour with anger. "Christ Almighty, clear out! Clear out!"

She turned and walked back to the door in silence, her hands clenched, her mind white hot. As she reached the door and her hand seized the knob her father shouted:

"Clear out! And good riddance!"

She stopped, very quiet, her quietness surprising even herself.

"That's done it," she said. "That's done it. I clear out."

Turk was suddenly quiet too. He made a single sound of inarticulate rage, but he did not speak. The cronies were very quiet, fingering their cards, embarrassed.

Seeing them, her rage shot up again. She turned and slammed the door without a word, going down the corridor in a frenzy of anger that did not begin to lessen until she was in the bar again, drinking a glass of port which she drew with her own quivering fingers behind the counter.

The port half-finished, she felt better. Her anger receded and a rush of recklessness took its place. She looked at the bar wildly, her lips tight.

A minute later she was standing over Tom Jeffery in the far corner of the bar, her eyes shining.

"Is that still on?" she said.

He looked at her heavily, in an excess of dumb astonishment, bewildered.

"Is it on?" she repeated.

"Is what on?"

"The boat, the boat."

He looked at her sickly, only nodding.

"All right," she said. "Be here tomorrow afternoon at two o'clock. I changed my mind."

Less than a minute later she was thumping the piano with a burst of muscular savagery, her lips tight, her joy gone.

CHAPTER III

I

DURING the rest of July Tom would wait about in the backyard of The Angel on Sunday afternoons, and soon after two o'clock Rosie would appear at the back door dressed all in white, from her white kid boots laced high up and her white dress full and flouncing in the skirt to her big leghorn hat and her white gloves skin-tight to her elbows, and Tom would hold her hand while she climbed down into the pub's best boat that Joe had moored in readiness against the jetty, Rosie steadying herself by pressing hard against the boat-bottom with the ferrule of her white sunshade. " 'Bout settled?" Tom would say and when Rosie was ready he would push off, rowing strongly but with restraint, the oars splashing softly in the deserted silence of the Sunday afternoon, Rosie opened her sunshade as the boat drew away from the jetty and went upstream. Straw hat level, coat buttoned, Tom would row as though by mechanical impulses, in and out, in and out eternally, without variation of rhythm or pace, and after a while Rosie would lie back on the boat cushions, her body looking splendid and in some way stronger and finer under the pure white dress, to watch him until the everlasting backward and forward rhythm of his arms and body and the soft passage of the boat through the water almost sent her to sleep.

Lying there, eyes half-closed, hearing the soft lap of water in the summer silence and feeling the sun hot through the thin white dress, she was conscious of

having gained an independence. Something had been
broken between herself and her father at last. There was
a split, a windening between them, that would never be
closed again. For years they hadn't hit it. For years she
had done the donkey work while he had fooled about,
laid abed, and lost money amounting to God knows how
much on dogs and horses. Now let him have the donkey
work for five minutes and she the pleasure. It would be a
change for everybody, and in the boat her thoughts
slipped through her mind idly, without malice, but with
new freedom, as easily as the boat itself slipped through
the water. And as the boat drew upstream she would feel
as pleased with her change of existence as she would have
been with a change of dress. Another three hours and she
would be back at the pub, changed into her black Sunday
evening dress, the afternoon gone, her white put away.
It was a flash of freedom only a mere flicker of change
in the flat day-in-day-out bondage. Yet, lying there, sometimes letting her limp hands run along the boat-side in the
cool water, she knew that she had gained something. Turk
was frightened. For a long time she had suspected it.
Now, recalling his shocked quietness in the back room
and more recently his totally unprecedented scuttles in
the bedroom when she called him of a morning, she knew
it without any kind of doubt. And knowing it, her mind
was made up. She'd had enough. It was the limit. Another
go like the one in the back room and she was finished.
The pub could go and she could go. There was an end of
all things.

Driven by Tom's stocky powerful arms that were
exactly the same colour as the outcrops of sun-red ironstone on the opposite valley-slopes, the boat would travel
so steadily and smoothly that she hardly noticed its

passage from one field to another. To her the meadows seemed all alike, the hay cut now and carried and the new grass sweetening into many flower-fringed lawns spreading over many pale green acres. Meadowsweet grew in fringes of thick cream feathers along the river-banks, in parallel and almost unbroken curves of blossom among the metallic spears of reed, so that the river seemed hardly to change either. It was a dreamy passage under a dreamy sky. Why did she come? What the pipe did she see in him? Always she was too content or sleepy to answer for herself. Once she had been, it had been very easy to come again. Now what? How much longer? And she would lie in the boat and watch him through half-closed eyes, attracted by the mechanical swing of his heavy brown arms as they worked out and in and out and back to his chest again, unceasingly, the stubborn rhythm never altered.

By the middle of August she was thinking of how she could break it off, finish it before it got too late. It had been nice enough as far as that went, but she was bored at last. That Sunday was very hot, the air full of the smell of harvest, the corn half-shocked, half-standing, white and golden, on the ironstone land above the escarpment. Better finish it. She lay wondering how to put it into words. "I ain't coming no more," – no, treat the chap decent. How then? It was always hard to start a conversation with him at all. Intent on rowing, he hardly ever spoke. Conversation spun between them on the thin webs of commonplace things, breaking easily, always brief.

"Nice up here, ain't it?"

"Lovely. I like it."

"Nice in summer. These're our meadows."

"All these?"

"One side."

"How many?"

"Six all told. Over hundred acre."

"Blimey."

The single word would finish it. After it he would row for a long time before he spoke again.

That afternoon Tom pulled the boat into the bank of the biggest Jeffery's meadow, splitting the reeds and shaking out the creamy powder of meadowsweet as he shipped oars.

"You better come home tea today, if we're going on with it."

"Going on with it?"

"Me and you."

She came to life, opening her mouth and eyes in bland astonishment.

"Who said we were going on?"

"This makes four Sundays you been up here with me."

"It can make four hundred for all I care!"

He said nothing for a moment. Then he suddenly got out of the boat and began to tie the painter to the field fence.

"Ain't nobody else, is there?"

"Don't make me laugh," Rosie said.

"Laugh, eh? That all you can do?"

"Oh! Cheese it! I never said I was laughing, did I?"

"Then why'd you come out wi' me?"

She sat silent. He finished tying the painter, swinging the boat flush against the bank with his foot.

Suddenly, half-angry with herself, she got up in the boat.

"All right," she said. "Look well, I should think,

59

─squabbling over why I come out with you. I come out, ain't that enough? Where's this tea?"

She held out her right hand and Tom took it without speaking. Then she struck the ferrule of her sunshade into the river bank and jumped rather heavily out of the boat, Tom catching her and holding her for a moment while she gained her balance.

His arm was still half round her waist when they began to walk up the meadow towards the farm-track. She looked down at it, pointedly. He took it away.

"All right, you can keep it there !"

But he hung it by his side, not speaking, and against her will she was quite touched, sorry she had been so snotty. Moses, what was coming over her?

They walked up the meadow and afterwards along the cart-tracks between the wheat-fields without more than half a dozen words. Even on the high slopes above the meadows, it was very hot, the sky like hot glass, the corn burning gold in the sun, the land silent everywhere under the heat. Drugged by the heat and the smell of almost ripened corn and the sun-baked earth, Rosie did not think much, and it was only when they reached the farmyard, where the many young calves of Tom's raising were snoozing in the shade under the fruiting plums and pears, that she woke up to the spaciousness and reality of the place. The shadow of the big stone house, lying in a dark wedge across the scorched-up yard and joining on the far side of the big balloons of chestnut shade, somehow magnified the whole place, giving the house itself an over-bearing and slightly sepulchral air. In this still and ex-pansive shade nothing was moving at all, the hens motion-less, cuddled together in many-coloured bunches under the fences, the white ducks pillowed on the pond edge, the calves drowsing, the leaves themselves unstirring in the heat of middle afternoon. And when Tom walked over the kitchen threshold and called once or twice into the house if anyone was there his voice, magnified also in the sleepy silence, had the booming echoing sound of a voice in a tunnel.

For a moment or two no one called in answer, but at the third shout Maudie, breathless from cycling home from Sunday school and from telling Ella and her mother that "Our Tom's finished with Elsie, it's all over the show", called from the front living-room in her high voice:

"Is that you, our Tom?"

"Ah, How about a drop o' tea?"

"It's Tom," Maudie whispered. "Don't say nothing. It's Tom."

"Eh? Who is it?" the old lady said, in a loud voice.

"Tom!"

"I never heard nothing."

"Be quiet, Mother, be quiet."

"What'd you say about Elsie?"

The two girls were still hushing her when Tom came into the room, followed by Rosie. The window-blinds were half drawn, making the light yellow, and the three women, all arrested in the act of looking at the door, were caught in attitudes of clay-like astonishment. No one moved for a moment until Frankie, lying full-length on the sofa with his boots and coat off reading *The Illustrated*, turned casually, and seeing Rosie, swung his feet to the floor.

For a moment the air was easier, the clay-like faces of the women softening a little but not warming, their eyes motionless with the composure of curiosity and resentment.

Then Tom walked over to his mother.

"This is Miss Perkins," he said, "come to 'ave a cup o' tea with us."

"Eh?" the old lady said. "Who is it?"

"Miss Perkins. We boated up and thought we'd drop in."

Maudie and Ella looked at each other. A boat. Sunday. Rosie stood still, very upright, and silent.

"Where's Elsie?" the old lady croaked.

Tom said : "These my sisters, Maudie and Ella." Rosie came forward a step, to shake hands, but no one moved, and Tom went on : "This is my brother, Frankie," and Frankie, shy and self-conscious in his stocking feet, stared at Rosie and nodded.

"I better get tea," Ella said, as though it were a task.

"Oh ! Don't worry," Rosie said.

She felt curiously unnerved, almost weak after the long walk up in the hot sun, and for the first time out of place in her white rig-out. She turned her sunshade round and round on its ferrule, at a loss. Her body, as she looked down at it, seemed very large in the shut-up sunlit room, her skirts too full and flounced, her long gloves rather flash, too flash, against Maudie's tight little ones of black cotton, which she had still not taken off. And she was glad, almost relieved, when Tom asked her to sit down. Then as soon as she sat down Maudie went out, putting her gilt-edged hymn book clasped by its black elastic garter on the under-shelf on the bamboo fern-stand in the window. After she had gone Tom said, "I gotta go out a minute to look at a calf. You talk to mother while I'm gone," and a moment later she found herself alone in the drowsy yellow light with Frankie and the old lady, in a silence that no one offered to break.

She broke it herself at last, saying to the old lady:
"D'ye feel the heat much?"

The old lady not hearing, did not answer, and Rosie, not understanding, did not know what to do. The silent confinement of the room crushed her. Used to an almost eternal racket of voices, she did not know what to make of a silence which she felt would stifle her. And she felt an absurd leap of relief in her heart when Frankie, leaning over from the sofa, said:

"Like to look at *The 'lustrated*?"

"Ah! Yes, thanks." She looked straight into his face. Very fair and burnt by sun, it went an even deeper colour as she took the paper from his hands. "Sure you finished with it?"

"H'm."

She sat with the paper on her knees, turning slowly pages at which she did not really look. After a time she heard the voices of Ella and Maudie and the jingle of crockery breaking the hollow silence of the big farmhouse. Soon Maudie came in to lay the large starch-stiff cloth on the heavy mahogany table, and then the cups and saucers of the best service, Ella following her with plates of food, the two filling the table gradually with an array of cake and jam and bread and lettuce and honey that was meant to impress her. All the time she sat not so much impressed as drugged. Now and then, looking up from the pictures she did not really see, she would gaze for a minute at some emblem of Jeffery prosperity, a cake on the table, the thick woollen antimacassars, knitted by Ella and Maudie, that lay like house-rugs on the chairs and sofa, the portraits of Alf Jeffery in frames that were like the gilded crust of great pastries, the big harmonium filling the whole of one corner of the window. She looked at them without thinking, her mind not doing its work, the heavy drug of the place robbing her of both thought and vitality.

And finally when Tom was back and it was time to sit down to tea she felt the flat weariness of feet and heart that she sometimes felt in the bar, on a bad day, after too much talk and heat and too little food and rest.

"You sit next to mother," Tom said. He bent over his mother, raising his voice. "You sit next to Miss Perkins!"

"What name is it?"

"Perkins," Tom said. "Rosie."

"Oh," a pause, a mumbling of teeth. "Where's Elsie?"

The question, unanswered, hung like an odd echo of some unpleasant sound above the tea-table. Maudie poured tea, the big silver teapot, unused for so long, pouring slowly from its clogged spout. Rosie, tired, sat with her hat still on, only taking off her gloves. Watching the slow stream of golden tea, she waited for her cup and then, when it came, took a long drink. The tea was good, and she drank quickly, coming to life.

"Blimey, I wanted that."

The Jefferys stared and listened, the girls aghast. They took her in under a kind of compulsion, scarcely speaking all the familiar little courses of conversation cut off, so that for long intervals Rosie heard no sound but the sucking-in of tea and the crackling munch of lettuce. Drinking and munching heartily, she recalled meals at home: snatched bits of bread and cheese, pints half drunk, lonely slices of ham eaten standing up in the kitchen, no proper table laid. She warmed up as she ate, her admiration explosive:

"Blimey, that dough-cake's all right. No flies on that."

"You like it?" Maudie said.

64

"Say when you've emptied your cup."

Rosie emptied it. "Blimey, I was hot. It's no naughty walk up them fields."

Maudie, pouring out, said : "It was hot work biking up from Sunday school." She gave Rosie her cup. "You're Church I 'spect?"

"Church?"

"You're Church, I mean. I know all the Chapel folks."

"Oh! I'm nothing," Rosie said. "My mother was Church."

"We're Methodist," Maudie said, stiffly. "Wesleyan."

"Whatever you are you can make damn good dough-cake!"

Frankie and Tom laughed, but Maudie and Ella sat rather straight, their half-smiles a faint condemnation. Fearful of missing something, the old lady croaked :

"Eh? What's that, Tom?"

"She says the dough-cake's good !"

"Who does?"

"Miss Perkins."

"Oh! Mother's a bit deaf," Ella explained.

The tension lessened. Ella cut the raisin cake. "There's half a pound of rasins in and a pound and a half of butter. Here, you'll try a bit, won't you?"

"Betcha life. Try anything once."

Eating the new sweet cake, Rosie said : "How much butter? It tastes like all butter. Butter and fruit." She turned to Tom. "You never said anything about this. Cake like this. Else I might have come before." She turned to Ella and Maudie, chattering, a little warmed up. "All he talks to me about is hay and corn, whether he's going to git a crop o' something or not. But no mention of his sisters' cake or anything, not as long as I've known him."

"How long is it you've known him?" Maudie said.

"Ask me another. He got fighting about me one night about a month ago, that's all I remember."

"Fighting?"

"Oh! That's nothing!" Rosie said. "They all fight over Rosie."

Sitting very upright, her shoulders back, her bosom smooth and splendid under the white dress, she looked until the end of teatime like a swan among a brood of brooding hens, too happy to notice the little slithering glances of Maudie and Ella at the stuff of her dress, the trim of her hat and the shapeliness of her small soft hands, glances of habitual jealousy, tiny and scarcely perceptible manifestations of the common family complaint. The eyes of Maudie and Ella soundlessly clicked and photographed her from many angles and in many attitudes. She suspected nothing. The cake was good, the tea lovely, the whole place something of a revelation. Nothing else mattered. At first a little suspicious, chilled and drugged by the shut-up Sunday air of the front-room, she arrived finally at a point where she felt warmed and almost touched, the spring of her good-heartedness welling garrulously up in spite of herself.

"It's all right up here, no mistake. You folks don't know when you're lucky. Oh! I'm about full up, thanks. Well, I'll try a mite more seed, just a mite. And a drop more tea to wash it down with. Blimey, I've never eaten so much in my life. Reminds me of that tale my dad tells, about the man eating so much they had to butter his belly. Lor' that always makes me crack a-laughing."

"Cowman's come," Tom said. "You better git off, Frankie."

"Oh, dear! Am I last?" Rosie said.

"We'll have a look round soon's you're done," Tom said.

And after tea she walked round the farmyard with Tom, the calves moving timidly up on their soft knees and feet from under the orchard shade as she went past, the hens beginning to stir from under the fences. The shadows of the chestnut trees and the house were now of great length, big steeples and towers of shadow enveloping the shade of the barns and fruit-trees and extending beyond them across the fields of cut and uncut corn that stood white and gold in the evening sunlight. It was quiet everywhere except for the stirring of the beasts in the milking sheds, the odd clank of buckets and the listless murmur of chestnut leaves. The late afternoon drowsed about her, the land sleepy and golden in the August light.

"How'd you like to live up here? Tom said.

"Ask me twice."

"Nothing to stop you."

"Be? Don't make me laugh. Who'd skim the froth off at The Angel then?"

He had no time to answer. From the house Maudie's voice squawked :

"Tom ! Mum says look round the pond for a duck egg or two."

Later, going back to the house with a dozen duck's eggs in Rosie's hat, they found Maudie in the kitchen, packing dough-cake and seed-cake into a basket in which there was still room for eggs.

"These are two little cakes I got over," Maudie said. "You can bring the basket back when you come again."

"For me?" said Rosie. "Starch and hair oil ! Blimey !"

"I'll just wash the muck off them eggs."

"The eggs for me too? Crikey !"

Half an hour later, overwhelmed, she began to walk

back across the fields with Tom to the boat, Tom carrying the basket, Ella and Maudie and the old lady standing in the yard watching them, each shading their eyes from the evening sun with one hand and lifting the other in a brief good-bye, Maudie running upstairs to straighten the back-bedroom curtains and get a last glimpse of them before they went from sight.

All that evening in the pub it was very hot, the air in the bar beer-sick and stifling. The August night fell in a thick breathlessness. Behind the bar Rosie served in a fever, like a crazy automaton, her thoughts making many constant swift excursions back to the afternoon, her mind snapping open like a mechanical shutter to reveal the farm again, to let in the smell of good tea and cake and corn and sunlight and the breath of unutterable and almost unbelievable quietness of the calf-sleepy shade under the chestnut trees.

Beside it, the pub was bedlam. Bitter, thank you. Two bitters. Change, change! Your *change*! Your head would never save your legs. Two porters, a mild. Thanks all the same, I'm taking nothing. Sorry, Takes me all my time to breathe, let alone . . . Four stouts, thank you. A whisky. A double whisky. Right. Hot? Hot ain't the word. I know words better'n that. Bitter, thank you, bitter, bitter.

By midnight, too tired even to wipe over the bar, she moved in a dream of exhaustion. Soon the barman had pushed the last sleepy drunks into the passage under the archway, the gas was lowered and only she and Tom remained.

"Come on, you get home yourself," she said.

"Rosie, I wan' ask you something."

"Don't ask me nothing. Not tonight. I'm whacked." She leaned her head against the bar half-door, slipping the bolt up with one hand and sleepily pushing Tom into the passage with the other. "There was something I was going t'ask *you,* but I can't remember it."

In the passage, Tom waited. And as Rosie leaned against the door, unbuttoning the neck of her dress, fanning her bare throat with her hand, it seemed as if the darkness dripped its heat in an invisible thundery rain. She put her hand to her head, wiping it backwards and forwards, her fingers oily with sweat, her mind sluggish and drowsy in its efforts of remembrance.

"No, I can't think," she said.

"Wa'n't about the farm?"

"No. I don't know." She drew a deep breath. "But Blimey, it was nice up at the farm. That cake, eh? It was nice."

He started to speak, but suddenly she spoke again, in a spasm of recollection :

"I know. I remember now. That Elsie. Who was that Elsie they talked about?"

"Nobody. She's nobody. I –"

"Used to be your donah? I know."

She spoke softly, teasing, her voice sleepily playful, and she was too surprised to speak again when suddenly he took hold of her shoulders and began to repeat : "That's all over It's all over. There ain't nobody now only you. Nobody. Nobody."

"Hold your horses."

"Rosie, Rosie !"

A moment later he let his hands fall from her shoulders and across her breasts and about her waist, drawing her to him in clumsy efforts to kiss her. Too tired to move or speak, she shut her eyes, lay back against the door, offered no resistance. The kiss prolonged itself and gradually the

little drowsy waves of passion rose up and up in her of
their own volition until she could not bear them any
longer. She pressed her heavy breasts against him and
responded, whispering with words of a fondness surprising even to herself :

"All right, I believe you. I know. I believe you."

"Straight?" he said.

"Straight." She felt him looking at her with a kind of
jealous tenderness. "Straight. If it's the last word I ever
say."

I I

THE same evening Ella biked at a great pace from Orlingford after chapel and half-threw the machine against the
yard fence and then burst into the front room of the farmhouse without rubbing her boots, a sin in that starched
and scrubbed household even in summer, to say in her
thin weasel voice broken by breathlessness and excitement :

"Maudie, Maudie. She's a barmaid !"

"A *what*?" Maudie stood up, kindled by Ella's horror
and pleasure.

"A barmaid. I know it's right. She works in The Angel.
I heard in chapel."

Ella sat down.

"I never stopped pedalling."

Maudie, mouth open, breathed for Ella as she regained
her breath, pedalling for her in her mind, a little jealousy
leaving the pleasure of astonishment.

The old lady was roused too.

"Eh? What is it? What she say?"

Maudie and Ella answered her almost together :

70

"She's a barmaid."

"Who *is*?"

"That girl. Woman." They spoke alternately. "Miss Perkins. That woman our Tom brought home. She's a barmaid."

The old lady nodded, grim.

"I knew she was *something*."

In a silence of common assent Ella unbuttoned her gloves and began to pull them off, trembling.

"And her father's no good."

"Well, you might know !"

"He fair lives on the racecourse. I found that out."

"What about her? How old is she?"

"Twenty-five. That's what I heard."

"And the band played !"

Then, since the old lady was not sure and must not be left out, they repeated it, punctuating each other with little exclamations of excitement, raising their voices, elaborating it all. "Her father's a bad lot. Ella knows that's right. Racing. Racehorses ! And she's twenty-five. Believe it if you like. She ain't a day under thirty. I do know. Thirty and in white, with a figure like that. White ! What? Where'd she hear it all? In chapel."

The old lady listened, grim, her mind deep and giving up its thought slowly but finally, only after rumination.

"Scented to death !" she muttered.

"Scent ! Call it scent."

"Eh?"

"I said call it scent !"

"Ah. Tainted my tea. Taint the house out. What pub did you say she was in?"

"The Angel. The little pub on the river."

"That's never been no good."

71

Their minds began to work together, the cogs of one thought and another racing in with each other, fitting.

"Think she'd never had a square meal in her life."

"That's what I thought. Seven bits o' dough cake I see her eat. And sat there with her hat on."

"What's our Tom seen in her? That's what gets over me. What –"

"Now I *know* why I never see Elsie at Chapel. I ain't seen her for weeks."

Then the old lady's thoughts came darkly up, like a full bucket from a well :

"He takes after his Uncle Eli. Eli Jeffery. He never had no taste. Aunt Em done cleaning."

"I never knowed that."

"I don't know as it wasn't hotels or pubs or something *she* cleaned for. She cleaned for *somebody*."

"Ah ! Yes, but cleaning. That ain't the bar. The beer and –"

"Oh !" said Ella. "Don't *talk* about it."

They went on talking :

"She didn't seem over particular what she said, neither. Notice that?"

"Notice it? Every other word. Blimey this, blimey that."

"Ella, you know what it means?"

"What means?"

"That word. Means God Blind Me !"

"You're sure she don't know else she'd never say it, saying it every other time she opens her mouth."

"Well, that's what it means."

The old lady explored her mind, mumbling darkly, saying at last :

"I'm trying to think. I got some idea I knowed her mother. What's her name, you say?"

"Perkins." Then with a kind of fatalistic darkness: "I shall think on it."

"Oh and I know," Ella said, "what else I was going to say. She —"

Her voice broke off abruptly as Frankie, unnoticed and almost forgotten on the sofa, threw down *The Illustrated* and got up in a fury that took them by storm.

"Like a house o' damn magpies !"

"Oh ! our Frankie."

He drew on his boots savagely and stood up, not troubling to lace them.

"Leave a gal alone," he said. "The gal's all right. What harm she ever do to you?"

He stormed out, his heavy unlaced boots clomping like carthorse hoofs on the front-room floor and the passage outside.

"I polished that floor !" Maudie half-shrieked.

"Nag, nag !" And harder clomps, marching away into silence at last.

A silence broken by a new flutter of excitement from Ella:

"I couldn't very well say anything while our Frankie was here."

"Eh?" the old lady said.

"Something else I heard. I couldn't very well say it in front of Frankie."

"About her?"

"About her mother. She wasn't married."

The old lady's face became alight.

"That's it," she said. "I knowed I should think on it. That's it ! That's what it was."

I I I

Rosie and her father became like strangers. She ceased to call him in the mornings. He overslept, putting on fat, and often, because she forgot to call him, missed trains which would take him as far afield as Nottingham or Worcester. "By God !" he would rave, helpless. "This is a nice house, ain't it? By God, it's a licker !" The train missed, the day ruined, he slouched about the pub all day in carpet slippers and his shirt sleeves, picking his teeth with a matchstick, serving odd drinks, saying very loud to cronies over the bar : "Races? Fat chance. Nice thing, ain't it, when y'ain't got nobody y' can trust for half a day? Moses in the bulrushes ! Poor old Turk !" The remarks, meant for Rosie to hear, had no effect on her. She went about with a kind of arch stoicism, shrugging her shoulders, her head up. If she responded at all it was indirectly, with the public across-the-bar manner of Turk's own sarcasm, but with savage sweetness : "Nice thing, isn't it, when you can't leave a dough-cake or a mite of anything safe in the pantry? I'm sure."

Then, on a night in September, Turk was not in when Rosie closed the bar. She split the cash-drawer on the bar-top and slid the takings into the cash-bag, too tired to count them. Bolting the bar door, she saw the big September moon coming up with orange fire in the east, beyond the river. She turned out the gas and the moon made dark gold slants of fire in the bar windows. She listened and when there was still no sign of Turk she went slowly up to bed, taking the cash-bag with her, locking it in the chest of drawers in her bedroom.

Half an hour later she heard him come home. She

listened, heard the familiar sounds of entry, the banging of doors, the scrape of boots on the brick passage, and then silence. It was a long silence. She became suspicious. Sitting up in bed, she could hear nothing. The moon was higher now, large and soft, the light flooding the meadows. Suddenly she got out of bed. A second later she heard a crash, and then another and another, as though Turk were overturning all the tables in the bar.

She went downstairs in her bare feet quickly. In the bar, Turk had the cash-drawer on the counter. In the moonlight she could see the chairs lying on the bar floor where he had overturned them.

"Well," she said quietly, "you trying to knock the house down or something?"

"I'll knock you down!" he shouted. "Where's this money?"

"Put that drawer down and get off to bed and don't act the jabey."

"What, what? What?" he roared.

"Don't act so big and silly," she said.

"By God!" he shouted. "It's a pity ain't it, when a man comes home and can't find his own money!"

"*Your* money."

"That's it. Chelp me! Always a back answer. Chelp me. By God. I don't know what your mother would of said."

"No." She found a box of matches on the bar and reaching up, lit the gas. The burner roared a little and she turned it down. "I don't know what she would have said, I'm sure."

He roared up afresh: "You're the spit on her. Big and brassy!"

She walked quickly up to the bar counter, her lips tight. Turk stood behind, the cash-till between them.

"You talking to me?"

"Talking, talking! Ain't I talked enough? Where's this money?"

"I don't know where you've been and I don't know what you're bawling about," Rosie said, "but you don't talk to me like that."

"I talk to you how I damn well like! It's my own house, ain't it?"

Her own temper flashed up before she could control it.

"Yes, blimey, it's your own house and in future you can run it!" She took the cash-drawer and banged it down on the counter with unexpected passion. "And see how you like that! I've finished."

Turk for a moment did not answer. For Rosie it was the end. She turned to reach for the gas. Turk stood behind the bar in a sudden inertia, big and greasy, his heavy face running with the quick sweat of temper, his lips pouched in sullen immobility. The moment of silence smouldered briefly and then flashed again.

"And good riddance!" Turk shouted. "Christ, good riddance!"

"You talk to me like that again," she shouted, "and I'll –"

She steadied herself. She suddenly spoke very quietly, sensing in him at the same time the fear that always overcame him when she spoke softly, with her old laconic downrightness.

"And if you *want* to know," she said, "I'm being married."

"Eh?"

She saw his mouth open. After his anger, there was something stupid about that open mouth and the inarticulate stare of astonishment.

"You heard what I said."

Before he could speak again she reached up, turned out the gas and left him standing there in the moonlight, stuttering feebly. "Eh? Here, here, Rosie, my gal. Here Rosie !" – words which she never troubled to answer.

It was the last flare-up between them, the end; but for her also, a beginning. A month later, at the beginning of October, she was married to Tom Jeffery and Jefferys from all parts drove in traps and buggies and even wagonettes to The Angel for the wedding, the big top-room more crowded than at any time since Turk staged a prizefight between a local heavy-weight and a travelling negro.

Rosie was splendid all in white and Turk, very drunk, kept shouting that she was the best gal in the world.

BOOK TWO

THE FARM

CHAPTER I

I

"OVER and then under and then back again." Maudie whisked the bedsheet and then folded it, in a demonstration for Rosie, who stood by the bed. "How if you took that side? If you took that side we could do it together."

Rosie took the sheet in her hands, standing on the other side of the bed from Maudie.

"No." Maudie took the sheet. "Over first and then under and then back again. Be better if you took it in both hands. That's it. Over then under, tuck it under. Then – no, leave a bit more. No, not so much as that. Be better if –"

"Think I don't know how to make a bed?" Rosie said. "Crikey, I made enough in my time."

"Well, that's how *we* make it."

Maudie smoothed the top-sheet with quick flat hands, until the bed was smooth as milk.

"Remember the time when we had six or seven lodgers in." Rosie flattened the sheet heavily, leaving it sulky. "I made beds for all *that* lot every morning."

"It's no more trouble, I always say, to make a bed properly than it is to make it anyhow."

"Think so?" Rosie said. "What's it matter anyway? Beds get some hard work, sometimes."

"Rosie!"

"Well, don't they?" Rosie gave the sheet its last flicks

81

and smacks into straightness. "Anybody'd think you thought they was only for sleeping in."

"Well, I only sleep in mine."

"That's it. You can afford to be particular. I can't."

"Oh ! Rosie, you do say some bits !"

"Well, ain't I right?"

Maudie, having finished smoothing the sheet, fussed along the bedside, crimping and tucking in the edges. "I like to see a nice clean bed," she said, panting. "You know folks are all right then."

Rosie stood silent, watching, not trusting herself to speak again, until finally Maudie stood up.

"We'll just give the bed-rail a lick with the duster," she said. "You can do it if you like, while I run round the skirting-board."

"The bed's only new a week."

"I know, but you could write your name on it !" Maudie, horrified, took a hairpin out of her screwed-up hair and going down on her knees began to scrape it along the skirting-board. "Enough muck here to sow carrots in."

Languidly Rosie ran the duster along the new iron bedstead, her hand slipping lazily along the rails, her mind and body heavy with the old morning drowsiness.

"Shake that dust out of the window !" Maudie panted.

Oh ! blimey. Shake this, do that. Whose room she think she was in?

Rosie went to the window, shook the duster and stood looking out. Here she was only married a week and no mind of her own. Her anger sprang up in her throat. Somehow she managed to choke it back again. Behind her she could hear the scratch of Maudie's hairpin along the skirting-board. Hairpin ! Blimey, hadn't the room been done up, all new paper, less than a fortnight? Hadn't Tom and Frankie themselves done it? Hadn't she chosen the paper herself? Standing at the window, she could smell the still new odours of size and paste, odours without which she never afterwards remembered her first days at the farm. And from the yards below she could breathe also the smell of corn, the sweet silky corn-odour of many stacks that towered up against the yard fence in a great barricade. Corn, in the rich autumn days, seemed still the whole life of the farm, the stacks towers of richness, the corn-smell everywhere. And looking at the stacks she wondered.

"Who are you looking at?" Maudie said.

"Me? I ain't looking at nobody."

"Oh! I thought you were *looking* at somebody. Standing there."

"Can't I stand here?"

"Well!" Maudie ferreted the hair-pin into the corner with triumph. "There's a cob-web for you! We don't get much time for standing about up here. Time's time, as Dad used to say."

Rosie flacked the duster and little dust fell and vanished in the soft air. Her temper flashed up silently but she controlled it, and stood by the window a little longer, looking out. Already the leaves were falling, little silent downward processions of bronze and yellow from the chestnuts and the willows by the pond-side, and there was quietness all over the farm and beyond it. Why was it so quiet here? Half the day, down in the pub, you couldn't hear yourself speak, and she had got into the habit of speaking with a high-pitched voice, a voice that shrilled through the quietness of the farm like the scratching of tin. "No need to shout, Rosie," Ella had already said. Well, very likely she did shout a bit, but she couldn't help it.

Blimey, there was nothing wrong in being natural, was there? Ella and Maudie would squawk sometimes like hens as they called in Tom and Frankie for dinner.

Suddenly Maudie came panting along the section of skirting-board under the window-sill, saying as Rosie moved back from the window :

"One thing we was always brought up to do in this house and that was keep things *clean*. You'd never credit the muck I'm getting out of here."

"You ought to see the muck I used to sweep out o' the bar every morning. That *was* muck. Fag-ends and spit and matches and I don't know what, dog-turds an' all."

"Rosie !"

"Well, it's right. Oh ! a bar's got to be kept clean. I used to be proud of the old bar. I used to scrub through every morning."

Maudie ploughed along the skirting-board, was silent for a minute, and then panted at last :

"Soon as I've done this we'll do our room, then mother's. Then we'll give Frankie's a look-over. I reckon to do the stairs down after and then polish the passage. Ella's getting the milk pans scrubbed. Time she's done that and we get the passage done it'll be tater-peeling time. I'm only giving this bedroom a lick and a look this morning. Friday's reckoned to be turning-out day. Day after tomorrow, that is. We give a thorough do t'everything Fridays."

Out of breath and at last triumphant Maudie stood up, unfolding her duster to show Rosie the teaspoonful of dust scraped from the skirting-board.

"There ! There's muck for you."

"Looks to me as if you're scratching the paint off."

"Better scratch the paint off than be mucky !"

She flacked the duster grimly out of the window and

in another moment left the room for her own, talking all
the way from one room to another, Rosie following.

"Once you let things go in a farm you're done. You got
to be at it all the time. There's muck and sludder brought
in every minute. And threshing-time, you should see the
chaff. That takes us a day to clean up. This is one of the
biggest farmhouses for miles round. Altogether, not
counting the dairy, it's got fifteen rooms. And there ain't
one you could say had above a day-old cobweb in it. Here
you take the sheet again. That's Ella's side. You can
always tell by the way she sleeps. All curled up, like a cat.
I'm always telling her she'll be curvatured."

"Don't we . . . don't you do nothing outside at all,"
Rosie said, "on the farm?"

"Hay-making and harvest we reckon to help. And roots.
That's next month. And always the milk, every day. And
chickens, and the bacon-salting when it comes. Then
bread-baking Wednesdays and Saturdays. I been harrow-
ing before now, too."

"About like the old bar," Rosie said, "allus a job for
somebody."

Maudie began again the process of fussing along the
bed, tucking in the skirts.

"Oh ! I do more now than I used to. I didn't do so much,
quite, when I was courting."

"Courting?"

"I went courting ten year," Maudie said. She spoke as
though it were some record performance. "But it's been
over and done with a good while now."

"A shame."

"Well, I don't know. Everybody always said I was too
good for him." She ceased to prattle for a moment. She
was standing by the chest of drawers now and suddenly

she bent down and opened the bottom drawer, calling Rosie to come.

"Look, look at that." Linen was piled solid white slabs on the newspapered oak of the drawer, aromatic virgin linen that had never been used. "Ten pairs of double sheets in that drawer alone, and ten more in the second. I think it's twenty towels I got in the top. Or else it's twenty table-cloths and only fifteen towels. I almost forget." She opened another drawer and another, each a kind of vault with its shrouds of untouched linen. "Not a brack in them. I don't know what I haven't got. Everything. Pillow-cases and blankets – a dozen blankets – besides knives and things. I was about ready when we broke it off."

"What made you – well, perhaps I hadn't ought to ask that."

Maudie slid the heavy drawers back into place, banging the last sharply.

"He over-reached himself !"

Grim, but now almost tearful too, she got up from her knees. "But I ain't crying over him. Take more than that to make me cry. I ain't throwing myself away."

She ran the duster along the iron bed-rails, her thin and no longer young arms tautened until they were like iron too, her lips a single line of bitterness and courage.

"I ain't heard Ella say anything about a young man," Rosie said. "Didn't she like the chaps?"

"She got served the same way too !" Maudie burst out.

"So you both had bad luck?"

"Bad luck?" Maudie said. "Good luck, you mean. You can make yourself too cheap. Anybody who gets Maudie Jeffery or Ella either, 'll get something worth having. We ain't poor. You needn't think it. Dad died worth something. You didn't marry into the workhouse !"

"Well, I'll very like land there yet," Rosie said. "I always say I'll try anything once." She was at the door now, making as if to depart.

"Going?" Maudie said. "But we got Frankie's room to do yet."

"I forgot. I always forget Frankie. The kid's so cussed quiet I never know whether he's about or not"

"A kid? You call him one. And see what. He's twenty."

"He's so quiet. Quiet and half-asleep somehow. Perhaps that's what makes him seem a kid."

"Frankie's the best of the family !" Maudie said stoutly. "Dad always said so."

"He's a nice kid," Rosie said.

In Frankie's room they went together through the old ritual of bed-making, Maudie prattling, the small single bed smoothly made long before she had finished her long rigmarole of speech. From Frankie's bedroom window the view was longer than from any other in the house, little gentle undulations in the land succeeding each other into the distance, the horizon crowned by the even rolling of larch woods. Church spires here and there pricked suddenly up from the land, more pasture there than arable, in dagger-points of stone. For Rosie it was a new view, a view of quite unexpected richness and distance, the horizon strange with unfamiliar points and spaciousness. Her lazy eyes travelled over it and back to the room again before she knew what pleasure it had given her.

A moment later, looking at Frankie's dressing-table, she had forgotten it.

"What's this?" she said.

"That? Oh ! that's Frankie's telescope."

Rosie picked up the clumsy brass-bound telescope and

turned it over and over in her hands, the brass as smooth as glass against her fingers.

"Don't you drop it! My word, if you dropped it. Frankie'd –"

"What's he do with it?" Rosie put the telescope down again.

"Sits up here for hours and looks through it. Looks at the view. On fine days he says he can see the weathercocks on the church spires. Dad used to have that telescope. He used to watch trespassers through it. He caught a woman stealing a sheaf o' beans once, saw her through the telescope. We never have folks meddling on our land."

The bed finished, Rosie said "Where's Tom? I meant to have asked him something afore he went out."

Maudie craned her neck out of the bedroom window. "Ella!"

The hen-squawk from Ella came up like an echo in answer. "Eh?"

"Where's Tom this morning?"

Ellas voice, clearer now, came back: "He's ploughing Top Land with Frankie."

"Ploughing Top Land with Frankie," Maudie said. "Which is Top Land?"

"It's our big field. Over the road, and then up by the fox-covert and it's on the hill."

Rosie untied her apron-strings.

"Your not *going*?" Maudie said.

"I want to see Tom."

"We got the passage to do!"

"I want to ask him something."

Maudie tightened, her face an image in hardened clay.

"We don't reckon to go gadding off of a morning!" she said.

"All right, I won't go."

"Oh ! go. I never said nothing about not going."

Rosie folded her apron, her mouth tight also. The antagonism between them was clear and hard, but still unspoken. Rosie held herself tightly back, with great physical effort, as she might have done if she were about to be sick. Maudie stood over the bed, as though there were nothing more she could do or say.

"I'll be back to peel the potatoes," Rosie said.

"I doubt it. It's no naughty walk up there."

Maudie waited, as though for an explanation of it all. Going out was enough, but not to say what she was going out for –

"I want Tom to run me down to Orlingford in the trap tonight," Rosie said.

"Tonight?" Maudie said. "It's weekly prayer-meeting. I as good as promised Mr. Hughes you'd come."

"I ain't so much on prayer-meetings."

She went downstairs without another word, and Maudie, watching her from her own bedroom window, saw her walk languidly across the orchard and over the road and up in the field-track beyond. In another moment Maudie was downstairs in the dairy, where Ella, sleeves rolled up to her iron elbows, was scouring the last of the milk pans.

"Don't even know how to make a bed yet ! And it's all what she done in the bar and what she didn't do in the bar ! She wants to forget that bar talk. And now she's gone running up to Tom on Top Land. And walking as if she'd got all day to get there in. And another thing. Prayer-meeting – she can't be bothered with that. Can't be bothered ! She's got to alter her ways a bit to suit me."

II

By late autumn, by the time that the Jefferys were
spudding their roots, Rosie had begun to adjust herself
a little to the new life. She did it more unconsciously
than not, falling into the new rhythm as an athlete will
fall without knowing it into the rhythms of a new performance. The autumn was late : to her the longest
autumn she had ever known, the leaves turning and
hanging on their branches like decorations in copper
and golden paper, the days like still periods of yellow
twilight. In the pub, down in the town with its narrow
streets, and the early mists coming up the river, she
knew that it must already be winter. She could see and
feel it all if she thought for only a moment : the fire in the
bar, the gas bubbling and hissing, the glasses cold as ice
to her hand first thing in the mornings, the smell of rain-
wet horses waiting against the kerb outside. There was a
thickening in the flow of the pub's life in winter. Whereas
on the farm, high up in the heart of a solitude only cut
across and broken by the road to Orlingford, a road not
much used at that, life seemed to thin and quieten and
almost, at times, to come to a stillness entirely, turning
in upon itself and coming to rest like a snake curling
in for winter. In late summer the clack of the binder
and a thousand sounds besides it had kept the air alive
and the life in motion; now if there were sounds at all
they were dying sounds, the somnolent fall of leaves, the
mournful moan of cows housed-in, the dull rumble of
muck-carts, sounds which sucked up and magnified the
quietness as the hum of bees had stirred and magnified
the silence of summer afternoons.

It was the quietness which troubled her. Like a dress which would not fit her, it fell about her in soft and too large folds, fretting her and keeping her restless. In early November the Jefferys began to lift their roots. She would spend the short silent afternoons with Maudie and Ella and their mother spudding swedes in the big fields beyond the road, under a sky that was sometimes as blue as spring, the men carting and clamping the copper-coloured loads in mounds that reared up like breastworks under the still haw-red hedges. And where, with the long passage of carts and the endless clatter of women's tongues as the spuds upheaved the swedes, there ought to have been for her a quickening of life, there seemed no life at all. Life hung suspended, flat and tranquil and unexciting as the sky. The silly prattle of voices, turning the churn of gossip over and over again – "You hear about Joe Norman's wife? – I don't say it's right – I heard in chapel" – drove her to a kind of inward distraction for which there was no outlet and no escape. And whereas her mind had felt drugged by the summer hay-time richness of the place it now felt caged up, cooped in by the thin wires of day-to-day circumstance. Feelings of an insufferable longing to go somewhere, do something, to hear a strange voice, to have a sing-song in the bar, would surge up in complicated agony. There was nothing beyond them but the evening and the night, the long communion of gossip and silence and gossip of women's voices in the lamp-lit kitchen and the final and almost mechanical submission to Tom in the darkness of the paste-smelling bedroom.

It was not that she had a grievance against Tom. She was sometimes astonished in fact that she had no grievance at all. She had existed all her life by feeling and she began, if anything, to live more than ever by feeling now, in a conflict of new feelings aroused, and of old feelings aggravated, by the life of the farm. But for Tom she could detect no new feelings and no change or aggravation or lessening of the old. He moved for her on a flat plane, in a straight line without change or subtlety. He got up, ate, went out, worked, ate, worked, came to her, slept. She measured out the day by his acts, and the week by the change of his shirt and suit on Sundays. The particles of his daily life crystallized into solid weeks, the weeks freezing into impervious months, the months into a single great mass of behaviour in which she could find no fault at all. She remembered how he would sit in the pub and stare at her, in solid entrancement, unperturbed by anything or anybody. All his life seemed like that, unified and imperturbable and almost, it seemed, unchangeable.

"Tom," she would say, "let's go out. Let's go down to the old Angel."

"Ah. Might do."

"Let's go down tonight."

"Ah, will."

And they would go down, taking the black trap and the old rough-handed mare that Tom had raised from a foal, and they would sit in The Angel for an hour, perhaps for two hours, Tom emptying two glasses of beer without comment or excitement; Rosie drinking one and exchanging a word with her father, a word with Joe, a word with the dozen or more people who remembered her, hadn't seen her for a month and who wanted to know how married life suited her. Except perhaps for a little giggle or two at a reminiscence of her days there, that was all. No one, now that she was no

longer simply Rosie but Mrs. Jeffery, asked her to play
the piano. The new barmaid was a woman of forty, a
widow with adenoids and, as Rosie observed, breasts
like stale buns, an efficient, garrulous woman whom Rosie
felt had designs on her father. With Rosie's going and
her coming the life of the place had lessened noticeably.
The piano seemed never to be opened. The old swaggering, bawling life was still strong, but seen from the other
side of the bar, The Angel to Rosie was very different.
It didn't seem so clean, either. Schooled by Maudie and
Ella, she could see the many cobwebs looped between the
wine bottles behind the bar, and sometimes the spittoons
were foul. It was a comment on Tom's company that she
had time to look for the cobwebs at all, and finally, after
an hour or two hours there, they would drive home
again, not speaking, for the almost inevitable submission
between the ice-cold sheets of Maudie's laundering.

And another day Rosie would say: "Tom, there's a
wild beast show down at Orlingford, tomorrow."

"Ah? I never see nothing about it."

"Let's go."

"Ah, might do."

And they would go, taking the mare and the trap
again, slushing through the mud of the menagerie tents
to see the beasts, to breathe the tang of bruised grass
and strange dung for an hour or so, to come out finally
into a night of frost or rain or stars and drive home to
supper, to the talk spun out by Ella and Maudie like
mechanical tunes of organ grinders, and upstairs the
same prelude to another day.

Until, after a time, she ceased to care whether they
went out or not. As winter came on and replaced the
misty-golden November days by days of half-light and

bitter spells of rain or frost, she felt her complicated desires to go out and laugh and shout and talk with fresh voices crystallize into a single emotion or bleak despondency. Against the tittle-tattling of Maudie and Ella she would hold herself in, as a man might hold a horse in in a fright or a temper, but against despondency she felt helpless and careless. She would look at her hands : small, still shapely but torn and disfigured now by contacts with earth. Once she had kept them nice. A man once had said to her in The Angel that her hands were like the insides of some shells his mother had. And now look at that ! Christ, look at them ! She saw in her disfigured hands something upon which she could seize, against which she could rail for a moment until stoicism rescued her. Oh ! blimey what was the use? What she expect, on a farm? – to be wrapped up in cotton wool.

And for a time, just after Christmas, she set all faults against herself. Tom was all right – what was wrong with Tom? Could she say he wasn't good to her? And in their own way Maudie and Ella were all right. Frankie was so quiet she hardly noticed him. Maudie and Ella would madden her often with the pettiness of vinegary ways and prattling spite, but if there were antagonism she never saw it. If they felt spite for her they nursed it secretly. It never broke out.

Yet for some reason, all through her first winter at the farm, she expected it to break out. She felt it instinctively. Having lived so much by feeling she had got into the way of trusting her feelings. And as she sat there sometimes with the family in the kitchen on winter nights she could feel Maudie or Ella looking at her, their eyes fixed upon her in a stare of dumb criticism or envy or simply wonder.

Down in the pub she had got into the habit of changing her dress in the evenings, to brighten up herself and the place in general. She would change from her black day-dress into a flowery mauve and purple or something scarlet that pulled as tight as skin over her bust. The bar liked it and she liked it herself, and up at the farm she went on with the habit almost unconsciously, putting on the bright red dress or the mauve or some other thing of gay colour and shape without thinking twice about it. And as they sat there in the evenings, the men reading, with their boots off, the old-lady half-dozing, Maudie and Ella knitting and chattering, Rosie would look suddenly up from the newspaper or some interval of mere pre-occupation, and catch the eyes of one or other of the two women travelling in unflickering and minute criticism over the lines and folds of her dress and the big curves of her own body. And it was then that she would feel that there was not only something there which was against her, but something there which must sooner or later come out or be forced out by a chance act or word.

And gradually she knew that it must come. Then when it did come, simultaneously with the spring, she was quite unprepared for it. It was as though the thought of it had never crossed her mind.

CHAPTER II

I

MAUDIE and Ella slept in the south side of the house, and their windows, unobscured by the big chestnut trees, gave a clear view of the road travelling along the open ridge on a course almost parallel with the river. And it was Ella, putting the bedroom curtains straight on an April afternoon after spring-cleaning, who saw Maudie biking up the road with that open-mouthed desperation that she knew by experience of years must mean a sensation.

Open-mouthed, too, she ran downstairs, meeting Maudie on the threshold, her face white under her veil, her breath in great labour.

"What's up? What is it?" Ella said.

"Oh, Ella!" Maudie sat down, and her words when she spoke at last, were pumped in great breaths.

"It's her. It's about her."

"I know," Ella said. "I know."

"Oh, Ella! It's worse than anything – she's got a baby."

Ella stood stunned.

"A what? Not her, not Rosie? *Got* one, d'you say?"

"Well, it's six. It's grown up. I know it's right, I know it's –"

"Means it's – means – oh! gracious Almighty, who told you? How'd you find out? It means it – where is it?"

"That's what I can't find out. It might be dead. But she *had* it."

"Means it's –" Speechless, Ella watched Maudie take off her hat and veil.

"Where's mum?" Maudie said. "*She* might know."

"Last I see of her she was in the wash-house."

At the door, Ella gave her hen-squawk: "Mum! You about, Mum?" answered by the croak of the old lady, and in turn by the shuffle of her feet across the yard.

"Eh? Either on y'call?" she said at the threshold.

"Mum," Ella said. "Mum, where's Rosie?"

"Eh?"

"Where's Rosie?"

"I don't know. I don't follow her about. That all you want?"

"No, Mum. It's about her, Rosie."

"What is?"

"Oh, Mum. Don't talk so loud. Listen. It's about her." Ella and Maudie spoke alternatively, in quick gasps of excitement. "It's about her. Maudie – Oh, Mum! she's got a baby!"

The old lady, hearing it, stood grim.

"Needn't wonder *what* she had."

"That's what I thought," Ella said, "but I never said."

"It's six!" Maudie said. "She had it afore she was twenty. That'd make it six."

"Getting on for seven," Ella said. "That's if it's alive."

And presently the old lady, too, fetched up her thought, the old dark grimness of comment:

"I ain't forgot about her mother."

"I never thought of that!" Ella said.

Maudie stood grim, too, thin-faced. "I ain't thinking about that. I'm thinking about what our Tom'll say. I warrant *he* don't know."

"Know? You think she'd tell him?"

97

"Eh?" the old lady said. "What?"

"I say you think she'd tell our Tom? About it, I mean?"

"Tell him? She'd tell him anything and he'd believe it. He don't see no wrong in her."

And soon, the bitter breath of comment exhausted, they could only stand silent, in horrified wonder, their minds alight with speculation. Maudie, genuinely upset, still sat in the chair, her hat and her veil in her hands, her face thin.

"Somebody's got to ask whether it's true or not," Ella began. "We got a right."

"I can't do it," Maudie said. "I feel bad as it is."

"Eh?" said the old lady. "What?"

"I say somebody's got to ask her whether it's right about having that baby or not," Ella said, raising her voice. "Maudie says she feels bad as it is, so –"

Ella was still speaking when Rosie walked into the kitchen.

Hearing all Ella had to say, she came in and stood stock still, her face very white.

"You talking about me?" she said.

Nobody spoke, and Rosie said, trembling, but very quiet :

"You were fast enough talking when I come across the orchard. I could hear pretty nigh every word you said. You were fast enough talking when I wasn't here."

Ella summoned courage and said :

"We had something to talk about."

"Yes," said Rosie. "I know. I know what it was too."

Maudie and the old lady were grim-lipped and silent. But suddenly Ella burst out :

"Well, is it right? That's all we want to –"

"Don't get over your collar," Rosie said. "It's right."

She stood for a moment after speaking, dead white and silent, whiter even than Maudie, who was now weeping a little, with short snivelling sobs that drove Rosie suddenly to fury.

"My God !" he half-shouted. "What've you got to roar about?"

"I ain't crying for myself," Maudie whimpered, bravely. "I'm crying for you."

"Eh?" said the old lady. "Wha –"

"Shut up !" Rosie shouted.

"Don't you talk to our mother like that," Ella said, dangerously. "It won't pay you. I tell you it won't."

"Who asked you to put your spoke in?" Rosie said. "If you can hold your damn tongue for two seconds, I'm trying to say something myself. You were so fast wanting me to talk, weren't you?"

"Yes, but –"

"Then shut up !"

"All I asked you," Ella persisted, "was whether it was right what Maudie heard, whether it was right you had a baby somewhere."

"I told you once it was right. You might know it was right if _she_ found out." Maudie's sobs welled up afresh, in still more bitter distress, at Rosie's words, but Rosie cried them down : "You were so fast finding out about it. You perhaps won't be so fast shouting about it when you get the kid here."

"Don't you say anything you'll be sorry for," Ella said. "You ain't bringing that child here, not if I know it."

"No?" Rosie said. "No? I'll fetch her tomorrow !"

"Her? Maudie sobbed. "Her?"

My God, what's wrong with that?" Rosie shouted. "I

couldn't help what she was, could I? I couldn't help it at all."

She was breaking down herself now, her tears coming quickly and bitterly and against her will, drowning in a minute all she had to say. With tears of anger running down her face she suddenly rushed across the room and out of it and through the passage and so upstairs.

She was still upstairs when Tom came home from the sheep-pens in the late afternoon. He went up to her. He had come in for a cup of tea and had taken off his boots and she did not hear him coming. Lying on the bed, she had exhausted all her tears.

"Summat up?" Tom said.

He closed the bedroom door and came and stood over the bed. She did not look at him.

"Ella started nagging soon's I got in, but I never took no notice," he went on.

Lying face downwards, she could not see him, but she could feel the unaggressive gentleness of his voice and hardly had he begun to speak before she felt her tears boiling up again.

Enraged, she sat up.

"Crying won't do no damn good !" she sobbed.

"What's up?" he said. "Ain't like you."

"I don't care whether it's like me or not," she wept. "It's done now. They done it this time."

"Done what?"

Suddenly she told him, and she could see his mouth open slightly as he heard about the child. Beyond that he did not move. He stood in a suspense of unbelief.

"Rosie, that ain't right, is it?" he said.

"Go on !" she wept, "say you don't believe me now. I was only a kid. I couldn't – I never –"

"I ain't saying nothing."

"Why d'n' you get on to me, instead of standing there?" she wept.

"It's done, ain't it, Rosie? A lot o' bawling about it won't do no good, will it? Where is it?"

"The kid?" she wept. It's with my aunt in Orlingford."

"Well –"

"I said I'd fetch it, tomorrow. Fetch it here, I mean. For good."

"For good?"

"They were fast enough finding out about it," she said passionately. "They can have it here and see how they like it!"

"I ain't saying nothing," Tom said. "Long as they don't plague the life out o' the boy when he gets here, I –"

"It's a girl!" she flashed. "Why'd the hell they all think it was a boy?" She began to sob again now, out of anger, and the depths of a new wretchedness, working herself up. "Anyway it was a girl the last time I saw it. I ain't seen it for so long and I don't know as I want to – Oh, I ! – Moses – !"

"Here, Rosie, gently." He bent down and put his arm about her with a wooden solidity and strength, comforting her with degrees of tenderness of which she had never believed him capable. "Here, Rosie, gently, gently. I ain't sayin' nothing," he said, "am I?"

II

Inexorable, Rosie fetched the child on the following day. Her aunt, a sister of her father's, did millinery in a front

101

room shop in an Orlingford back street, in a museum of hat-frames and snipped stuffs and ribbon rolls. The child looked thin, in some way stretched out, and white. "She don't eat a mossel o' nothing," the aunt said. Made all the difference, Rosie thought, when you had it to eat. The kid looked starved. "This all the clothes and things she's got?" she said. She felt grim herself, hardened. She picked up the thin chemises and bodices and scanty bits of dresses that lay ready packed in the open black leatherette case. "They're good yet," her aunt said. "Ain't a brack in 'em." Like her father, mean as old Nick ! Rosie shut the leatherette case. The child stood ready. The aunt took off her spectacles. "You'd better give Aunt Ada a kiss," Rosie said. Obedient, almost negative, the child craned her thin neck and kissed the aunt. Her long legs, as she reached up, seemed so gawky and thin that Rosie was touched. The kid was like a skeleton. Suddenly, the close air of the curtain-dark shop with its smell of stuffs and dust choked her and she seized the child's hand. It was thin and cold, nothing but skin and bone. "Well, we'll say good afternoon," she said shortly. Then she remembered something. "I hadn't ought to forget," she said, "but I just forget her name." The aunt said, "I always called her Lily." With grim humour Rosie opened the door. "Another flower in the family," she said, and a moment later she and the child were out of the shop.

It was evening when they reached the farm. They walked. The child was tired. On the way Rosie tried to interest her in things – "The farm's a very big place. Ten or fifteen horses. Pigs, a lot of hens. The primroses are about as nice as they will be now in the woods. You'll like that, shan't you?" but Lily, walking on the grass-edge, only nodded, said "Yes" or murmured in a response that

─lacked all life. "You'll soon get used to it," Rosie said. The child said nothing. What was wrong with the kid? Rosie, in spite, of a lack of affection for the child, felt worried. She glanced sideways at the thin long face as they walked along the ridge. Thin wasn't the word! And looking at her, she would look for a sign of resemblance to herself. She could see nothing. There was nothing of her big, plump, frizzy-haired self in the straight-haired dark child with the bone-white hands and face. She was looking at a stranger. No use trying to think about the father either. She couldn't remember a lot about a commercial who had stayed two nights at The Angel and – oh, cheese it! She'd cried all she was going to cry over that.

And all the time the child walked along as though it had ceased to matter. She began to walk with great effort, wearily, long before they reached the farm. Tired too, Rosie saw the chestnut trees, the house and the tracks with relief, her grimness softening away by the time she led the child by the hand into the kitchen, where Maudie and Ella were waiting.

And while Maudie and Ella waited she took off her gloves and the child stood by on weak legs. Tea was laid. Maudie had put on a Saturday dress, Ella a new pinafore, and they stood ready, as though to take the child.

"Well," Rosie said, "this is her. This is Lily."

She had expected some remonstration, a scene, some kind of snub for the child, something – she did not know quite what. But nothing happened.

"These are the Miss Jefferys," Rosie said, grudgingly. "Ella and Maudie."

The child did not speak. Together, Maudie and Ella stared at her.

103

"Why didn't you take the trap?" Maudie said. "The child looks worn out."

Rosie did not speak. The child stood silent. Rosie put the leatherette bag on a chair. Ella unfolded her arms and said:

"We got the old apple-room ready for her. We thought she could have that."

"Shall I take her up then?" Rosie said.

"I'll take her up," Maudie said.

Maudie took the leatherette bag off the chair with one hand and took the child by the other. "You're cold," she said, with horror. "Ella, boil that kettle up. This child's cold. I expect you want some tea, don't you."

"Yes."

"Could she eat an egg?" Ella said.

The child, uncertain, did not answer. And Maudie said, kindly:

"Aunt Ella says would you like an egg?"

"Yes," Lily said, and a moment later she went with Maudie upstairs.

Five minutes later, when they came down again, Maudie was saying: "You'll try to do what Aunt Maudie says, won't you? Keep your things straight. It's no more trouble to keep your things straight than it is to have them littered all over the place. But I expect they learned you that at school?"

"I haven't been well," the child said. "I haven't been to school a lot."

"Been to Sunday school?"

"No."

"Ttck! Ttck! Well, here's your egg. Do you want salt on it, can you cut it yourself?"

"Yes."

104

"Say please and thank you."

Taking off her hat, Rosie sat down and ate with the child. Ella and Maudie hovered over the table in an attendance of genuine concern, pouring tea, handing plates. Puzzled and tired, Rosie scarcely spoke. Lily, tired also and now nervous at the largeness of the farm kitchen and the sharp rattle of Jeffery voices, could not finish the boiled egg and Rosie finished it for her.

"Anything else you'd like?" Maudie said. "Doughcake?"

"She's tired," Rosie said.

"Bed's her best place," Ella said. "Don't look to me as though she's been getting enough rest."

"Soon as she's washed," Maudie said, "I'll get her off to bed before folks come in."

Folks meant Tom. Rosie said nothing and after a few moments Maudie took Lily upstairs, with Ella calling after them : "I'll bring hot water up in about a minute."

Upstairs in the small bedroom that still smelled with the musty sweetness of old apples, the sun was still shining slantways on the child's undressed figure, made her seem thinner and more stretched out than ever.

Washed, the girl stood at last by the bed, in her night-gown. The nightgown had a hole in it.

"This is best nightgown you got?"

"It's the only one."

"I never did in all my life. I never did."

The child, in a moment, began to climb into bed.

"Don't you say no prayers?" Maudie said.

"No."

"No prayers at all? You won't go to heaven if you don't say your prayers. Don't you *know* a prayer?"

"Our Father which –"

"Our Father."

"Let me hear you say that." Her voice was firm and gentle. "No, kneel down and say it. It's best to kneel down. Aunt Maudie kneels down."

Lily knelt down by the bed and her voice faltered.

"Art in heaven. Well, go on. Hallowed be Thy – Your feet are not very clean," Maudie said. "I never noticed that. That's another thing we must see about tomorrow. Well, ain't you saying it?"

"Thy kingdom come –"

Lily faltered again, there was a silence and finally Maudie began to say the prayer in phrases, so that the child might repeat it after her. "I'll learn you another tomorrow night," Maudie said when it was finished. " 'Gentle Jesus.' I'll learn you that. That's a nice prayer, and very easy."

And downstairs Maudie said to Ella :

"Well, it may be a bad thing in one way, but it's a good thing in another. The child ain't fit to send out. Nightgown ain't fit for a dishcloth. No decent shimmy, her feet not clean. Never been to school. Don't say her prayers. I don't know, I'm sure. What'd you do with them old nightgowns of ourn we put by? They'll cut up. Good thing we saved them. It never does to throw anything away. And what about them vests? Couldn't we undo them and knit them up again? She needs *something*.

III

And gradually, that summer, the child was taken out of Rosie's hands. At first through pity, then out of a fretful fussy kind of affection, Maudie and Ella took charge of her. They cut down for her their old, thick and generous nightgowns of flannel, unravelled the wool of many under-

106

vests and knitted it up again, stitched new dresses out of their own and bought others. Lily would go with them to Sunday school, sit with Maudie among the sopranos of the choir, and treasure her Bible with its pressed flowers of poppy and cowslip and silver paper and bright texts with scenes of Bethlehem and Galilee. She altered physically also. Though she was always thin, with the sharp nose and skimp cheeks and pinched up air, and though Maudie's comment, "Ain't a mossel o' flesh on her, all legs and wing's was always true, she gradually lost the look of fragility. It was only the air of acquiescence that never altered, the feeling that the child was spiritless. Like Jesuits, Maudie and Ella took her and moulded her, the child's mind and will so soft that they could knead and shape it by their words and acts more easily than they could knead and shape their dough for bread. So if Maudie said, believing it herself, "Jesus is watching you all the time, there's nothing. He don't see. It's no use your hiding either. He'd see you even if you hid behind them stacks," the child would believe not only that Christ was all-seeing but that Aunt Maudie was all-knowing too. Her trust in Jesus became great, but not greater than her trust in Aunt Maudie and Aunt Ella. In turn they saw this, and it gave them an odd satisfaction. "Funny how she took to us from the first." And as though feeling, deep-down, that time had almost finished their own chances of making any adventure beyond virginity, they seized upon her as a last hope and as one of their own. All this zeal for the child increased also when they remembered Rosie. Though they never spoke it, the thought was always there in their minds that "Bad as her mother was, that's no reason why the child should be anything like her," and out of it the old jealousy sprang up with righteous vigour, solidifying stoutly into a pillar of care and protection. So that years later they could say with truth and pride in which there was only a trace of asperity, "If we hadn't seen after her, heaven above knows what *would* have happened."

And Rosie let them take her. The child meant so little to her that she regretted bitterly, often and often, ever having fetched her. For that action she was bitter not only against herself but against Tom. "I didn't want her," she would say. "Why'd he take it laying down like that and let me fetch her? He should of gone for me and given me what I asked for." His very goodness of heart enraged her. She saw in him all the solid exemplification of the farm, the steady comfort, the soft, too-rich air, the feeling of earth and earthy things that she could not escape. She longed for something, even anger, to bring him to life. He was never angry. "I ain't saying nothing. Long as nobody interferes with me, I ain't saying nothing." And that lack of all anger in him never brought her own to life. She raged inwardly and was helpless. So much that was solid and essential and natural in the life of the farm seemed to her foolish and infuriating. Nothing but work, work, work. Why didn't he take a rest? One thing after another – lambs and calves and hay and harvest and ploughing and roots and seed-time. Why did it bind him so completely? Why couldn't he break it? What about her? She had a thousand grievances against him that she never spoke.

He in turn had only one grievance. Children – what about that? He rarely spoke of it, but clearly enough the feeling was there with him, and Rosie sensed it. It was the old lady who spoke of it. Deafness kept her world narrow, a world to which she never admitted the child and still less Rosie. "Funny. Been married near enough two year and don't have no children. Eh? I wouldn't say so much if –" Deaf, and having the idea that no one else could hear either, she spoke in a kind of public hen-croak, without secrecy, for all to hear. Relatives strange to Rosie would often drive over from distant villages on summer Sunday afternoons, and for them also the griev-ance would come out, croaked aloud, between pauses of grim lips – "No, been married here two years, and no sign on it. Fast enough having 'em the wrong time, but –" until even Ella and Maudie would quieten her, and Tom would say :

"Mother, I won't have it. Why're you so dead set on her?"

"Dead set on her? I wonder you ain't dead set on her yourself."

"Never you mind me."

"Mind you? I minded you times anew, didn't I? Nussed you for long enough? That's what *she* wants – a little nussing and carrying. Be more like it. Eh? You speak?"

"No. And I don't want talk like that. I won't have it."

"Well, if you won't say summat, other folks must. Enough t'urge anybody to death, both on you."

So that at last, under that constant bitter pressure, Tom was moved to talk of it to Rosie.

"Well," she said, laughing, "I do my best."

"Don't seem hardly good enough."

"Like quarrelling – takes two," she said, good-humour-ed.

"I wouldn't have said nothing," he said, "but Mum keeps on."

"Mum !" Her fury leapt up. "What the hell's it to do

with her? What she think I am? A cow or something?"

"Rosie! Rosie!"

"You're against me, the whole damn lot of you are against me!"

"Nobody's against you, Rosie. I ain't against you."

"You're not *for* me."

"How – what you –"

"If you're for me, why don't you show it?"

"How, Rosie. How d'ye expect me to show it? How –"

"Oh! I don't know. I don't know," she said bitterly. "I don't know what I want at all."

In the end her anger and resentment, her own sense of disappointment and her feeling that they were all against her fused into a single inarticulate misery. The life of the farm, with its solitude and silence, it's rich hummer air, its almost ceaseless work, seemed like a world so complete in itself that it had no outlet. Cut off by some inexplicable barrier from Lily, usurped by Maudie and Ella, half-hated by the old woman, she longed to turn back and escape the way she had come. She half-longed for the pub, for the smell of grass and corn to be replaced again by the smell of beer and smoke, for the fixed existence of the farm to be swept away by the shifting passage of the old bar life. And once or twice during that summer she went back to The Angel, dropping in alone, half hoping to find escape there. But it was no use. It was different. The change in the place was painful, the bar dirty, the class different, and the woman with busts like flat buns and her hands closer than ever on her father seemed almost to resent her coming there. And gradually she gave up going altogether.

BOOK THREE

FRANKIE

CHAPTER I

I

SOMETIMES on winter nights Maudie would light a fire in the parlour – "Jus' so's things shan't get damp" – and the family would sit there. And as on other evenings when they sat in the kitchen, the clack of gossip went on unchanged, Ella crouching by the fire like a cat, Maudie twitching everlasting needles, the old lady munching and straining to listen, Rosie herself bored to silence. A change came only when Maudie, dusting the harmonium with the pinafore she still wore in the evenings, tried the week's anthem over with one finger, labouring hard with her knees to keep the wind going while she found the note with her finger, her knees failing often and the harmonium squeaking like a dying balloon before the note could be born. Until at last she would beg : "Rosie, would you mind coming and play a bar or two over?" and Rosie, glad of anything to break the monotony, would sit on the plush revolving piano-stool and work the pump with her feet and knees and play, very slowly so that Maudie could follow, and pianissimo, in order not to wake Lily in the bedroom above, the notes of the anthem or perhaps of "What a friend we have in Jesus," Maudie's favourite hymn.

And as they sat there one evening in the January of that winter, Maudie squinting at the music copy, Rosie holding the note so that Maudie could hear and find it, Frankie burst into the room, cutting off Ella's horrified : "Not with them boot in here !" with a half-shout :

113

"They're a fire! Orlingford's afire!"

"Oh?" Tom said.

Rosie, excited, leapt up off the stool, the wind dying in the harmonium with a groan.

"Where, where? Who says so? Who told you?"

"You can see it!" Frankie said. "You can see the sky."

He began to lug back the curtains, Maudie shouting, "Not them curtains! I only –" the boy not heeding her, drawing them back at last so that the family could see the black January darkness and the great radiance of the fire glowing orange in the valley.

"Half Orlingford's afire," Frankie said. "I see a chap going by on a bike. He told me."

"That's furnaces," Maudie said. "That's th'iron furnaces."

"Furnaces! Don't be so wet! Furnaces! I'm going down and chance it. Is anybody coming?"

"I got my shoes off," Tom said.

"I'll come," Rosie said. "I'd like to come. I'll come."

"Rosie, you ain't –"

"Shut up, our Maudie! You git a coat, Rosie, while I git the trap!"

A minute later, outside in the dark yard, Rosie could hear the jangle of Frankie harnessing the nag and could see the light of the fire over half the sky. Then as she stood at the stable door, her eyes not accustomed to the darkness, and waited for Frankie, she could smell the fire coming over the damp fields, a wild smoky breath of burning.

"You can smell it, Frankie! Come out here, you can smell it!"

And he came out and stood in the yard with the bridle in his hands and they stood together and breathed at the night air, catching the smell of burning in sudden waves. Then Frankie ran back and threw the bridle over the nag and brought him from the stable, half-running. In another minute they were driving out of the farmyard, not seeing until they were already far down the road, beyond the farm, that Frankie had forgotten the lamps. And then it no longer mattered. "Go on! Go on!" Rosie urged. "What's the matter! What's a lamp? You can see to read a book!" And Frankie drove wildly, the horse smelling the fire and frightened, the glow in the sky widening and brightening terribly until the night-clouds were like red smoke over the town and Frankie and Rosie could see the black river shining red and tawny in the meadows below. And soon, before ever they reached Orlingford, they could see each other's faces, stark in the strange light, and the horse's ears cocked up with fear like the steeple above the town, and the fields and the road as clear as though under a stark moonlight. The stink of smoke came stronger. From yellow their hands grew orange finally a smoky crimson in the strange lit-up darkness.

In Orlingford they could get no farther than the bridge. The fire roared across the roofs and the whole street was alight. Houses were smoking just beyond The Angel. And suddenly Rosie saw the frantic running of figures to and from the door of the bar, figures carrying chairs and tables and boxes, her father among them. And after that she remembered nothing but a frantic running to and fro herself, carrying furniture, shouting to her father, gabbling desperately to Frankie. Voices shouting and jabbering. "It'll be all right if the wind turns!" meant nothing to her. From the first moment she had a feeling, an odd tight secret feeling of her own, that the pub was doomed. She ran and worked like an automaton, feeling nothing but that, so sure of it that when at last the pub was burning like the end of a great torch above the river she had no surprise or even regret. She could only stand with Frankie and stare, worn out, the sweat drying cold on her body, and wonder vaguely where her father was. "Frankie, you go and look for him," she entreated. "Tell him I want him," she entreated. "Tell him I want him. Tell him I want to know where he's going." She spoke quite calmly. It was only when she had lost sight of Frankie in the mass of people jammed across the bridge that her fears sprang up, fears which she had not time to explain before Frankie was back and which rushed from her then with an unexpected fervour that was almost desperation :

"Where have you been? I thought I'd lost you. I thought I'd lost you."

"He's down at the end of the bridge."

"Oh ! All right, all right, only don't go away again. Stay here. Don't go away again."

And still later, with the pub still burning through the skeleton of the roof and the river still softly hissing with falling sparks :

"What time is it? Let's go home. We can't do anything. Let's go home."

Driving back in the midnight blackness, Frankie would halt the trap and they would lean back and look again at the glow of the fire. And up there, on the deserted road shut in by the deserted fields, it seemed as though they were in another world. They hardly spoke. Driving on again, they could still smell the smoke of the fire in the cold air, but in front of them nothing of the glow was visible, only the still blanket of absolute darkness over the sleeping country, without a prick of light at all. And

Rosie, now that the crazy tension had passed, sat in a mood of abandoned relief. "Don't drive so fast," she begged. "There's no hurry." And Frankie let the nag fall into a walk, and it was well on into morning before she got down to open the gate of the yard under the still chestnut trees so that Frankie could drive quietly through.

And having driven in quietly they were quiet in the stable and quieter than ever as they went into the house. They did not speak and in the dark house only Rosie's soft breathing broke the silence. From the kitchen Rosie, a little cold after the drive, groped her way to the parlour, the room dark except for the tiny fire-glow. Behind her she could hear Frankie searching in the kitchen for matches, then the rattle of the matchbox and finally the noise of his feet coming along the passage towards her. At the door he spoke : "Where are you? Rosie?" and she answered his quiet voice with a whisper : "Here, here I am," a whisper almost of excitement. Then she heard him strike the match and saw the flame burn up and then go out again. "Don't light the lamp," she said. "There's no need. Don't light the lamp." She heard him move about in the darkness, then felt him come towards her. She was standing by the fireplace, her coat undone, her hat off. He was coming towards her with his hands outstretched a little, groping, and suddenly she put hers out, too, and touched him. "Steady, here I am. Don't knock anything, don't make a noise." In a moment she was catching hold of his hands.

"Rosie," Frankie said. "Rosie, Rosie."

Almost in fear, she stood motionless. Jesus, what was up? And in a moment she knew what was up. His hands were trembling so hard that he could not hold them still. Frankie," she said. "Oh, Frankie! You silly kid," and

117

except for the sound of his own voice murmuring in answer it was the only sound between them except the sound of her breathing, quicker now, almost desperate, as he ran his hand over hers and her arms and across her full breasts. She stood for a time in a weakness of sudden ecstasy, trembling. Jesus, how was it she – ? Then suddenly her strength rushed up. She caught hold of Frankie passionately in the darkness, and he held her with sudden fierceness in the silence, for a long time.

It was a silence broken by feet on the landing above and then by the creak of stairs as someone came down. Standing still, together, in the almost fierce silence, they waited without moving for the feet to come down and the chink of candlelight to lower and enlarge and brighten.

The light widened and halted at last. Frankie knelt down, untying his boots. Rosie stood quiet, breathless, hooking her dress.

Above and behind the candlelight Maudie stared and moved her grim lips:

"Oh! You are back." She held the candle forward and higher, so that its light fell on them more brightly. "I just *wondered.*"

CHAPTER II

I

"Put your left hand farther along. Farther. You ain't holding it straight. You can't look through a telescope like that. Rosie, oh ! Rosie, you ain't looking. Rosie."

"Lie down. I don't want to look."

"You said you wanted to look."

"Come here. Lie down. There's better things to do than look through telescopes."

It was the beginning of a new existence, the end of an old. In Orlingford the skeleton of the pub's roof stood like a broken ship, the timbers charred to strips of funereal silk. On market days, when Rosie went past, she could see the ruined bedroom she had slept in almost all her life, the blue wallpaper singed and naked to the street, the door blackened and crooked on its hinges. Already, early that spring, houses were going up again after the fire, rows of yellow-bricked uniform houses in drilled lines along the high causeways, all ugly to see, the brick bilious. Only the pub stood derelict. Standing at the water edge, beyond the bridge, it still remained like a wreck thrown up and upturned.

And with the pub, for Rosie, something else had gone. While it remained some chance of escape remained. The pub was a kind of comfort. If something should happen, if the life of the farm should break up or change or in some way reject her, there was always the pub. For more than a year she had used it as an excuse. "I'll just drop into The Angel for five minutes," or "I'll just walk down to

The Angel," or "Tom, let's go down to The Angel for an hour and pass the time away." And now that also was cut off. Not only the pub, but all it stood for. She felt it bitterly. It was something she could not express in words. She could not even gauge it. Just under the skin she felt a current of bitterness, of anger she could not explain, of vicious misery for something lost. On top of it all she felt reckless. The old passion for escape sprang up afresh, but now in earnest. It was no longer a mere fretting for something without knowing what or why it was, but a new ache, conscious and positive, a longing for some mad counter action to the passionless sour life of Maudie and Ella, the narrow pinch-gut life of the farm, narrow and pinched for all its richness. And after the night of the fire she had never any doubt about what act it should be, or what course it should take. She went straight into it deliberately, her eyes open, her passion from the first more reckless than Frankie's, she careless where he at first hung back. "Did Maudie see? Did she notice, d'ye reckon?" he said. "Damn Maudie!" she said, wildly. "What do I care?" From the first she was a challenge to him. Didn't he dare? By God, he wasn't frightened, was he? Then in a minute, seeing that he was half afraid, she would pity his fear, be tender with him, warm and ease him with words which were all feeling, the full flowing rich feeling that welled strongly from her heart like oil.

Then there were times when, knowing how far the eyes of Maudie and Ella could see, she was almost afraid herself. But it was a savage fear, a kind of nervous rage against them in her heart. "If Maudie watches me about like that much more I'll give her something to watch for!" Then to Frankie, with almost savage tenderness: "And you too. By God, don't look at me across the dinner-table like that again. I can't stand it. Frankie, don't look at me like that again."

From the first they could hardly meet. For all her recklessness, she knew it quite well. The farm was big, the stacks and the barns seemed to be hiding-places, but Maudie and Ella or the old woman were for ever prowling round the corner. And there was scarcely any splitting up of the family. Where one was, the rest must be. On the other hand, the farm must never be left. So if Maudie went to chapel in the morning, Ella went in the evening, and the farm, for all its sleepiness, never broke the rhythm of its life. Something was always happening, somebody always moving, everything ordered. There could be no secrecy.

"Ain't there somewhere we could go? For five minutes?"

"Might try the loft. Above the big barn. I s'll be sorting seed taters there s'afternoon."

"All right. Anywhere so's we can meet a minute. Anywhere."

And Rosie would go up to the loft, secretly, only to find Tom there, or Maudie, or even the old woman. It was the same in the stables, behind the stacks, in the cart-hovels. There was never secrecy for a second.

So she startled Frankie's heart into great bounds of fear by saying at dinner one Sunday :

"I'm always hearing a lot about Frankie's telescope. But I never had a look through it yet. When do folks get a chance?"

"Oh, Frankie's jealous of his telescope," Maudie said.

"Never let's me look," Ella said. "Afraid folks'll drop it or something. That was our Dad's telescope," she prattled

121

on, "he used to watch folks in the field, trespassers. Catch 'em an' all. I remember – "

"You're going to let *me* look?" Rosie said, "ain't you?"

His heart almost still, Frankie could say nothing.

"See," Maudie said, "he don't let nobody look."

"Oh, he'll let me look!" Her voice was soft, offhand. Underneath the table Frankie clenched his hands like iron. "I'm his sister, after all, ain't I?"

"Sister!" Tom roared. "That's a good 'un. Sister. Like as two peas in a pod, too! Ha! Ha!"

"She means in-law," Maudie said.

"Eh?" The old lady, fearful of missing something, and the laughter in all faces but Frankie's, leaned forward, cupping her ear, and Tom bawled:

"Rosie says she's Frankie's sister. About as like as two peas in a pod, I says. Ha! Good 'un, aint it?"

"Eh? Nothing funny in that, is they?"

"What? Nothing funny, eh?" Tom roared. "Nothing funny? 'Bout as good a bit as I heard this turn! Ha!"

Then when the new wave of laughter had passed, Rosie said: "Don't say you ain't going to let me look now?" Her voice almost bantering, as though the telescope were childish.

"All right," Frankie said.

"When? This afternoon? Sure nobody's intruding?"

"Sisters allus welcome!" Tom roared. "Long as they don't upset my nap. Ha!"

And somehow, what with Tom's laughter and her own off-hand manner, it passed off as she had wanted it to pass off, as something not quite serious, so that afterwards, if she seemed bored, Tom would say, "Loose-end? Whyn't go up and have a look through Frankie's spy-glass? Ha !" Or if she were missing : "No telling where Rosie is. Lookin' through Frankie's spy-glass, shouldn't wonder !"

And that Sunday afternoon, after Ella and Maudie and Lily had cycled off to Sunday School, she went up to Frankie's room quite openly, even calling to Tom as she went, "I'm only going up to Frankie's room. Just to try that that wonderful telescope", her heart beating wildly in spite of it, all her banter dropping away the instant she opened Frankie's door and found him there by the window, hands clenched as she sat on the bed, with the telescope beside him. "Oh ! Frankie, Frankie !" she said then, "Frankie", and for a time they sat together on the bed in the anguish of joy and relief, not speaking, the spring, sunlight just warm on the bed, the spring afternoon golden and sharp outside, a March cloudlessness everywhere, the telescope forgotten. Rosie had on a dress of plum red, with a high neck and big sleeves, that hooked down the back, and Frankie began to try to undo it, fretting and trembling at the hooks, until at last, without a murmur, she undid it for him, slipping out her arms and letting the dress fall away from her to the waist, so that her neck and arms and chest were naked, her breasts like strong pears under the white bodice, the fine nipples thrust up to him. When he kissed her the breasts were a challenge to him, her mouth was open, soft and moist, and she locked him against her with soft big arms that had in them a power of strength and passion that took him altogether by surprise. And she, in turn, seemed to feel that he hung back, that he was not ready for her. "You wanted me to come?" she said. "You want me, don't you?" But even when he said "Yes" she was not sure. It seemed as though she were too strong for him. "They won't come." she said. "Nobody'll

come. It's all right, Frankie. Nobody'll come," and she let
herself go completely, tenderness transfusing her passion
until he, too, was overcome and began to kiss her breasts
and take her at last.

It was only afterwards that they went through the
pantomime of the telescope, pretending : "Put your hand
farther along, farther. You can't look through a telescope
like that," when Rosie, holding the glass to her eyes saw
for a moment the distances of the valley lose their spring
brightness, the horizon rainbowed and misty, she threw
the telescope on the bed again and said : "Come here. Lie
down. There's better things to do than look through telescopes."

And it was while she still lay there holding him, but
only after what seemed a long time, that she heard the old
lady's voice, a mere croak in the passage below.

"Lie still !" she whispered. "For God's sake, lie still."

Listening and lying still, they heard the clop of feet,
then the voice.

"Rose, Rose !"

"It's you she wants."

"Be quiet ! Listen !"

The feet were on the stairs, coming up, the voice rising
with them. "Rose, Rose !" The hostile single syllable that
the old lady always used, the name skinned of all friend-
liness.

"She knows, she knows !" he whispered.

"Shut up !"

"Rose ! You there?"

He struggled up, and then Rosie, hearing the voice
again, felt panic too.

"Hook my dress. Quick !"

And while she slipped her arms back into the dress and

'smoothed the stuff with her hands and Frankie hooked her up, Rosie called:

"You want something? What is it?"

"Somebody called to see you."

"Me?"

"Eh?" The footsteps had ceased.

"Wants me?"

"Somebody came hammering front door and I went and he says he wants to see you."

"I'm coming." She could feel the old woman waiting, suspicious. "Smooth the bed. Quick. Frankie, Frankie." She smoothed her hands over her bust and arms and waist for the last time and called, "I'm coming!"

"'Nation long time."

Rosie opened the bedroom door and went out on the landing upright and neat. Halfway up the stairs stood the old lady, waiting and listening.

"Who it is?" Rosie said. "You sure it's me they want?"

"Eh?"

"You're sure it's me?" She felt furious, her tenderness snapped in half, the course of her passion changed to hatred. Eh? Blimey, pretending not to hear. And all the time stand there catching every damn whisper! She half-ran downstairs, saying in a loud voice as she went, "You be careful you don't slip backwards!" her heart black.

"Eh! Tom's asleep," the old lady croaked. "Clattering about," and then upstairs, still suspicious: "You still telescoping or summat, up there?"

Unheeding, Rosie went on downstairs and through the house, to the front door.

"Oh! It's you is it?"

Under the porch, in a check suit and bowler hat, stood her father.

"What do *you* want?" Her resentment at the breaking up of her passion rushed up now against him.

"Thought I just drop in."

"Oh, did you?"

"Things ain't too sparklers."

"I thought you were after *something*."

She stood fully in the doorway, rather proud in her anger, her cheeks flushed, her eyes splendid with resentment.

"Well?"

"The shoe's pinching, Rosie. They ain't going to rebuild the pub."

"No?" That too angered her. Why shouldn't they rebuild it? "Why not?"

"Dunno. Say it ain't worth it. Trade gone down or something."

"What was wrong with the trade? It *used* to be all right. Who killed it?"

"Dunno. All I know –"

"Don't talk out the back of your neck. You know who killed it."

Turk stood sheepish. "Well, it's gone somewhere, and they ain't going to rebuild."

"Well, what can *I* do?"

Nervous of her, he took off his bowler and wiped the sweat off the inside band.

"Help your old dad, can't you?"

She stood silent, splendidly arrogant, showing no sign.

"I got nowhere, y'know, Rosie. Nothing."

"I thought you were living with Aunt Ada?"

"She wants summat."

"You got *nothing*?" she challenged. "You mean to say you saved *nothing*?"

He did not answer and it was only out of the hardness of knowledge, of long experience with him, and bitterness, that she persisted :

"You can stand there like that and say you saved *nothing*? Can you?"

"Well, it's gone."

"So you come up here to see if I can feed and clothe you for nothing, eh? Is that it?"

"Well, not exactly," Turk said. "I want a job. Work."

"Work!" Funny! Her father working! Turk, who'd never done a decent stroke in his life! "You?" she said. "What can you do?"

"I'm good with horses."

"Very!"

Bitter as she was, she broke into a roar of laughter, her strong white teeth shining, her voice sounding richly over the farm. And while she stood laughing and her father waited, discomfited, Tom came out sleepily from the parlour in his shirtsleeves and stockinged feet, with his thumbs in his braces.

"What's a' matter?"

Half asleep, his hair shocked up, his bootless feet splayed a little, Tom looked quite old. She wondered in that moment what she had ever seen in him. She was caught up by a great rush of new bitterness.

"Oh! you'd better talk to him!" she flashed.

Tom came forward, hands in his breeches tops now, to lean on the door-post.

"What's up, Mus' Perkins? Trouble?"

"Down on me luck," Turk said.

Rosie flounced off into the house, her head up. Luck! Horses! By God, why'd she ever marry into this house? The chaps she could have had! The chances! She began to lay tea in the parlour, dragging out the big mahogany table so that the feet rattled, brandishing the cloth, clattering the cups. "Early gettin' tea, ain't y'?" the old lady croaked. Talk to yourself! Furious, Rosie stormed into the kitchen. The fool she was, oh! the fool she had been. Where was Frankie? She stood on the threshold of the back door, looking out over the still sunlit yard, her heart full. In the spinney, blackthorn was beginning to shine snow-white against the gold flower-clouds of sallow and hazel. She wanted a word with Frankie. She walked out into the farmyard, into the sunlight, shading her eyes with her hand. A moment. Not seeing him, seeing only the dry empty March world and hearing only the thrushes breaking the hollow Sunday silence, she almost called. Then, quite suddenly, full up, she turned and went into the house, and it was only then that she remembered that he might still be in his room. She ran upstairs, hearing her father and Tom still talking by the door. But the room was empty, the bed smooth, the telescope neat on the dressing table, as though nothing had happened.

Half an hour later, at tea, she felt that for a word or a look she could have cried. Somehow, that Sunday, the table seemed extra full, the prattling of Maudie and Ella extra loud, the talk more stupid. She could not look at Frankie. Tom had invited her father to stay for a cup of tea and that too infuriated her. Why should he come sponging? To have him sponging all his life and then when – Why should he come with his lies and his sponging and his wheedling? Why should he? By God why should he?

"Mus' Perkins tells me he's handled horses, Frankie," Tom said.

"Never handled a horse in his life," Rosie said.

"Ain't I?" Turk said. "I was under-groom to Lord St. John two year – afore your time though."

"It would be."

She stirred her tea savagely, in silence, and Tom went on :

"What dy'e think, Frankie? Summer's comin' on and I reckon extra pair of hands wouldn't be in the way, would it?"

"Too many damn folks about this place already!" Rosie flashed.

"Rosie !" The family came down on her in a broken chorus. "Rosie ! Sunday an' all."

"Sunday be damned !"

She sat through tea without another word. Wretched at heart, she listened without a protest to her father wheedling the Jefferys – "Don't seem to have had no luck since Rosie's mother died. Then Rosie gits married. Then the pub gits burnt down. What with one thing and another . . ." Oh ! let them, if they were such fools, let them ! It was all she could do to nurse in silence her own inexplicable wretchedness.

After tea, she missed Frankie again. Ella and Lily cycled off to chapel and Tom, with Maudie and his mother, still sat in the parlour, talking with Turk. The cows had long since come in, the cowman gone home again. Rosie walked across the orchard. Everywhere there was a rousing-up after winter, the earth in the fields almost white from wind and sun, the catkins honey-bright in the spinney, the thrushes singing high up against the cold blue evening sky. She walked round the stack-yard and back through the big barn and the stables, halting at odd places, whistling quietly. But Frankie never appeared.

129

Back in the orchard, there was nothing she could do. She stood for a moment under the bare trees, at a loss. Then, as a last hope, she walked down through the spinney. Under the trees it was almost dark, the earth black, the young primroses flaring everywhere like pale fires. Walking down the path she halted at the stile and leaned on it, smelling the strong primrose air. She put her hands on the high stile and then her head in her hands. And almost without knowing it, she began to cry. Her tears flowed with bitter quietness, her big body listless and scarcely moving. Never in all her damned days had she cried for anybody, never in – She cried until even her anger no longer meant anything, until she was drained of everything but the bottom dregs of wretchedness.

And while she stood there crying, Turk had gone from the house and Tom to the gate to see him off, and in the parlour Maudie was saying to Ella :

"Don't you think she's a bit hard on him? You think she'd show a *little* Christian charity to her father, wouldn't you? – if he *is* her father."

I I

By midsummer Maudie was suspicious. "I know," she would think, "I seen 'em !" From her bedroom she could look down on the fields and the farmyard. Fingers itching at the curtains, she would watch for the flutter of Rosie's dress among the thickening trees and for Frankie to follow it, her anger at seeing them almost joy. If Rosie appeared and Frankie did not come she would twitch the curtains into place and flatten bitterly her already ironed-out lips and think in consolation : "Well, if he ain't there, he ain't *far* off. If I don't see 'em *Somebody* does. And One they little think. *He* sees 'em." She crept about the place on quiet feet, standing often to listen. She gained a sour but precious joy from the sound of her voices together. Little acts of significance electrified her, a glance of Frankie's, a wave of Rosie's hand. "Waving hands. *That* don't mean no good, I know." In the afternoons Rosie walked into the orchard and set the corn-bucket down on the grass and clapped her hands for the hens to come, raising her voice in a loud "Chucka! Chucka!" that echoed back from the spinney and the barricade of barns and down across the fields. At that hour Frankie would be fetching the cows up, raising his voice "Hup! Hup! there! Coo-ah! Coo-ah! Hup! Hup there! Hup!" and the exchange of voices echoing one against another in the afternoon silence would charge the moment for Maudie with new significance. "They don't call for nothing, I know."

And lastly, and with real anger, she would think of Tom. "Ain't he got sense enough to know? Don't he see 'em?" She went about in a continual angry anxiety. She ached to tell him, the perfect moment for telling him for some reason never realized. "I know, I seen 'em," she would think. "But if I could *catch* 'em." Then she would go about in fear that Tom, or perhaps Ella or even her mother, might catch them before her. She would lie awake in the almost never dark summer nights and think of it. Hearing strange sounds, she would interpret them according to her thoughts and her mood of bitterness or anger or shame. "No telling," she would lie and think, "no telling but what this *minute* she's –" and she would listen with her ears strained towards Frankie's room – "no telling but what they –" until with a dry snap of horror she would break off her thoughts and try at last to sleep. All the time it was something she kept altogether to herself, not even

131

Ella sharing it, nor her mother. "I'll tell 'em as soon as I can *prove* it." And she would lie awake in the midsummer warmth and silence and wonder how proof would finally come and what form it would take. "Like or not I shall catch 'em redhanded. And then –"

One night she dropped to sleep against her will and woke later, startled. The wind had risen. She thought for a moment that the noise of it was the noise of someone walking about the house. She sat up in bed, listening. Even when she knew it must be the wind, she still sat there, straining her ears, her mouth tight, her breath coming in uneasy gasps. Finally she got out of bed. "I'll just see. I ain't so sure even now." Her eyes on Ella, curled up like a cat on the far edge of the bed, she opened the door a thin crack, holding the breast of her night-gown with one hand on the door with the other. She listened : no sound but the wind, nothing. But something made her open the door wider, go out on the dark landing and listen again. The wind made noises that went all through the house, echoing. Then after a moment she walked along the landing, the floor-boards creaking under her slow feet. Frankie's door lay at the farthest end of the landing and as she went towards it she came suddenly to a dead stop, startled by some sound behind or below her. "I ain't so sure even now." Going on, she came to Frankie's door and stood by it for a long time, listening. Almost in horror she thought : "Supposing she –" one part of her mind instantly cutting off the hope of the other, until, finally, she put her hand on the latch and lifted it. It snapped up in the darkness before she could control it, the iron click like a shot, her heart leaping up with it.

She tried to stop. It was too late. And she heard the whisper of Frankie's voice :

"What? – Who is it?"

She stood in a sickness of terror, trembling, not knowing what to do or say.

"Rosie, is it you? Rosie?"

Mechanically Maudie opened the door a little wider, and said : "It's me, Maudie. Your door was a-banging in the wind and I couldn't get off, the words running off her tongue almost as quickly as her feet scurried her back along the dark landing.

In bed she lay trembling, her heart thumping. "What I said all the way along. He thought it was her. What I said all the way along. What I thought." Her mind had only the single thought, repeated in an endless rhythm. She lay triumphant but shocked. She knew, but – Turning, lying on her face, she tried vainly to think of some Biblical utterance to fit it all, but the recurrent whisper of Frankie's voice, alert and astonished, asking "Rosie, is it you, Rosie?" shattered the structures of all other thought. She turned and lay on her back, shocked, her face burning with excitement, and then over and on her face again, in a suffocation of too much emotion.

Until at last Ella stirred and threw back her hands and woke :

"Ain't you been sleep?"

"No." The desire to confide in Ella sprang up but went unfulfilled, and Ella said :

"Hommacking about. Why can't you lay still?"

"I thought I heard somebody about." Should she tell her? What if – "Somebody going downstairs."

"It might be Rosie's father." Ella said. "I reckon I heard him one night."

"Him? Can't he sleep? What's he? –"

Before she had finished speaking Ella was asleep again

and in the silence Maudie lay occupied with the new thought. Turk? Why should he prowl about? That summer Turk had come finally to live with them. At first he had come to work, as odd job man, cleaning the stables oiling the harness, chopping the kitchen wood, sleepy-blooded in all he did. Maudie remembered him panting to Tom : "Ain't as though I was a young un. A colt. I'm fifty. Another thing – a bit of exertion, Tom boy, anything sudden, and I might be a dunner. Heart." Then taking in the kitchen wood, he would sit down for a moment, his big face like an over-juicy plum, and talk to the women as they cooked or made the bread. "Never known what home was. Bread like that, now. Never seen bread like that. Starch and hair oil, if we got as much as a yesterday's crust at the pub, and a bit o' dripping we was lucky. Another thing. I ain't bin well for years. Heart as big as two. Rush for a train, and Moses, I might drop down." And the women took to him, pitying. They saw him as a creature of fate, as one deprived of marital and maternal comforts, a big orphan. "It seems a *shame*. No decent life. And only half well." So he got into the habit of appearing in the kitchen on baking days, and Maudie would set aside a loaf for him. Then Maudie remembered him saying, excusing himself : "You ladies won't mind if I don't come in? The seat o'me trousers is half out. The last I got." And Maudie was full of pity and succour. "Oh ! I'm sure our Frankie's got a pair he's done with, or if they ain't big enough we got a pair o' Dad's. He was a bigger man. Not your size, but we could let 'em out." All the spring he had lived with Ada, his sister in Orlingford, walking to the farm day by day. Then as hay-time came on and work began earlier and went on till darkness Ella said : "It makes my heart *grieve* to see him. No sooner home than he's back again. And so hot, panting down that road. And the rooms we got, surely we could give him one?" And so by midsummer Turk was established.

But as Maudie lay in bed, her heart still thumping, the old pity for him was charged with suspicion. She lay wide awake, her nerves stretched. The sound of the wind seemed very often like the sound of feet – Turk's feet, perhaps, going downstairs? Who knew? That was it. You never knew. Prowling about – you couldn't trust nobody, nowhere. Then she would lie and listen and think in the softer key of concern and pity. Supposing he was bad? His heart was bad. If he was bad in the night and nobody to help him? What then? What time was it? It must be one o'clock, past. The worst time for folks, the lowest ebb. Lying in the darkness, she could hardly bear to think of him in trouble or pain, and even the thought of Frankie receded.

Then as she lay thinking, troubled, she caught the unmistakable crack of the wooden stairs beyond the landing, the cracks repeated and diminishing. She sat up, cautious. "I bin had once," she thought. "I bin fool enough for one night." But after a minute she slipped out of bed, her thin legs as white as her long nightgown, and went to the door. "I'll jus' make sure." And opening the door she saw weak rays of candlelight coming from downstairs, throwing up the shadows of the stair-rails.

"That's *somebody*. No mistake. *Her* perhaps. Excited, she opened the door and stepped out. In an instant she was back in the bedroom, searching on the floor for a stocking to tie round her waist. "Be decent. In case it *is* him." She tied the stocking round her nightgown like a black girdle, her hands fumbling.

Going downstairs, she was trembling. The light was in

the kitchen. Half suspicious and now almost frightened, she halted in the passage. Turk's shadow lay in the shape of a stooping tree on the kitchen wall, and a moment later she saw Turk himself. He was at the cupboard, beyond the fireplace. He was searching for something. He had something in his hand as Maudie walked in, but what it was she never saw. Her voice staggered him. He shut the cupboard door as though her "What you up for, Mister Perkins?" had shot him.

"Moses, you frit me."

She was sorry at once. In the candlelight he looked as white as his night-shirt, his heavy eyes scared.

"I didn't mean – I heard somebody about and –" She looked at his white face more closely. "You don't feel very grand?"

"That's what I come down for."

His night-shirt was short, so that she could see his legs. She took an almost scared look at the thick hair on the naked flesh before looking swiftly up at his face again.

"You ain't – you ain't going to be bad, are you?"

"Moses, I'm –" Turk stood limp, his body a flabby balloon of white. "You ain't got no – nothing – no –"

"Brandy?" she said.

"Ah!" He ran one hand over his hair, weakly. "Anything. Whisky or anything. It's me heart."

"I'll see," she said. "I'll get it."

As she went by him to the cupboard she was conscious for the first time of her condition, her night-gown. A current of altogether unknown emotion ran up her body, a spasm of fear that was almost pleasure. A good thing she remembered the stocking. With the stocking she was –

"I often git it," Turk said. "At nights."

She took the whisky bottle from the cupboard and set it on the table by the candle before answering.

"Good thing I heard you," she said. "No telling what –"

"Bin like it for years," Turk said. "Since *she* died. Y'see, sleeping by yourself, that makes a difference. A man don't –"

As she set the glass on the table, her hand trembling, Turk stretched out to take the bottle and the brushing of sleeves almost paralysed her, so that the wineglass spun and staggered on its slender stem.

"I should git a bigger glass," Turk said. "Summat as won't tip over."

"Perhaps I'd better."

Reaching up to the cupboard for the tumbler she felt quite weak, and she pressed herself against the table edge, holding herself rigid, while Turk poured himself the whisky.

"You have a drop?" he said.

"Oh ! no, not me. Not me. I'm a –"

"Signed the pledge?"

"Yes."

She watched the rise of the pale gold whisky in the glass, afraid for a moment to look at Turk himself.

"Water?" she said. "You want water?"

"No. Don't do you no good wi' water."

He drank. Concerned, she watched his heavy chest panting and his heavy neck bulging with the effort of drinking.

"Any better?" she said as he finished drinking. "Feel any better?"

"Bit." He looked at her, licking his lips. "You look a bit dicky yourself. Did I fright you?"

"A little. I –"

"You have a drop. Go on. Here –"

"Oh ! no, no. No –"

He was pouring whisky into the wineglass before she could protest, saying at the same time, his voice louder : "I'd put a drop o' water in. Water it down. It'll do you – Here –"

"I shan't drink it," she said. "No, I can't. I shan't drink it."

"It's medicine." He turned to the sink and held the wineglass under the water tap and then went to her. "You know the pledge don't count if it's medicine." He was talking more loudly now. "Eh, Maudie, you know that, don't you?"

"Sssh !" she whispered. "Don't talk so loud. Sssh !"

"Moses, I forgot," he whispered.

The sudden lowering of his voice and the effect of hearing him speak her own name sent her whole body weaker than ever. A faintness of fear that was also excitement ran through her. She stood chilled and faint, her bare feet cold, the rough nightgown pricking her skin.

"I'd have it if I was you," Turk said, "and then git back to bed."

She took the wineglass without thinking or speaking. Drinking, she had no sensation but the sweetness of the whisky until she felt the warmth of response it excited in her throat and chest. As she drank, Turk filled up his glass. In a moment they were drinking together, the whisky seeming to burn her slightly, deep down, under the tightened stocking, just below her breast.

"Here we stand," she marvelled in a sudden whisper. "Boozing."

Turk laughed. "Look well if somebody come."

"Don't you talk so loud then !" she whispered. "In *case* they do !"

"I forgot."

They stood in silence, nightgowns yellowish in the candlelight, Turk's lips wet and shining, her own dissolved by the whisky into a slightly parted line.

"It burns you," she said.

"What does? Oh ! – feel better?" He reached out, took the bottle and filled up her glass again. "Didn't I tell you you'd feel better?"

"Yes. Do you?"

"A bit. But whisky ain't everything."

She had no sensation that her body, inside, was being burnt up. She felt a fierce vein of pleasure from her throat downwards. Her heart itself was on fire. Her lips had fallen slightly open, and she felt she could not shut them again.

"Whisky ain't everything," Turk said again.

She did not speak. Her lips seemed to have fallen under a paralysis.

"Is it?"

Suddenly she conquered the immobility of her mouth and said, hardly knowing it, almost laughing at the same time :

"Funny, us being down here."

"Yeh !"

They were laughing together, almost soundlessly, as Turk moved round the table and stood heavily against her, the movement of his body flickering the candle-flame.

"You know what I mean, eh?"

"What?" She was trembling in a conflict of extreme, almost fierce pleasure and fear, transfixed, her mind weak. Turk, though so near, seemed a great way off.

"You know what I said? Whisky ain't everything?"

Maudie did not speak and suddenly Turk stretched out his hands and ran them down her thighs, smoothing the nightgown against the flesh. She wanted to scream out. It was as though her legs were dissolving away. All she could think was "The stocking. I'm all right if he don't touch the stocking", the thought finally dissolving away also, leaving her with nothing but a sensation of weak sublimity coupled with a far-off idea that she ought to move or speak in protest.

Instead she did nothing. Her mouth parted, but she did not speak. It was Turk who moved and spoke, pressing her back against the table, whispering : "You're all right. I shan't hurt you. You're all right. I got you. You're all right."

I I I

NEXT day the big meadow was mown, the grass in a maze of pale green circles, the sun white hot. The family moved across the field like a small platoon, drilling with rakes, the line at the diagonal. It was the women who fell slightly away, Rosie behind Maudie and Ella, the old woman last, in a world of feeble rhythms all her own. Working together, not speaking, Frankie and Tom were leaders, Turk coming behind them, wearing a sweat-stained shirt, trousers and panama of Alf Jeffery's. "I'll git you a hat," Maudie had said that morning. "You want something on your head. I don't like to see you —" Then, "All right after last — You know?" Turk had said, but Maudie signalled him to silence, too overcome to speak. And in the field, caught up in a vortex of heat and altogether staggering emotion, she was almost overcome to think. She could

140

only work her arms in automatic obedience to the family
pattern and move mechanically across the hot grass,
looking from Turk to Frankie and from Frankie to Rosie,
and wonder at them almost as much as she wondered at
herself and what she had done.

Whenever he saw her uplifted face and her gaze
swivelling blankly over to him Frankie's heart would stop
dead. His rake seemed to move of its own accord. The way
the glance swivelled away again roused him to inward
panic. His fear crystallized to something tight and brittle,
to an emotion so highly charged that he felt that it would
explode and shatter him. Frightened, he would move his
rake faster, without knowing it. "Gittin' on with it?" Tom
said. Frankie could not answer, but mechanically he
slowed down, his fingers glued in his hands. And then,
after an interval, he would look up again, and now at
Rosie. Once she made signals with her lips. In fear he
made signs back to her, little shakes of his head. She
opened her mouth, questioning, troubled. Her face was
very brown, the skin of her arms golden, almost wheat-
coloured. She had on an old blouse of washed-out cotton,
with a black belt. He could scarcely look at her face, but
only at the blouse, tight over her strong breasts, and the
belt. She had filled out, got stronger. In the sun, she
looked splendid. It was an agony to see her.

When Tom called a halt it was almost four o'clock.
"Wind a minute," Tom said, "under the tree", and the
family went out of the sun in a straggling troop, to sit in
the ash-tree shade, the old woman last. "You come out o'
that sun, mother," Tom called, and she came deafly across
the hay-rows, at her own will, to hand out the cold tea and
buttered slabs of bread, the butter like yellow oil in the
heat. This year the air was still rich but dry, and there

141

could be no fear of rain. But the meal was gulped, every drink and bite a sip and a slice out of the day's precious daylight, the talk running on the old lines. "Don't seem five minutes since last year. Weather holds, we s'll git all in by Saturday. If we look sharp. And have good luck. And nothing don't happen." Then new glances at the sky, and the uneasy prattle of the old woman : "I don't reckon we git such good crops as we used to git. Don't seem like *half* crops. Not a quarter. Eh? You speak?" nobody troubling to answer.

Frankie drank but could not eat. The sunlight hurt his eyes and matched the tensity of his fear and exhaustion from the stained brim. In turn Maudie and Rosie sat in wonder, Maudie worked up, Rosie troubled. Tom and the old woman and Turk alone sat relaxed, Turk breaking up the tension at last.

"Nice filly running tomorrow. Lady Nicotine. Moses, if I'd got the spondoolicks."

"Shut up !" Rosie said.

"I ain't asking you to put nothing on it, am I?" Turk said. "I only said she was a nice filly."

"Don't jump down his throat," Maudie said.

"Oh ! him and his fillies ! I've had some."

"She's forty-to-one," Turk said. "Was. She might be fifty-to-one, starting. More. What I was thinking was —"

"Eh?" the old woman said. "What's he say?"

"Bit more bread? I was saying," Turk shouted. "For you, I mean."

"Eh? Thought you said summat about a horse."

"I said give the bread to the horse."

"Eh?" she snapped. "Don't you waste bread here !"

Tom lay back on the grass, laughing. "That's a good un,

142

Mus' Perkins. Ha!" Tom's throat, thrown back, swelled like a pouch of sun-coloured leather. "Ha! That's a winner!"

"And so's this filly. I'm tellin' y'. I know. I'm serious," Turk said. "If we was to put a quid on, that's – four, five, six, count the gal, eight – half a dollar a piece, and she come up forties, only forties, we should draw a fiver apiece."

"If," Rosie said.

"I'm *tellin'* y'," Turk said.

"Tell me the old, old story."

"Look –"

"I wouldn't mind half a crown," Maudie said, "would you, Tom?"

"Me?" Tom said. "Not me. She's a lady. I know 'em. Ha!"

"It's five pounds for half a crown," Maudie said. "It's a lot. Me and Ella will, if Frankie will."

"It's gambling," Ella said.

"Well, so's everything," Turk said. "Y' put money in shares. That's gambling."

"Well –"

"What about Frankie?" Maudie said.

Frankie hesitated, thought a moment. Best not to upset her. Supposing she –

"All right," he muttered.

"That's only four. That makes –"

"Let's have five bob on," Turk said, enthusiastic.

Rosie stood suddenly up.

"You start any o' your damn games here," she said, "and you're finished."

"Here, Rosie, what –"

"You heard me."

Maudie was standing up too.

"Interfering," she said. "Why're you –"

"Because I know. I've had some !"

"It's our money, our business."

"Well, I'm telling you. Any betting here, and he's done. Besides – you, chapel folks above all !"

"You're jealous."

"Jealous ! By God !" Rosie stood furious.

"Steady, Rosie," Tom said.

"Shut up !"

Turk stood sheepish. Rosie's "Hear what I say?" startled him like a shot into decision :

"All right," he muttered. "All off."

Back in the hay-rows, Maudie was black with jealousy. The sun seemed to wither up her mind to a crabbed and twisted knot of bitterness. Her coming here, interfering. Always interfering. They was all right till she came. Always something, always interfering. And now Frankie. Under Tom's eyes. His brother under his own eyes. Interfering with him, making trouble. She heard again, as she had heard all day, the voice of Frankie whispering as she stood on the landing, and her mind knotted itself up more fiercely, her hatred of Rosie a clot of blackness. And now interfering with her, with Turk, with her own father. She wouldn't stand it. She needn't think it. Always interfering, always on to somebody. On to her father. A sudden tenderness for Turk, a kind of maternal pity, asserted itself and coloured for a moment the blackness of her hatred. The warmth of sunlight became the warmth of the whisky sliding in a burning vein through her body. She clutched the rake almost as she had clutched Turk in the darkness by the table, fiercely, in possessive panic, hardly knowing what she did, the field of white sun and

144

whitening grass swooning away for a moment as the darkness had done.

Almost calm again, she looked up to gaze at Turk. Her eyes instead went to Rosie. She was resting on her rake almost upright, in alert suspense. Her brown arms were folded one over another, an almost golden cross of sun-browned flesh on the white rake-stale. Looking at Frankie, she made signs, slight motions of her mouth, her teeth shining.

Seeing it, Maudie brought up her rake savagely, the knot in her mind at breaking point. Standing there, doing it in front of folks. No shame, nothing, just standing there doing it in broad daylight! All the pent-up concentration of her jealousy suddenly broke like a fester. Think she was somebody standing there, showing herself off. Thinking she was somebody! Look at her! Hair all over the place, ear-rings on. Ear-rings in the hay-field. Ear-rings! Be more like if she'd wear her corsets. Did she think nobody could see? Didn't she ever *think* of being decent? She looked with envy that was almost cankerous at Rosie's breasts, corsetless under her working blouse, the big curves clearly lined in the tight cotton. Why couldn't she dress herself properly, dress herself decent? And looking at Rosie, she could marvel at Tom. Why didn't he see? She saw him suddenly as a creature of stupid slavishness, a blind mole working in the earth of the farm, as someone who could not or would not see. And thinking of him, her mind clarified, the hatred replaced by a passionate vehement anxiety to speak to Tom. If he don't see, somebody's got to tell him! If he don't know, then somebody must tell him as does!

But when, almost four hours later, the field was turned

145

and the rakes shouldered and finally hung away, it was not to Tom she spoke at all but to Turk.

"It's a sovereign," she said. Loose-sleeved and still in a sweat, Turk was in the garden behind the house, pulling young supper onions. "I want you to have it. I want you to put it on."

"A thick 'un?"

"You put it on."

"For you? For yourself?"

"You put it on and what there is we'll share."

She spoke low, in agitation. Turk, astounded, held the sovereign in his hand, staring at her thin face. Her eyes seemed startled. He remembered how hard she had been, her flesh so thin and unyielding that it scarcely softened the bones. She had clutched him as though she were drowning. Before the point of relaxation she seemed like a doll of wire and wood, with a virginity as hard to break as oak or iron. Her chest, hardly breasted at all, had pressed against him like some stout basket of bone, her heart caged and fluttering madly within it. She was the hardest, oddest one he had ever had. But, as he held the sovereign, he told himself that he could change that. "She'll soften down," he thought. "She ain't so –"

"And if that comes off," she said, "we could – I got some to spare. Plenty put away. Plenty."

"Right, right. You can trust me. I know 'em – every jack one, seen 'em. Moses, there ain't a horse in this country I don't know."

"It's just between us two. Only us. You know that?"

"Betcha boots it is, sure. We'll mint money."

She looked round the garden, alert. The shadows of the walls and trees were already emptying it of sunlight. Nobody was about, and she spoke rapidly.

"You better git in now and change your shirt before supper."

"Ah." Turk put the sovereign in his pocket. That's what I'll do. And get the spondoolicks on afterwards."

She fingered his shirt-sleeve.

"I could find you a better shirt than that," she said. "Shall I? Shall I, and bring it up?"

IV

"You were dreaming," Rosie said.

"No. It was her. She come along the landing and opened the door. And I said, "Is it you, Rosie?" I know. I wasn't dreaming. I know."

Sun-brown arms folded on the gate-top, Rosie stood and looked without speaking over the big wheat acres of Top Land and down to the farm and the hay-meadows beyond. Frankie stood looking at the stone-hard earth of the track. The land on either side was wheat. Stray fronds of wheat had come up in the fissures of the track and were fattening for ear.

"What did he say?" Frankie said. "Tom. What'd you tell him?"

"I said I'd lost a chicken and was coming up to find it."

"What'd he say?"

"Nothing."

"He'll know. She'll tell him. You shouldn't of got mad with her in the meadow."

"Oh ! What do I care?"

Suddenly Rosie moved her hands, flattened them out on the gate-bar, tip to tip, making a smooth place to rest her head. "Come here, Frankie." Turned sideways, her throat shone white under the chin, where the sun had not caught it. Her hair frizzed over her hands and the gate. "Come here," she said. "I want you, come closer." And almost sullenly, too, Frankie leaned his arms on the gate.

"You don't love me."

"Yes." He was not looking at her.

"Then why're you frightened?"

He moved his hands, brought them unconsciously together, fingers locking. "I ain't frightened. Who said I was frightened? I ain't frightened."

"You are," she said. "You're frightened. I know. I can feel it. I felt it all day. I know."

"She'll tell him."

A white hot stab of exasperation shot up at once and she could not speak. She simply stood there with fingertips pressed against each other, her head hiding them, her mouth tightened up.

"I s'll go off," he said. "Go away from this damn place. New Zealand or somewhere."

"Don't be silly."

"I mean it, I –"

"Oh, don't be silly! Don't make me laugh. Frankie. Honey. It's silly to talk so."

He put his hands on hers, hammering the flattened knuckles with his palms, gently, but in agitation.

"You don't know Tom. He's like Dad. Dad was like that – never say nothing, never notice nothing, and then – Once when I was a kid I lamed a horse. Dad never said nothing. Never done nothing for weeks. And then when I thought he'd forgotten it he half-killed me. That's how Tom –"

"It's me he'd half-kill," she said. "Not you."

148

He could say nothing. He was astonished that she could take it so easily, almost lightly. He looked up, away from her. The sun was down. The young wheat waved like dark green water. Among the chestnut trees the farm stood solid, impregnable, a block of stone. As he looked, someone moved across the orchard, a swing of white shirt-sleeves, the white almost candescent in the darkening air.

"Somebody in the orchard now," he said.

"Never mind. Never mind." She spoke almost wearily, but suddenly she lifted her head off the gate and stretched out her arms and put herself between the gate and Frankie, her breasts pressed up to him. She was obsessed suddenly by a sensation of carelessness. It rose up in her like a current of heat. Anger and impatience were absorbed in it, burnt up. She held him with a strength that was bitter and tender, a challenge and a comment on his weakness. Beyond the cart-track, far up, the horizon was darkening. She kept her eyes fixed on it while speaking. "Now listen to me, listen to me." Her passion was released. "Frankie, Frankie, if you go away I'm done for. You know that. If you go away I shall have nobody, nothing. The whole damn lot of them aren't worth – Oh Jesus! you know what I mean. You know!" It was her turn now to be upset, to be afraid but not frightened. Her fear was so bitter and the expression of it so strong that Frankie could feel her arms locked together like a vice of bone behind his back. "It's only you who's kept me from running away myself." She spoke quickly, almost savagely, but her words were wooden beside the feeling of her body, the feeling of anguish uncommunicable except through her body, the relentless tightening of her arms in the strength of passion and agony.

149

"There's somebody still in the yard," he said, "prowling about."

She was not listening. "Don't do anything silly. Say you won't do anything silly."

"I don't know what you mean, silly."

"Silly, like running away, like –"

"It's Tom." He put his hand on Rosie's shoulders, trying to push her away. "Rosie, it's Tom. It's Tom, all right."

"I'm not looking. I don't care."

"He's looking for you."

"Let him, Frankie, Frankie."

But even as she spoke she had a feeling that he was greatly troubled. She let her arms relax. And looking up she could see his face quite pale.

She did not know what to say or do. Then she looked up in the direction he himself was looking, at the farm-yard. She could see Tom vaguely in the twilight. In his shirt-sleeves, hat off, and with his hands thrust idly in his belt, he was going from object to object in the orchard, from one tree to another, from the wood-heaps to the chicken house. Every now and then he would stoop and peer about and at last call "Chucka! Chucka!" in a fal-setto imitation of Rosie's own voice, calling the lost chicken. Rosie watched him. Tom walked heavily. His feet, even on grass, were set down with preponderant effort. They seemed to carry a great weight of earth. They were the feet of someone who had conceived of life as being a journey that must be taken at unalterable pace, as a long and steady progression to a given end. "Hurry?" Tom would say, "I wadn't born in hurry." Coming to the last chicken coop he halted and, the chicken unfound, stopped to light his pipe. The slow clockwork pressure of thumb on tobacco, the upward flicks of match flames in the twilight, and the first smoke puffs, made a slow and, to Rosie, a maddening ritual. She remembered him rowing like that on what seemed already distant Sunday afternoons. She saw his stocky arms, ironstone coloured, making their given rhythms, wooden as the oars they pulled. No excitement, no passion in Tom, nothing but the solid performance of fixed tasks, the unswerving and unexciting resolution of fixed ideas. And even as she stood watching, her arms still half round Frankie, Tom completed the circuit of the orchard and went back into the house.

But the sight of him reminded her of something. Before Frankie could speak she said, "Let's go on the river on Sunday. A boat. Just us."

"With her knowing? With Maudie knowing? —"

"Damn Maudie !"

"Maudie's like Tom. If she sets her mind —"

"Oh, if she knows, she knows ! What difference will it make? What difference? What matter?"

And gradually, too strong for him, she coaxed him into it, petting him, breaking up his fear, saying at last : "We'll tell him we're going. Wait till Maudie goes to Sunday school and then tell him."

"Ask him to come, I would."

"Well, ask him to come. Anything. Say we're going on the river and we don't suppose he'd like to come, but —"

"And if he did come?"

"Can a duck swim?"

"I don't know. I can't. I never could. Tom can. He persevered. He *would* learn."

"You can't swim?" she marvelled. "I'll teach you. I'll teach you," she joked. "Sunday afternoon."

V

And on Sunday afternoon, after Maudie and Ella and Lily had gone off to Sunday school, Rosie walked into the front parlour and spoke to Tom. Boots off, his grey woollen socks stained walnut colour by sweat, he sat in one chair with his feet on another, the Sunday paper limp in his hands, his mother sitting opposite, hands locked on her black lap, sleeplessly staring into space, the room stale with heat.

"Tom, we thought it'd be nice on the river, me and Frankie. I don't suppose you'd want to come?"

"Eh?" the old lady said. "Who?"

"Nothing. You wouldn't like to come, I suppose, Tom?"

Tom moved the paper, looking up. He sat for ten seconds or so in vague regard of her. She was all in white, in the carefully preserved white dress of her barmaid days, the sleeves a little by-gone in fashion, the bust too tight for her. To Tom she was like a spectacle conjured up out of memory. And when he looked at her it was with a memory of former admiration. She stood so white and fine that he was proud of her.

"I ain't got a collar on," he said.

Her heart began to race at once.

"You ain't all of hurry, are you?" Tom said.

"We were –" She could not go on. Tom stood up. The old lady was looking, first at Tom, then at her, with inquisitive grimness. Tom said, "If you ain't all of hurry, I'll git a collar on and come. Bin years since I had a boat out." The old lady croaked, "Ah? What say?" and in another moment Tom had gone from the room, his stockinged feet on the stairs sounding to Rosie like im-

152

mense and in some way ominous echoes of the racing of her own heart.

In the kitchen she waited, sick. Outside she could see the trap waiting, Frankie's straw hat shining white in the fierce sunlight. She smoothed her long white gloves, not thinking. Helpless and impotent, she heard Tom come down.

"Got the trap?" Tom said.

"Frankie's got it."

She walked vaguely out into the yard, Tom following. Outside she looked only for one thing, the look on Frankie's face. She saw the instant flash of astonishment, the stare of unbelief, and finally the bitter clenching of the mouth in jealousy. She dropped behind Tom as they walked. The sun came down with full stabs of heat through the thin stuff of her dress. Vaguely at last she climbed up into the trap and sat between Tom and Frankie, neither she nor Frankie saying a word.

And afterwards she did not recall that Frankie spoke more than half a dozen words between the farm and the boathouse by the bridge, where The Angel had stood. He drove rather fast, the reins tight as a stretched catapult, his hat savagely angled. She felt helpless. It was a situation altogether beyond her control. She sat most of the time silent herself, in a pretence of serenity. It was Tom who spoke.

"What we want, this weather. 'Nother week like this, that's what we want. Git that bottom meadow turned tomorrow and we shan't hurt. Hay ain't going to be so good this year. I bin keeping my eyes open. Grass is middlin'. If we git that bottom meadow in all right we shall do well. If we have good luck, and nothing don't happen."

And when finally they got a boat it was Tom who rowed. Jacket off, his arms almost the colour of cow-hide in the sun, his hat back, he rowed upstream past the breweries and the last houses with the same stocky rhythms as ever.

"Remember when we used to come boating, Sundays?" he said. Rosie kept her eyes on the water. Tom turned to Frankie, explanatory: "We used to come boating, Sundays, afore we was married. Time the pub was still all right." He spoke as though remembering occasions of terrific excitement. "They was days, if you like. Some sense." He spoke until he was hot, until the sweat dewed his forehead and face.

"Let Frankie row," Rosie said.

"I'm all right. I'll row up. Frankie can row back."

Ten minutes of Tom's unchanged rhythm brought them to the first of the Jeffrey meadows. All along the river the hay-scent was strong, a rich cloudy drug of sweetness. Unmoved by wind, like picture-flowers, creamy billows of meadowsweet feathered the dykes, the air sicklied about them. The valley held the heat as though in a cup.

Tom rested his oars. The boat drifted. "There's grass for you," Tom said. The grass in the big meadow lay creamed and frothed in sun-whitened circles. "I doubt if there's another meadow o' grass like that between here and Stamford. Very like between here and anywhere." He licked his lips and then his hands. Paddling one oar, he said: "I'm glad I come. It's worth coming for. Ain't every day you can see th'old meadow from the river. Eh, Frankie?"

Frankie did not answer. Reluctantly Tom rowed on, his eyes still on the hay. Proud of it, he had no eyes or ears for the sullenness of Frankie scorching on the boat seat or for the odd quietness of Rosie sitting in the stern. He rowed with controlled heartiness, the stiff leather of his Sunday braces creaking in time with the knocking of the rowlocks.

Until Rosie could stand it no longer. She felt she could cry out in fury, in fury not so much against Tom as against herself, against the turn of things and her own stupidity.

"Let Frankie row a bit," she said. She put into her voice a kind of careless solicitude. "Let Frankie row a bit."

"I'm all right."

"You've had a fair whack. Let Frankie row." She wanted to shout it. "Let Frankie row. Let Frankie have a turn."

"Want a row, Frankie?"

Frankie nodded, took off his hat. His face was oddly sullen, charged heavily with an accumulation of jealousy. Sitting, he took off his coat, dropping it on the cushions. Rosie took it and folded it and laid it down again. It was warm, the armpits moist with sweat. Tom ceased rowing. He shipped oars as Frankie rolled up his sleeves.

Then Frankie stood up. He stood up abruptly, with unexpected energy, almost savagely. Tom, half standing, slipped from his own seat to Frankie's sitting down as Frankie moved up the boat. For a moment the boat rocked. Frankie stepped over the boat seats, to one side, almost too far. Suddenly the boat came back with a great lurch, lapping the water, the balance broken, the gunwale down and in the water and up again before Tom could shout: "By God, steady! Steady, what you're doing on, Frankie!" the boat skewing into the final lurch before the shout had finished.

Screaming, Rosie went over the boatside heavily, her

frock parasolling out before it touched the water. The full light stuff of the frock floated out and down, dragging her. She swam at once, striking away from the boat. Strangely cold, the water half-paralysed her. Then Tom shouted. She turned, swimming back, her clothes like lead. Tom was duck-paddling, keeping afloat. Suddenly she saw him dive. There was no sign of Frankie.

In a minute Tom came up. "He's can't swim!" she shouted. Tom looked wild, scared, and for the first time in her experience afraid. "He'll come up," he shouted. "Bound to. He'll —" She dived before he could finish speaking. Her clothes were like skeins of water weed on her legs. She could not stay under. She came up almost at once, swimming to the bank.

She went in again without her underskirt, diving straight down. The boat had drifted away. The water was empty except for the three hats, the two straw hats and her own big white one, idly floating. When she came up again they were all she could see. She felt blinded. The sky seemed metallic, the sunlight a dazzle of quicksilver.

Then Tom came up. He was holding Frankie with one arm and making his stroke with the other. Frankie made no movement. Tom looked about him desperately, signalling her, shaking his head. She swam towards him at once, with terrific strokes, with the strength of terror, knowing even then, long before she reached him, that it was all over.

BOOK FOUR

A HOUSE OF WOMEN

CHAPTER I

I

In the summer of 1914 Tom had barley in the twenty-five acres of Top Land. Sown late, it was very good. In the heat of July it came on quickly, sturdy and sweet-eared, the long beards pale emerald. It began to turn by the month's end, a big lake of ears, pale gold, not quite white. Hearing of it, men came to look at it. From a trap seat a man could get a good view of it, an impression as of looking down a field of white water. It was a beautiful piece. It looked in some way inviolable, virgin. "That *is* barley : I don't know as I recolleck seeing a better piece. Seems a shame to cut it." And Tom, seeing the barley, thinking of it and hearing the comments of neighbours, was phlegmatically proud. Family satisfaction, which had not been shaken since Frankie's death, stood once again as solid and sturdy as the barley itself.

And on the still hot July evenings Tom would set out, between supper and darkness, to look at the barley, Rosie with him. Across the orchard, over the road, up the cart-track and finally in the pause by the gate to the barley field, they went together through the acts of a performance which meant nothing to her. Tom walked slowly, with unaltered deliberation. Without thinking, she was glad of it. She had gone rather thin. She was harder, less florid. Still big, without any of the drawn skinniness of Maudie and Ella, she looked strong and gaunt. Her arms were like wood, very hard and sun-stained to a white line above the elbows. She had given up her ear-rings; she looked older. Her hair alone had not changed; it frizzed in handsome and irrepressible curls, thick and brown, toning down and softening her look of rather arid sobriety.

"Weather holds, I s'll cut about the second week in August." Tom would stand critically at the gate, hand among the barley ears perhaps, his mind on the crop. "Git th' oats and the wheat knocked down and then see. Live and have good luck, that'll be about the best piece o' barley we ever growed. Live and have good luck and nothing don't happen."

She would not answer. There was nothing to say. For almost ten years she had heard the same voice, deliberating, in the same accents, on the promise of one crop and another, voicing the fatalistic dependence on fate and weather. Unchanged, Tom also seemed changeless. He stood as sturdily as the farm, absorbed in it and by it. Crops might fail, even had failed, and members of the farm's body, as Alf Jeffery and Frankie, might be cut off, but Tom remained unaltered, the backbone of it all. Rosie saw changes in Maudie, in Ella. in Lily, in the old lady; she felt changes in the world outside the world of the farm; and there were catastrophic changes in herself. But there was no change in Tom. The death of Frankie had disturbed him momentarily, but not ultimately. In a house of shaken women he stood by contrast almost unemotional, a rock of comfort, impassive. The farm without him, was beyond conceiving.

August broke hot. On the open hillside, the barley came on quickly, shining and candescent in the white noon heat. On the first Sunday morning of August, after pig-feeding, Tom went to look at the barley, starting out alone. Crossing the road, he met Will Middleton, his neighbour on the Orlingford side, and Will said, looking at the barley :

"Rum goings on. Seems like war, Tom."

"Ah !" Tom said. "Paper hadn't come when I started."

"Yis, be all accounts. Talking about it long enough. Too late to git out on it. Proper serious."

"Never s'thing in me life," Tom said.

He went on and looked at the barley. It seemed to have come on, to have whitened perceptibly, in the night. He rustled his hand among the ears against the gate. They were dry, the beards crisp and soft. Across the field there was a spasmodic talking of wind in the white ears, a whispering current of light and shade. And as, in almost thoughtless meditation, Tom looked at the barley and listened to the wind in it, the fact of war had no place in him or even near him. In his world, just then, the barley was paramount. He was faced by the crisis of harvest. He was about to direct an attack beside which the rumours of war were less important than the prattling of sparrow flocks on his early wheat. Then, still looking at the barley, he remembered that he had no string in his binder, and slowly, without any haste at all in the morning heat, he went back to the farm and tinkered with the binder until dinner-time.

At dinner he picked up the Sunday paper. There it was, as Will had said : War. Will had voiced the rumour of weeks; the paper seemed to make it a truth, a fact.

"Rum 'un." Tom said. "You seen this?" he said to the women.

The women had seen it. They had been aware of it for days. Already disturbed, they felt vaster implications. And they put up a pretence of being slightly impatient, unbelieving.

"Want something to do," Maudie said. "Putting it in. Scaring folks."

"Anything to fill up. They got to fill it up with something," Elia said. "More peas, our Tom? Be about the last bait."

Absently Tom held out his plate for the peas, reading the paper at the same time. It was an act almost unprecedented : reading the paper at Sunday table. And Maudie was impatient.

"Put that paper down, Tom. And cut me a thin mossel o' meat. Only thin."

Carving the meat, Tom said : "Don't like the look on it." It was a pronouncement, almost oracular. And the women, for all their unbelief, sat more deeply disturbed.

"Just at harvest !" Maudie snapped.

After dinner Tom absorbed the news. The paper, in turn, was his own oracle. He read slowly, with credulous sobriety. The front-page headlines had for him a character of hard fact, of almost biblical truth, that was powerfully impressive. He could not do otherwise than believe it. There it was in black and white : war. His mother sat opposite him, eating an early pear, scratching out the flesh with a bone scoop, sucking and licking, the juice oiling her fleshless chin. And when, about three o'clock, she ceased eating, let the scoop fall into her black lap, and dropped to sleep, Tom felt himself dropping off too and they dozed together, the pear core slipping off her knee and the paper off his, the war drowned in the mists of sleep.

And afterwards, for more than a month, it did not trouble him more than that. Relatively, beside harvest, it was a little thing. When he woke in the morning his first thought was of corn, his first act a glance at the sky. He remembered war as a hideous after-thought, an unncessary evil in what was for him already a time of trouble. Men he had known all his life enlisted; soldiers went past the farm. They were no more than figures in a peep-show. The barley sheaves were more real, more living. Carried by moonlight at the end of August, the barley represented for him something more than all conquests. It was a victory won by his own hands, out of the earth, against all adversities of wind and rain. It seemed ultimate. He did not ask for more : the aisles of white shocks in the moonlight, the clack of carts, the sweet corn-smells everywhere, the solid piling up of many house-shaped ricks in the yards between the barns and the chestnut trees. They were the manoeuvres and fruits of a campaign not less important to him because he had made and won them before.

By the middle of September he had executed almost the final manoeuvre, had dragged the stubbles, had removed all but the gleaming shocks. In the Jeffery fields nobody gleaned but the Jefferys. "We got hens to feed, well as other folks, ain't we?" So the last shocks, the warning that the field was not and in fact never would be ready, remained until the month's end, while Maudie and Ella and Rosie and the old woman gleaned all day and on into the mild damp evenings, pinafores swollen with a rich pregnancy of corn, hands stubble-torn, figures moving unrestingly over the now empty and soft-lighted stubbles as they plundered the last ears before the plough began.

The gleaning finished, Tom made a pronouncement.

"War goes on, looks as if we might ha' to 'list."

"Our Tom !"

"Ah !" Tom said, "it's serious. Serious thing. Rum go."

"And what should *we* do?" Maudie said, in a panic.

"Squawk about. I ain't gone yit."

In October, Tom did some shooting, stalking the stubbles in the hour before twilight. He read the papers avidly, linked himself in conversation with neighbours, with men passing the gate, laying down a dispassionate law, a law which finally became a creed, the creed passing finally into a new pronouncement:

"No good. If we don't stop them – this is how I look at it – they'll stop us. Things ain't no better time we git the roots in I must go."

And in November, after the last burnished vaults of roots had been earthed over, all his pronouncements became a fact. Ponderously, without fuss, he clipped his moustache, washed his feet and went.

The evening before his going he walked with Rosie across the stack-yard, across the orchard, through the spinney, making a last circuit of the farm. He was thirty-seven; with moustache clipped he looked younger. As they walked Rosie was seized by an intolerable panic, an inexpressible agony of many fears, that left her inarticulate. She could say nothing, could scarcely think. She was caught up by the sheer power of emotions for which she had no name. Her mind felt dumb and wooden. Her heart lay like iron, heavy beyond all experience, an indefinable weight of misery. She listened to Tom's words with scarcely a word of her own in answer.

"Only one thing" Tom said, "as you need worry about. Anything happens to me and you gotta git rid of anything, any land or anything, keep the meadows till last. Grass'll keep the cows and the cows'll pretty nigh keep you. But that's all if – I dare – say I shall be home for Christmas."

II

The death of Frankie had narrowed her ways and chances of escape to the littleness of a pin-prick; the enlisting of Tom seemed to close them up altogether.

Except for Turk and the cowman, Amos, who had been with them for thirty years, they were a house of women. Of Frankie no one ever spoke; but of Tom they could speak freely now, and Ella and Maudie began to lard him with undreamed-of virtues. Enlisted, he became something far more for them than a mere soldier; he became a symbol of the whole army itself. Just as, in peace days, the farm and Tom had been synonymous, one with another, unthinkable without each other, so with the war and Tom. The unit and the whole were one, the same, inseparable. So that when Maudie, after some reported atrocity or the death of an acquaintance, or at the mere thought of blood and barbarism, raised her voice and said with almost religious fanaticism : "The dirty Germans ! The dirty Huns ! Wait till our lot git going. They'll show 'em !" she meant, "Wait till our Tom gits going ! He'll show 'em !" seeing Tom alone, gigantic and imbued with the hot spirit of her own fanaticism, as the solitary conqueror of enemy battalions. And at night she cast the molten spirit of her hatred and worship into the clumsy iron of her prayers, praying in bed, with her head under the clothes, winter-fashion, the fashion of praying on her knees being only for summer : "Lord who this night are watching over all of us, keep us safe, guard us against all evil. Keep our Tom safe this night, wherever he may be. Succour him and keep him. And if need arises, O Lord, let him give it to 'em, as Thy servant knows he can give

it to 'em, in Thy name and for Thy sake. Our Father ..."
And now that she slept alone, having tiffed with Ella,
who curled like a cat and now slept in Frankie's room, she
was free not only to pray as she liked but to come and
go as she liked, her prayers cut short sometimes into hasty
incoherent splinters of words by the heat of her desire to
have Turk come to her. And when, by prearrangement, he
did come, she put into the fulfilment of her desire for him
all the anguish of her hatred against the enemy, coupling
it sometimes with not a little of her unforgotten jealousy
against Rosie, so that Turk, caught between the forces of
her double rage, was often staggered to impotency.

So Maudie had ways of escape. Rosie had nothing.
Frankie's death held her in an unrelaxing trap of anguish.
The war tightened it. She went about with a feeling of
bitterest emptiness. Unconsciously, not knowing it, she
had replaced Frankie by Tom, just as, in the beginning,
she had replaced Tom by Frankie. And she began, after
a time, to miss one as much as she had missed another, but
differently. If, as she sometimes felt, the best of her had
drowned with Frankie, what remained of her seemed to
be lifted into a suspense of nothingness by Tom's de-
parture.

She began to work, at once, very hard. The family, less
now than ever, could give her nothing. She felt also, as
always, in some way outside of it. More even than Turk,
she felt that she was the outsider, the usurper. The shell
of family clannishness, petrified by time, infinitely harder
to break than Maudie's iron virginity, offered no crack of
comfort. There remained only the farm, the land.

And when Christmas passed, and the New Year drew
out coldly to spring and Tom did not come back, except
for week-ends of leave, she took on the responsibility of

the place not merely as a chance of comfort but almost as the only chance of existence at all. Without it, she felt that she could have died, petering weakly out. And since the bitterness of things against her had been uncompromising she was bitterly uncompromising herself. She began to look rather hard. She got into the way of saying a thing, meaning it, and leaving it, in spite of all family argument and reproach, at that. For all their zeal, Maudie and Ella were capable only in the house. They could glean and bond sheaves and turn hay, but they jibbed at a plough. So, in the spring, with Amos at the lambing, Rosie herself struggled with one plough, relentlessly driving Turk into a struggle with the other. "Git that damn plough and for once in your life *do* something!" Turk, flabbier than ever, almost moaned the old protests : "Moses, one bout and I should drop down. I never ploughed in me life. Straight, Rosie, straight." She looked at him with impersonal determination, relentless. "You git that plough and never mind whether you ever ploughed or not. Nor did I." And together, all one wretched February day of wind and scuttling showers of rain, they ploughed what remained of the last stubble, the land scarred by them into dark bands of jagged steel, Turk's courses more zigzagged and drunken even than her own. But it was done, and she was proud. And when, that evening, Maudie protested for Turk's sake, she flared up, not with the old volatility, but with a new and hard-lipped determination.

"He'll do as I tell him. Who's in charge? Who's farm is it?"

"Ourn," Maudie said. "It's ourn."

"Oh, is it? And whose is it if Tom gits killed?"

This new aspect of things shattered them. It almost

167

shattered herself. Consciously she had scarcely thought of this. The farm had seemed so inviolate, so much a tradition, belong only and unalterably to the family, that she had not thought of it, as by some act of fate, ever belonging to herself.

And at once, seeing it consciously for the first time, too, Maudie was enraged. So long dormant, all the old bitterness of jealousy sprang up with sharper power, her mind cat's-clawing Rosie in vicious silences. The thought of Rosie as loving Frankie had been intolerable, but it was nothing, a mere pettiness of memory, as compared with the thought of Rosie owning the farm.

"What right's she gotta say that? It's our farm, always has been, always will be. Ain't as if we were tenants. We own. It's ourn. She ain't got no right at all. If everybody had their rights we should own it, mother should own it. Ain't that so, Ella?"

It was hard for Ella to argue, to summon anger. Frankie's death had drained her of much spirit. Perpetually tired, she continued to be dumbfounded, discouraged by little things, crying much by herself in Frankie's bed at night. She could respond only with the petulance of the sick, her pity of Frankie mixed with pity for herself.

"I don't know. I know one thing. It would have been different if – it'd been a different tune then."

"Eh?" The old lady would be drawn into it, her old steely eyes drawn by the magnetism of spite. Old, but not aged, she was a creature of wire, of some imperishable time-hardened metal that nothing could loosen or mark. To Rosie she seemed not to have changed at all under the racket of years which had changed herself out of all belief. "Eh?" she would say. "What say?" Her eyes were like old weather-keened bullets of steely brightness. "You speak?"

"We were saying about her. About Rosie –"

"Eh? About who?"

"Her. Rosie. What d'ye think now? She says –" Maudie would speak with difficulty, her throat contracted like cooling iron, "– she says if anything happens or if Tom should happen – she says the farm'll be hers."

"Depends." The thought came darkly up, a weight of significance.

"Depends on what?"

"Eh?"

"Depends on what, I say?"

"Tom. Depends how he's made his will." She gave up a grim secret. "I know how I made mine."

"Yes and I know how I made mine, and Ella's!" The thought was a mouthful of comfort to Maudie. "We made ourn for each other. She don't git non o' that!"

"I made mine for the gal. For Lily."

"Oh!"

Surprised, almost shocked, Maudie for a moment did not know what to say. That money ought to have been hers, Ella's, somebody in the family. Still, it wasn't as if – well, Lily was a nice child, a good little gal. Thanks to them. And after a moment's pause, taking a phrase of Tom's, she said :

"Well, I ain't saying nothing. Better Lily than some folks. I ain't saying nothing."

Lily was growing up. Too old for the village school, she had begun, at Maudie's insistence, to attend High School in Orlingford. Rosie had argued against it, weakly, and Maudie and Ella, as always, had triumphed, paying the fees as the price of their satisfaction. And now every morning Lily cycled off at half-past eight on spindly black-stockinged legs, straw-hatted, with trim satchel, and thick worsted gloves of Maudie's knitting, her fair hair plaited into the limp double tails of respectability. More than ever now, Rosie would feel that she did not belong to her, that she was the fruit of some ghastly mischance. And in the evenings, as she sat at the parlour table and struggled with algebra, with French, with signs and wonders of which Rosie did not know even half the meaning, it would seem not only that she did not belong to her, but that she belonged to a different world. Milk-veined and nervous, she carried timidity nakedly in her face wherever she went. She seemed in some way damp and soft, her pale melting eyes a skim-milk blue, almost characterless. Rosie found no contact with her. Once, soon after Frankie's death, she had tried to teach her the piano, teaching her the first keynotes in the harmonium. "If she'll learn," Maudie said, "we'll git rid of the old harmonium and have a proper piano." But within a week, driven to the verge of rage by the child's milky hands straying abstractedly, without point or spirit, over the yellowing keys, Rosie had given it up. And thereafter Maudie and Ella took her back absolutely into the straight folds of their own care, helping her as best they could with her lessons; curling her hair, making her dresses, moulding her mind into the blameless shape their creeds demanded, warning her at last, in due time, of all the terrors and discomforts and darknesses of coming womanhood.

So that soon after the beginning of the war, Rosie saw them ranged against her. Oddly, it did not perturb her. The bulwark of their jealousy seemed less than paper against the stone-hard towering fact of war, the absence of Tom, the tension of loneliness, the imperishable memory of Frankie drowning.

Then, unexpectedly, Tom arrived with kit-bag, and twenty-four hours leave before he left for France. It was April. Warm rains had brought on the wheat, the pastures were vivid. Disciplined to a greater deliberation than ever, Tom walked with Rosie about the farm, spoke of what she must do and what she must not do. "Keep th' hoes goin' in the wheat. You women can watch that. The hay'll pretty nigh take care of itself. And don't let the wezzles git too big afore y'thin. Y'understand?"

And then finally, just before sleep.

"Summat I wanta say. Chaps git killed, and I might. Anything happens, the farm's yourn. I spoke to mum. She knows. She's lived her life."

"I don't know as I –"

"It's done with now. I made the will."

He departed the following morning. Hardly had he gone before Maudie prattled bitterly to Ella :

"He's left her everything. Everything. Made the will. I *know*. I heard 'em. I heard 'em talking in bed."

"In bed?"

"I happened to be on the landing," Maudie explained. "I had to git up. I didn't feel very grand." It was a precious opportunity for allaying suspicion and fear. She took it. "I don't feel very grand in the night sometimes. I git up and go down for a drop of brandy."

III

Money easy, Turk made nightly circuits of the bars, oiling himself against the harsh graft of daily existence, staggering home in the late hours. Fighting against sleep, Maudie would hear him come in, miserable for him, offering perhaps a fluttering prayer for him before tossing to unsatisfied sleep.

And suddenly Turk had news, gleaned in one bar and confirmed in another :

"What d'y' think? They're going to build The Angel again."

"And the band played," Rosie said.

"Had it straight!" Turk insisted. "First hand. Stable information."

"Well, whether they do or not, does it concern us?"

So Turk took his secrets to Maudie. No gettin' over Rosie. No diddling Rosie. No help from her, nothing. Hard as nails, treat him like muck. And see all he'd done for her !

"They're goin' to rebuild the pub, The Angel," he said to Maudie. "My old pub. That's a good thing, y'know. A cert. Look where it stands – just on the bridge. Catch all the traffic – soldiers, everything."

"When?"

"Y' won't tell anybody if I tell y'summat? Y'won't split?"

"You know I wouldn't. Oh ! You know that."

"There's a chance for me. To git back, see? I got it straight from th' horse's mouth – they'll consider me fust."

"You? You'd go back?"

"Oh ! It ain't sure. Nothing fixed. One thing, I should want money."

"Money? Much money?"

"I don't know. I'll tell y' later."

In his mind the fantasy grew that he might go back. He saw himself established. Swaggering in the soldier-crowded bars, he belched invitations, issued challenges, took bets. It seemed to him that, in the old days. The Angel had been the finest pub in England. "Worked meself to the bone in that pub. Served in the bar of a Saturday till I was silly. But Moses, it was worth it."

He took the fantasy to Maudie: "It's a dead cert. They're only one runner, and that's me." That spring soldiers had been billeted in Orlingford and rush-work was already beginning on the pub, the fire-scorched skeleton, so long bill-plastered, vanishing at last, the empty river echoing with the dong and clatter of transformation.

"Why do you want money?" Maudie said.

"A guarantee." He sweetened her with explanations, professing surprise. "Didn't you know that every publican has to put up a guarantee? So much per cent?"

She did not know. She knew only that she was greatly perturbed, deeply afraid that he might leave her. She had come to a point of utter folly in her thoughts of him, to a point of almost childlike trust. Clay-like, her mind softened and moulded itself as she knew he wished it, taking wonderful and sometimes almost wicked shapes that shocked her. She lived a kind of double life: the passionate softened life, responsive as clay, for Turk, the habitual existence of iron behaviour for the family and the rest of the world. Its duality at times astounded and even frightened her. She was frightened at the thought of misadventure, suffering recurrent terrors. She was astounded that she could go on, until she remembered that she had gone too far ever to think of going back.

Sometimes it eased her own sufferings if she burdened herself with Turk's. Pity was a lovely antidote. Almost knowing she was foolish, she had long given him money: odd silver, occasional sovereigns, little extravagances for

the big races. The giving eased her wonderfully. Good
Samaritan-like, she found excuses that were righteous. "If
we can't help folk not so well off as ourselves, it's a pity.
And that's what we should do ! What do I want with a
lot o' money? Who could I leave it to? Nobody. Not her !"

One afternoon Turk said : "I should want a hundred."

She was shocked : so much that she could not speak.

"Oh ! I'll pay interest," Turk said. "Bank rate." That
made it seem safe.

Intuition, an inborn Jeffery regard for a good deal, held
her back. But already Turk had worked it out :

"We'll do it properly. Business. A proper agreement –
I agree to pay you so much per cent and so on."

That satisfied her. She kept her money upstairs, the
cashbox imprisoned among the linen of her courting days.
It was almost milking time as they stood in the kitchen
talking. She was to milk. Rosie and the rest were
thistle-pulling on the arable between the house and the
meadows. The house was quiet with the drugged summer
quietness that suspended all motion and almost all sound.

"You want it now?"

"I gotta place it with the solicitors pretty soon."

She seemed to hesitate. It was a lot of money, an awful
lot of –

"It's the chance of a lifetime," Turk said. "A snip."

"All right." She succumbed. "I'll get it."

She went upstairs. At the landing-head, faint with
excitement, she called down :

"You can come up if you like."

Events had suppled her body a little, and when Turk
entered the bedroom she seemed, as she bent over the
open chest of drawers, almost girlish, her body easy in
the cotton working frock, her face flushed. She was

174

trembling with the secrecy and the importance of the occasion, and putting her hands on his shoulders and rubbing them passionately up and down the leather of his flesh-tightened braces, she said :

"I only want one thing. I only want to ask you one thing. Don't tell anybody. It's between us. Don't tell a soul. Promise me."

"Cut me throat. All you need do is git the paper ready."

Afterwards, a little troubled, thinking much of the money, she was fretted with secret uncertainties. Until suddenly something happened to make her forget it almost, but not quite, altogether.

Taken suddenly ill in the hay-field, Ella died. Thin, dried up, lacking passionate escapes, she seemed, as she lay in Frankie's bed for the two days before her death, as if she had surrendered all excuse for living. In the hour or two before she died she rose beyond and above the obsession of her loss. "I s'll see Frankie," she would say to Maudie, until the bitterest tears of all, the fusion of the old and the new grief, ran hopelessly down Maudie's face and dissolved into anguish, and the fears that had seemed so important seemed nothing at all.

It was only afterwards, in the late summer, as she straightened and sorted Ella's effects and counted the two hundred pounds of her legacy and locked it away with her own silver and notes and her few precious sovereigns, that she remembered the causes of Ella's grief, which seemed in turn the causes of her death.

"That's her ! That's what she's done !" Her thought was beaten by grief and rage to a bitterer, harder shaft of hatred than ever. "That's what she done for us !"

But always, whenever she felt such passionate physical hatred, some turn in the war, some new abomination of

her creeds of patriotic decency, would offer a larger and
more realistic target for her wrath. She worked off her
feelings on the war, on the invisible enemy, as a man
might work off a rage by beating a horse. Hands clenched,
she lamented bitterly the misfortune of her sex. "Only
I'd bin a man, I'd ha' shown 'em! Me and our Tom, we'd
ha' shown 'em!" Underneath it all ran the current of fear,
the deadly terror of loss that was almost expectation. She
lived wrought up, a little abnormal in her hatred, the
temperatures of her mind quivering at breaking point, her
body wired with a system of nerves dangerously charged.
Ella dead, she took upon herself, as a kind of duty, Ella's
work and the discharge of Ella's emotions, almost living
the life taken away from her. "Like Ella'd said, like Ella'd
done. Same as our Ella, my blood *boils* when I think on
it!" Drawing heavily on her reserves of strength, she
scarcely rested. Up at five, she sweated through summer
heat or sluddered through winter muck like a creature
of iron. She seemed unbreakable. Her dark hair, thin,
straight, uncurling, would rat's-tail over her bony face as
shse worked, taking away the look of rather grim decency.
As though remembering Ella again, she cycled twice on
Sunday and once in mid-week to chapel, praying with
unashamed heat for vengeance on whoever might kill or
injure Tom. Endlessly knitting scarves and socks, and
baking cakes for him, she packed up each week a parcel
which she grimly posted off as though it were a bomb.

And all the time she kept up the secret play of existence
with Turk, giving indefatigably and even joyfully what
was left of herself, and almost what was left of her money.

"Y'see," Turk said, in early autumn, "it's a game. What's
a hundred? Afore the war if a bloke wanted a pub he
took it. Had done with. But the war's changed all that.

176

'Money for this, money for that, prices enough to break your heart. Brewers as hard as nails. Solicitors diddlin' folks. For two pins I'd give it up. Chuck it. Bung in."

"Oh, don't give it up !"

"Well, what can I do?"

"It seems a *shame*. After you set your heart on it, after we –"

"They don't stan' about hearts. Nothing else either, come to that. They want money."

"What is it this time?"

"They say I gotta buy the furniture."

That day she gave him thirty pounds. "On account," Turk said. On account of what she did not know, and was too grieved by the prospect of Turk's going to think.

"When'll you go? You won't go yet?"

"Depends. Soon's I can get the deal through and the furniture."

"Where'll you get the furniture?"

"Wholesale somewhere. Mean a day in London."

"So it won't be yet?"

It came sooner than ever she had dreamed or expected. Harvest, late for lack of labour, had been gathered in, and the stubbles stood white, only half-gleaned, in the October sunlight, when one morning Turk departed. Fat, toffed up in best bowler, check suit, and light brown boots, he took the morning train, looking like the bookmaker Rosie had always declared he ought to have been, promising easily and lightly : "Be back by the ten if they don't kidnap me."

By eleven, when he had not come, Maudie was in secret panic. "Oh, I know him !" Rosie said. "I'm used to him," and went to bed. Following her, Maudie could not sleep. Towards midnight she went downstairs and stood at the open kitchen door and stared across the black October

177

darkness of the fields and shivered and wondered. At two she was in Rosie's room.

"Your father ain't in."

"Blimey, what if he isn't? Like as not got boozed and missed it."

"I feel so lost, somehow," Maudie said, "without a man in the house."

"Oh, get to bed ! You'll catch your death."

And the next day, when Turk had still not come, it was as though she had, in fact, caught her death. She went about chilled, the life gone out of her. It was not until evening, when she ran suddenly upstairs and began to turn out the chest of drawers with frantic hands, whimpering, that she knew that he would not come back at all. Too shocked to cry, she stood with the empty cashbox in her hands.

Days later, Rosie too gave up hope. Stoical, very embittered now, she could only repeat :

"Skedaddled. And no more than I expected. Didn't I always say? By God, didn't I always tell you? That's his lordship all over. Didn't I tell you?"

There was nothing at all that Maudie could say in answer to that. Only in her own heart, in the privacy of her bedroom, as she unbelievingly turned the cashbox over and over in her hands, could her emotions find anything like their full expression : old emotions, but now more bitterly expressed :

"Her again ! If it hadn't been for her it wouldn't have happened. That's what she done for us. Coming here. Look what she's done for me now ! Look what she's done for me !"

IV

To Rosie the war was like an evil necessity. All through
it she clung hard to the farm. She began to be conscious
of a foreshortening of life, a hardening and sharpening, a
narrowing to a point. It began to seem like a wedge
driven into the dark stuff of time, and she herself the
hammer which drove it. And since the wedge and time
itself were hard it behoved her to be hard too. The war
forged and beat her out.

By the middle of the war she was thirty-five. There
were days when she felt older, and hours and times in
every day when, pig-mucked or sun-tired or wet or
fighting with her wind-strangled hair, she looked much
older. She was still handsome, but work had coarsened
her, her forearms sack-clothed by wind and wet, her
winter face bone-hard, her gait knocked graceless by conflict with the yard's muck. She still walked well : but no
longer superbly, only in a splendour of larger and harder
strength. Her eyes were no longer arrogant, only defiant
against the coarse cow-mucked serge of her dress. She
worked hatless, her brown hair rain-frizzed or wind-torn
or bleached by sun. If she stood still, with arms folded,
bare flesh locked over her still strong breasts, her mouth
went straight, almost hard, in listening or reflection. It
was her mouth which gave her away. She kept it shut so
much, going about in the silent musings of bitter recollection, that it was shaped by all the emotions she could not
or would not express, the lips hardened and whittled
down by repression and conflict.

And inevitably her mind hardened. Bitterness covered
it with a shell of protection, which time and the war

thickened, which every scare of war enamelled over with terror and stoicism. And over and above it all she had a reason for being hard : the farm.

Supposing Tom should catch one? What she had once said to Maudie in a moment of temper she now believed in earnest. Supposing Tom should not come back. No use snivelling, no good being soft then. The farm was all she had, her only fortification against time or poverty. And not satisfied, leaving nothing to sentiment or chance, she built up about it the further fortifications of reason. If Tom died, then, she reasoned, the farm died with him. She was adamant.

And, clinging so hard to the thought of the farm in secret, she became almost attached to it in reality. Since it was all she had she was almost jealous for it. She squandered her passions on it, her last atoms of strength. She worked as she had never worked at the pub : the day as long but more exhausting, the whole conflict harsher and deeper. And now, beside the farm, the pub seemed a little thing : the swilling of beer into bellies something of no point at all beside the swilling of pigs and the tilling of land. Looking back, she would wonder how she had endured the pub, with its stifling stench and shifty life of men and beer, as once she had looked forward and wondered how she could survive the farm, with its too-rich solitudes and muck and winter darknesses. The thought of going back, now, to the pub, was almost a nightmare. Whereas the thought of the farm had grown to be a comfort : the kitchen a comfort against the winter nights, the chestnut shade a comfort against the sun, the earth itself a large and enduring comfort against the terror of war.

And hardly knowing it, she would be as jealous as a

Jeffery herself at any trespasser. "Folks in that bottom meadow? You let me see 'em. Blimey! I ain't got that grass laid for nothing." And when, on winter nights, Maudie cycled to Orlingford for week-night service, for Band of Hope, or even, at Lily's coaxing, to the pictures, she was not only jealous, but resentful.

"Pictures! What again?"

"Well, I don't know. You must do something. Times are terrible enough. You take and come."

"Me? I should like. Think I got nothing better to do 'n look at tarts on a screen?"

And she would stay savagely at home, ironing, sewing, reading the newspaper, writing letters to Tom; always some unluxurious task, done, as it were, as a kind of penitence, inexorably. "Orlingford! What you see in Orlingford I don't know. Thank God I'm shut of it." And always, as she sat there reading or working, the old lady would be with her; deaf, dried-up, seemingly imperishable, sunk in the grimmest meditation of Rosie's face in the firelight, her time-yellow face inscrutable as wood and as hard, her eyes wet with the pale blue acid of her ancient jealousy.

"Eh? You speak?"

"No, I'm reading. I never spoke."

"H'm. When d'ye say Tom's coming home?"

"I never said he was coming home."

"Eh?"

"I never said a word about he was coming home."

"I know you did."

"You dreamt it."

"Eh? You said the war was pretty nigh finished and Tom'd be home. I know you did. I heard you. Speakin' to Maudie."

"You just imagined it."

"Did I? H'm. Another thing. I ain't had a letter from Tom about a week."

"You had one the day afore yesterday."

"Eh?"

"I say you had one the day afore –"

"You did. I never."

"You had one! It was in with mine. Two letters in one."

"You kept it then. I ain't seen it."

"Put your head in a bag."

"Eh?"

And finally Rosie would take refuge in silence, the feud between them going on without words, the old acid eye burning in the kitchen lamplight with a resentment that had behind it the accumulation of muddled spite, of past bitterness, even of past tragedy. Maudie might work off her jealousy in toil and passion; but not the old lady. She lived in inexorable enmity, her mind grim and as sharp as a splinter of rock. Unclear about the passage of time and the magnitude of war, she was forgetful of much but never forgetful of Rosie. She saw her always as the stranger, the dolled barmaid of a distant Sunday afternoon, the seducer of Tom and the threatening usurper of all she had and almost all she had ever known.

And as they sat there one night, alone, in the lamplit security, a knock came on the front door, the hard tap of a stick.

In a moment the old lady was up in her chair, alert.

"Somebody, ain't it?" she listened, her face as sharp as a dog's. "Front door an' all."

Knitting in hand, Rosie went and came back in a moment, sticking the needles into the wool-ball.

"The parson. Mr. ——. Well, I'm afraid I don't know your name," she apologized.

"Franklin." He came just behind her, a big man, red-faced, a sort of ecclesiastical prize-fighter. "I came to see Miss Maudie, really."

"Maudie's out. Gone to the pictures."

"H'm." He looked at the old lady. "And how are you, Mrs. Jeffery?"

"Eh?"

"Bawl at her," Rosie said.

"How are you, I say?"

"Oh! I don't hurt."

He held the old lady's skinny right hand in his big dark-haired paw, his black trilby hat still on.

"Won't you take your hat off?" Rosie said.

"Eh? Oh! Yes, I will."

He sat down, hat on knees, walking stick crooked across one thigh. Sitting at the table, idly counting the stitches of her knitting, Rosie resented him bitterly: the big meat-red hands and face, the godly black hat, the thick pugilistic lips with their soft shine of fleshiness.

"Cold out?" the old lady said.

"Bitter. A bitter night."

Arms extended, he rubbed his hands before the fire with a great harsh sound, as though he wore gloves of sandpaper.

"Like anything to drink, eh?" Rosie said.

"I mustn't stay." He went through a little pantomime of protest. "I mustn't stay. No, no. How long will Miss Maudie be?"

"Oh! No telling about her," Rosie said. "If she gets worked up over some daft kissing slop she'll very like see

183

it through twice. But she's generally home by ten, anyway."

"Have something to drink," the old lady said.

"Oh ! I –"

"A glass of wine," Rosie said, grudgingly.

"Well, I –"

"Oh, say whether you will or whether you won't !"

Without waiting for an answer she took the candle off the mantelpiece, lit it at the fire and stalked off to the cellar, coming back with the wine bottle two minutes later to find the minister warming his backside by the fire, his heels sing-songing up and down, on the hearthrug.

"And very tempting that looks !" he intoned.

"Wait'll you've had a drop."

Unsmiling, Rosie poured out the thick grape-red wine into three glasses.

"What kind? Your own make?"

"Elderberry. Yes, we made it. And be careful if you don't want to be flat on y' back."

He took his wine and sat down. "Won't you come nearer the fire?"

"I'm all right."

They sipped and sucked at the wine without speaking, the old lady cupping her glass in thin fingers of fire-reddened bone, her lips sucking and smacking at the wine-taste with the sound of too rich kisses.

"Very good." The minister made wry shapes of his thick lips, as though the wine had stung them with sourness.

"Want it hot," the old lady croaked. "Little in a pot and hot it, with a drop o' beer. She knows. She'll tell you."

"Who?"

"She will. Rose. My daughter-in-law. She's hotted it times anew."

"You seem to be something of an expert." He laughed, fleshily, the heavy professional laugh of politeness.

"Well, I ought to know. I was born and bred in a pub. Spent more than half my life in one."

"Oh!"

She flared up a little. "Anything wrong in that?"

"Oh! I didn't –"

"And a good pub too. The Angel."

He licked his lips, and made a surprising statement:

"I was in The Angel myself, only last Saturday."

"You? In the new Angel?"

"Yes. It's part of my campaign. To go into the pubs. Among the boys."

"Blimey!"

"We have pub discussions. Pub sing-songs. I read poetry to them, Shakespeare, Masefield."

"Well, that's one on me."

He took more than half his wine at one gulp, the glass a red thimble against his huge mouth. With the wine he took courage:

"Why don't you come, some time? Just come and watch. See what the Church can do."

"Me? And bring a tambourine? Like the Salvation Army?" She laughed strongly, her teeth a white circle, in soft derision. "Some hopes."

"Eh? What y' laughing at?" Fearful of missing something, the old lady hooked her body forward, her ear cupped. "What –"

"Your daughter-in-law was saying –" he went through it all with the deepest intonations of his best ecclesiastical voice, "and finally I invited her to come too."

"Where? Come where?"

"To The Angel."

"Nice thing. You ought to know better, if she don't!" And she relapsed into silence, the acid eyes pinked with firelight, her lips jealously straight and savage, her hatred of Rosie something that could be felt in the air.

Uneasy, the minister said: "Miss Maudie doesn't seem to come."

Rosie looked at the clock. "Going uphill for ten." She felt the wine firing her chest. "I should say she'd clicked or something perhaps if she hadn't got Lily with her."

"Ha! Hardly, hardly." He finished his wine. "Lily's a nice girl. A nice child."

"H'm."

"I say child. I dare say I ought not to. She's growing up."

"Seventeen. And like a kid of seven. No go, thin as a rake. Blimey, when I was seventeen, I had – well, never mind. Two men half killed each other, anyway."

He looked at her, sidelong, warmly, with veiled, rather fleshly admiration. "I can well believe it."

She looked at him fiercely. "Was that a compliment?"

"Well –"

"Stuff your compliments up your waistcoat!"

In the silence which followed, he draining his wine, Rosie defiantly staring straight in front of her, the old lady fuddled up from her chair. "I'll git my candle," she muttered, and she took the tin holder and lighted the wick with feeble independent fingers and then went off, her slippers slipping harshly on the bare wooden stairs, her good night a tart good riddance.

"Now you come nearer the fire," the parson said. "Take the old lady's chair."

"You ought to be getting home to your wife."

186

"Me? A bachelor."

"Oh!" Rosie said, "that explains your pub goings on."

"Don't call them goings on. They're done in the Church's name."

"I dare say. Another glass o' wine while you're waiting?"

She poured the wine into his glass, gave it him, filled her own and sat in the old lady's chair.

"You're very bitter," he said. "Is that quite necessary?"

"I didn't know I was bitter."

"You haven't got anything to be specially bitter about?"

"Nothing that you need trouble about."

"There you go again. Bitter as gall."

"Well!" she flared up. "What the hell does it matter to you?"

Confused, he said nothing, but drank his wine, slowly, as though preparing for the task of fresh argument. Rosie sat silent, rather relishing the course of conflict between them. It was like the best of the old days; the flint and steel of back-chat in the bar, the feminine against masculine contact that set the sparks flying. And the wine had warmed her to defiance, so that she was ready for anything.

Franklin leaned forward. "Why don't you do as I say? Come down. Join us. If not to the pub, then the chapel. Come once and give it a chance."

"Take your hand off my knee."

Shamefaced, he sat back, clumsy in actions, and guilt alike, his neck burning crimson like raw beef, his clerical balance aunt-sallied, so that for a moment she felt sorry for him.

"That was meant harmlessly," he said.

"I've had all kinds do it," Rosie said. "Soldiers, prize-fighters, all sorts. But you're the first parson."

"Parsons are only human. It must be the wine."

"I daresay. Only I'm a married woman, remember."

"That makes it worse."

"A lot worse, if my husband happened to be here. The Jefferys are devils for jealousy, don't forget."

So he sat silent, subdued, trying to reinstate himself by silence, to regain some decency of balance. And after an interval he tried another tack.

"You don't do any war-work?"

"I slave from dawn to dark, if that's anything!"

"Always? No days off? No break?"

"Once in a blue moon."

"Why?"

"You ask some damn silly questions, don't you? Why? What else could I do? What'll happen to this farm if I neglect it? What'll happen to me if my husband gets blown to smithereens? This farm's all I've got."

"Don't talk like that."

"How must I talk? By God, he might be blown to bits while we sit here."

For a moment he was beaten. Then he came back to the argument softly, to soothe her :

"That's just what I say. You should come down and join us. We're all in the same boat. It's a time of national as well as personal anxiety. The Church stands for that."

"Does it? You want to make an angel of me?"

"Not quite, but – there's comfort in human companionship. In the company of others."

"Sewing-meeting teas. Magic lanterns. I should like. I know."

"There's more in it than that."

"Not for me."

And suddenly they heard the tinkle of bicycle bells

188

in the farmyard outside and said : "That's Maudie," not
realizing till that moment how long they had talked or
how fiercely.

"A glass o' wine and I get worked up," she apologized.
"Been years since I had an argument, too."

"I enjoyed it." He respected her.

And when, finally, he took his hat and stick and departed with fussy "Good night, sirs" from Maudie, she
felt tired, limp after the stimulation of wine and argument.

"Fancy you and the parson," Maudie said.

"Oh, you never know with me !" Fuzzy with wine, she
lighted her candle, realizing for the first time how lonely
the war had been for her. "I'll try anything once."

V

And after that, during the last spring and summer of the
war, Franklin would often come up to the farm. Lily
apart, they were almost at the end of their tether :
wrought up, constrained, trapped in a triangle of tension
and bitterness and anxiety. Wind-reddened, no overcoat,
clerical collar discarded, a cattle dealer to look at, Franklin would come up in the evenings at first, ostensibly to
see Maudie, to discuss anthems, good works and classes,
but in reality for the glass of wine and Rosie. And at first
Rosie, seeing through it, would have none of it. Stand-
offish, she swept past him like some fierce broom. Hearing
him knock, she would get up and take on some stony task,
sleeves up, apron tight, clothes-folding or ironing or
stitching, in frigid efforts to shut him out. But always
without success. Sooner or later the wine, the talk, a

sudden feeling that she was too tired to keep it up, would
thaw and soften her. Until at last, knowing him better,
she came out with ironic banter : "Hullo, *you* here again?
Moses !" drawn into argument and intimacy by his fleshy
good-humour, his effervescent little eyes, so worldly and
unparsonic, glittering like lights in their heavy setting of
flesh. So that in time she tolerated him and then, out of
sheer perversity, was angry if he did not come. "Ah !" she
would say. "How's it you didn't come last week? Did I
scare you or something? Nice thing. Frightened of the
truth?" And he would grin, bantering back : "Oh, I've
other fish in the sea !" Rosie flashing at once : "Damned if
I didn't think so !" until Maudie prattled her horrified :
"The bits you say to Mr. Franklin ! You don't git a bit
better. I wonder he ever comes again."

And then, as summer came on, he dropped the evening
visits, and began to come in the afternoons, cycling. And
they having no time to stand and talk in the rush of hoeing
and hay-time, there was nothing for it but that he must
give a hand. Stripped, sleeves up, he showed the physique
of some craggy stoker, arms coppered and shiny, his pelt
coal-black. Buckled in an old belt of Tom's, he did the
tasks which Tom had once done and which the women
could no longer do, hauling and axing and lifting, a living
epitome of the Church militant. Then, as the rush of
summer increased, he began to come up before noon, his
bread and precious meat sandwiched in his pocket, to
work at self-set tasks, or at the hay, always a power of
energy, working and talking and finally eating at midday
on common ground with them, without uneasiness or
snobbery; so that even Rosie was drawn to admiration at
last.

"Well," she would say, as they sat in the hay-field shade

or in the kitchen, eating : "Seems a parson can be *some* good after all. I should never have believed it if I hadn't seen it."

"Don't be too hard," he said once. "I wasn't always a parson. I was the biggest blackguard in Christendom not twenty years ago."

"Oh ! Until what?"

"Until I was converted."

"Betcha life there was a woman in *that*."

"Not altogether. Mainly Christ. Doctrines of John Wesley," Franklin said. "For want of a better way of putting it, I saw the light."

Still Rosie bantered. "You're sure they weren't the sights that dazzled?"

"Oh, no ! I'd seen *them*. That was the trouble. I was blinded with them – beer and women, gambling, all the low life." He clenched his hands. "I was a regular rip-roaring devil. A boozer. Soaked in it."

"I bet they all loved you."

"They did. For a good reason. I had money. That's why. I was earning good money. I was a handsome chap and –"

"Oh !"

"Well, anyway, gang-foreman. Railroad work. We were laying new sections of rail in South Wales coalfields. And there I was, a single chap, with plenty of money."

"And no sense."

"That's it. No sense at all. A walking liquor-barrel."

"Awful. And then you saw the light?"

"Yes, and then I saw the light. And it's no fairy tale either. It's true. And I'm never tired of telling of it. I tell it over and over again in every circuit I go into. How I turned and made a fight and won and educated myself –

191

Miss Maudie has heard me tell it, haven't you, Miss
Maudie?"

"Yes," Maudie said. "I've heard it. It's exciting."

"I use it as a sermon," Franklin said. "I shouldn't say it
– but it's a better story than the conversion of St. Paul."

"He takes his coat off," Maudie said, "and rolls his
sleeves up."

"Well, it sounds exciting," Rosie said. "As good as
Maudie's pictures."

"Better. A lot better. And I'll tell you something. If
you'll come down to chapel, one Sunday evening, I'll tell
it again."

"All for me?"

"Yes, for you."

"Your coat off and everything?"

"Yes, coat off, sleeves up, everything. Imitations of myself drunk and everything. That's a fair offer, isn't it?"

"It's a dodge. You just want to convert me."

"No, I don't. But if you're afraid of –"

"Afraid? I'll afraid you in a minute. You'll be asking me
to sing the solo next."

"Well, you might do worse than that."

"All right. I'll come and sing 'The Old Bull and Bush'?"

"Rosie !" Maudie said.

"I don't care what she does," Franklin said, "so long
as she'll come."

And more than half that summer he schemed to pene-
trate her iron indifference. He worked insistently, painfully, as a man might seek to pierce an oak-tree with a
gimlet. And all the time also he worked for them, his big
raw figure in its element, his presence an antidote to all
the acid of womanish fears and jealousies that had threat-
ened to eat their life utterly away. That summer he saved

them from themselves. With a passion of energy he schemed and worked and advised and solved their problems. "I know they say," he said, "I should be in France. But you mustn't forget that I'm nearly sixty. And one day I shall crack. The rip-tearing boozing body that I was so proud of will have its revenge on me, I know. All boozers crack in the end."

"Don't kid yourself," Rosie said. "My father's been boozing for forty years, and looks as fat as butter."

"Wasn't there some trouble," he said one day, when they were alone, "about your father?"

"Oh! yes. He bunked," Rosie said. "Went to London one day and skedaddled. And good riddance."

"Wouldn't you like me to find him? I could trace him."

"Not me."

"Miss Maudie was asking me. I would try to trace him if you liked."

"You trace him, and see what! I was never so glad in my life as the day he went."

And sometimes, as they stood talking together, alone, she could feel a sudden rise of the inflection of his voice, a rise of passion, that was almost infectious. And she would see his struggle to keep it back, the inward fierce conflict of creed against passion, his eyes alight. Until almost in pity, and for her own sake, she would say:

"Well, talking don't get that barley down."

Then, harvest over, he surprised her.

"There's something special at chapel next Thursday," he said. "I want you to come."

"Your sermon? The strip-out affair?"

"Well, I'll do that if you come. But there's something else. A special mid-week musical service. Lily is taking the solo."

"Singing?"

"Yes."

"She couldn't sing pussy."

"Oh! yes she could. I've coached her. She's got a nice little voice. She's singing a Handel aria, 'I know that my Redeemer Liveth'."

"Blimey."

"Say you'll come."

She hedged : "I never knew she *could* sing."

"But she can. And a sweet little voice too."

"It's a new one on me. Lily singing. You could knock me down with a quart-mug."

"I want you to say you'll come."

"Oh, blimey, I don't know."

But all the week it was as though she were between nut-crackers, Franklin on the one side and Maudie the other, both seeking to snap her resistance. "After all," Franklin would say, "look who she gets it from !" And Maudie : "I should think you *will* come. A big do like this. If it were one of mine I should die with excitement."

"It's a dodge," she would say. "A dodge to get me there."

But in the end she went. It was late September, the mild evenings darkening early. She put on a plum-red dress, and wore her ear-rings. "Want two or three pepper-mints?" Maudie said. "I always take a pepper-mint or two. If I slip one in during the second prayer it lasts through the sermon." So she took peppermints, tucking them in the palm of her glove, with her collection money. "There'll be a lot there," Maudie said, excited. And the chapel was crowded, the pine seats warm-smelling in the close air, the crowded faces greenish in the gaslight. Rosie sat alone, far back in the gallery, and Lily sang her solo between the second prayer and the sermon, the sweet Handel aria milky and delicate, almost negative in its softness, like the girl herself. It was like the singing of a doll : just so meek and virgin and white, a voice of china. And all through it Rosie crunched her peppermint hard and, in spite of herself, was almost touched, singing the notes for Lily in her mind, feeling the way for her, glad when it was over.

After that Franklin preached. The pulpit was like the wooden prow of a ship, and Franklin stood raised up, a watcher over the ocean of faces. Sun-scorched, he looked out of place, a savage, his hands big and primitive as they clenched themselves on the pulpit top and finally on the Bible. He held the Bible aloft. "Tonight I do not need the Bible, nor," he said, "do I need my coat." He put the Bible in the preacher's seat and took off his jacket and laid it on the Bible. Then he unfastened his cuff links and rolled up his shirt-sleeves, steeling his muscles. "My heart is my Bible. And in my arms is the strength of the Lord. And my opponents –" he took up guard, crouching his raw fists clenched "– are the devils that were the evils of Sodom and Gomorrah ! The heavy-weights of vice and devilry. The welter-weights of boozing and blasphemy. The sparring partners of Satan himself !" He brought round in the empty air of the pulpit, terrifically, the left of an imaginary knock-out. It seemed to inspire him. He went on to preach for fifty minutes : a sermon of muscle and fire, his big raw face sweat-oiled with the passion and heat of force and anger, his eyes righteously fired and strangely uplifted to the gaslight. Until in the end he stood in a trance of passion, exhausted, limp after an orgasm of fury and godliness, his face transcended, the congregation shattered.

In spite of herself, Rosie was moved. She never forgot it. Afterwards, as she waited in the chapel-yard for Maudie to leave by the choir-door, Franklin suddenly came out to her.

"Mrs. Jeffery," he said.

"Hullo," Rosie said. "Blimey. It was hot stuff. No mistake. A teazer. There was some sense in it. I liked it."

Suddenly she stopped. His face was white.

"What the matter?" she said.

"Will you come into the vestry a moment?"

In the vestry Maudie was holding a telegram in her hands. Franklin took it from her and gave it to Rosie. "They had the sense to bring it here. The postmaster is a chapel steward," he said. Maudie was crying.

The telegram said :

PTE T JEFFERY CRITICAL CONDITION WEYMOUTH VAD
ADVISE COME IMMEDIATELY MATRON

Rosie stood dumb.

"There's no train tonight," Franklin said.

VI

"Have you got your money all right? And your clean vest?" For the first time for many years Maudie was speaking with kindness in her voice, the kindness of fear. "And the telegram? Because that's got the address on."

Rosie had the telegram in her handbag. She had her handbag in turn clutched tightly against her hip. In her other hand she had the family straw travelling bag. Without her ear-rings, wearing a grey costume, with black gloves, she looked oddly sober.

"And the sandwiches?"

"I put the sandwiches in the case."

"In the case? The mustard won't get on your under-things will it?"

Rosie climbed up into the carriage. And then for a minute she leaned out of the train window, Maudie on the platform, and they talked of the mustard, fearfully, magnifying it, glad of it, making it an outlet for their fears. Until at last doors banged, and Rosie, trying to make light of it all, said : "There's a chap next door giving me the glad-eye already," and laughed faint-heartedly, Maudie remembering just before the train moved, to say :

"Telegram us when you get there ! Telegram us if it's all right."

And in another moment Rosie had gone, vanished for the first time beyond her world. It was a going whose significance never crystallized. Fluidly, her fears ran hot and cold, drowning and chilling her. She never reached the hard stark core of terror. She kept her mind on little things like the mustard, wondered if Maudie knew the hen maize was running short. In London she had a glass of beer. That, and the silly mustard, was almost all she afterwards remembered of a journey that took her the better part of a day. Of Tom she scarcely thought. Tom, as always seemed inviolable, as firmly socketed in life as the farm itself was set in the landscape above the river. She remembered that he used to boast of never having had a day's illness in his life. It was as though nothing could happen to him. And when she consciously thought of the telegram, the hospital, the whole shocking business, it was paradoxically to be angry. Why hadn't they let her know sooner? How long ago had it happened? Chaps

197

half-dying and they couldn't let you know about it until it was perhaps too late!

She was back within a week; glad to be back. She telegraphed, and Franklin met her at the station with the trap, Lily with him. But Rosie scarcely noticed it.

"Are things all right?" Franklin said.

"As right as they'll ever damn well be in this world!" she said passionately. And then, as they drove along: "Don't ask me too much. I'm whacked. For two blessed pins I could bawl like a kid."

And at the farm it was the same: "Give me a cup o' tea. Don't ask me anything."

It was only when she had drunk her tea and Franklin had taken Lily into the orchard, that she could bear Maudie's questions and the dazed deaf catechism of the old woman, who only half understood.

"Eh? How d'ye say Tom is?"

"Tom's all right. I seen him, and he's all right."

"What is it?" Maudie said, in fear. "How bad is it?"

"He's wounded. Bad: in the back." Telling it, she felt hard and cold, her heart stony. "He's ain't goin' to get over it in a hurry. If he gets over it at all."

"He's all right. I seen him. I know. He's all right."

"With *that*?"

"I shouldn't have come back unless. They didn't expect him to live a day, let alone a week."

"Eh?" the old lady said. "Tom say anything about me?"

Rosie cupped her hands and spoke louder, in a great effort: "He's all right. He don't think about us. Too busy gettin' off with the nurses!"

"Ain't much wrong with him, then?"

Rosie never answered. Maudie, fainting, staggered back across the tea-table like an iron nine-pin, her stiff body

198

smashing down on the world of cups and chairs as the news of Tom had already smashed down, catastrophically, on the world of the farm.

BOOK FIVE

CHANGE AND DECAY

CHAPTER I

I

"LIFT me up," Tom said.

"I'm sure I shan't. It ain't been five minutes since I lifted you up. Is that all you fetched me traipsing up here for?"

"Damn y', lift me up! Give me holt o' that bloody telescope!"

Tom lay in bed, in the big room overlooking the yard and the road and the fields beyond, helpless, sick beyond all recognition. Rosie stood with folded arms, her lips sewn tight to a single line. Tom's hair had begun to come out, thinning back from the temples in seams of white baldness, and his voice had some of the same thin nakedness, his words shorn completely of all easiness and quiet.

"Get me that bloody telescope!"

She stood hard, not moving. It was July, a month past midsummer. The windows of the bedroom were thrown up, so that his voice lashed out into the open air. And while she still stood there, adamant, arms and lips folded in refusal, Maudie heard the sick yell of Tom's voice from the yard below, and rushed up, frightened.

"What the matter? What's he want? What is it, Tom?"

"Lift me up! Lift me up!"

Maudie was hardened into righteous antagonism. Turning on Rosie at once:

"Why couldn't you do what he wanted? Ain't the poor chap –"

"It ain't been five minutes since I lifted him up. D'ye think I want that wound running again?"

"Blast the bloody wound and you an' all! Lift me up and let me see that wheat! Lift me up!"

"As if it'd hurt him," Maudie said, "for two minutes. Quiet now then, Tom. Quietly. I'll git y'up for a minute."

And Rosie stood by, unmoving, while Maudie lifted him up, first back and then up, mounding the pillows under him, the bulges made by the wound-pads shifting slightly upward, the motions screwing him with new pain, until, thin wrists pressing down on the bed for leverage, he could just raise himself enough to look through the window, his face fierce with agony and triumph. And propped there, waiting for Maudie to get the telescope from the chest of drawers, he shot one look at Rosie with eyes that were momentarily like his mother's, acid and prematurely old and burnt up, full of pain and a new anger against her, a strange look of corrosive bitterness and joy.

Until at last Maudie came with the telescope and held it for him and almost crooked his fleshless fingers round it, standing by for fear of catasrophe while he focused the ragged sections of Top Land that were visible under and between the full chestnut leaves, a yellow rent in the green fabric of afternoon, the wheat just turning colour. And then, having focused, he looked for a long time. The telescope was never still, always trembling. Tom's mouth was shut in savage determination, his clenched teeth cemented together between his stone-hard lips, the sweat pricking out on the patches of bone-white baldness.

He spoke at last with anger that was really against Rosie, the telescope clenched at her like a weapon.

"You call that a bloody crop?" he raged. "Christ! that won't be above a quarter!"

"How can you see," she flashed, "from here? How do you know?"

"Know? Know? A kid would know. I ain't blind, if I did get my guts shot out! I know what –"

"Tom, Tom," Maudie said.

"Shut your chops!"

"Tom, Tom, you must lay down. It's no good you gittin' obstrocklous. Wheat ain't no good nowhere this year. It's poor stuff everywhere. And it wants a month t'harvest yet. You must lay down."

"Lay down. Damn wonder as I don't lay down and die after that lot. Wheat! God, I never see nothing like it."

"Cover up now, and lay still."

And while Tom was lying back again, the telescope lay on the bed, and seeing it, Rosie moved for the first time. She reached forward for it, snatched it, and put it back on the chest of drawers.

"Leave that telescope here!" he raved.

"I ain't forgot the last time I left it." She stood relentless.

He lay helpless, raging against her, futile. Then weakness checked him. He lay still, bone-white. And when he spoke again it was with a quiet that, after the futility of rage, seemed dangerous.

"Now both on you git out," he said, "and send Collins up."

"Anything else?" Rosie said. It was almost dangerous too.

He did not speak, and the women went to the door together, driven out, Maudie first, already on the landing, when Tom fetched Rosie back with a half-shout:

"Wha'd' them pigs fetch yesterday?"

205

"Twelve pound odd." She lied, adding the two pounds, her eyes dead straight.

"Christ." He gave bitter groans. "Who took 'em?"

"I did."

"And you let 'em go for that!" he raved.

"Pork ain't fetching nothing. July. You might know that."

"Then why the hell didn't y' bring 'em back?"

"You said get rid o' the pigs. The whole blamed lot."

"Who did? Who did?"

"You did. Raved and put yourself out and said get rid of 'em."

"Never said a damn word about it!"

"You don't know what you do say!"

"Who don't? My God, you wait till I *can* get out o' this bed. Somebody's for the bloody high jump, that day."

At a loss, abashed into silence, still staggered by the new turn in him, she went out. And when she had gone he lay quite still, staring at the ceiling cracks, waiting for Collins, the new man, to come up. As he lay there, half-bald, his face almost fleshless, the eyes fixed, he looked extraordinarily old, a man old before his time, a human apple withered on the tree. He could feel no pain : only the heavy revolving engine of his heart pumping excited blood through his weak veins, his shattered stomach dead, his legs wooden with paralysis from the hips downward. And on top of it all the rage of his own mind : infinitesimal cog-wheels of hatred and impatience tearing their teeth into one another, a concerted cry of bitterness against his own impotency. He had only one thought of anything like pride and satisfaction.

He was home; he had made them send him home. At least he had done that much. He was viciously proud of

his triumph against doctors and officialdom and adversity.
"They wanted to keep me there!" he would say. "In that
bloody hospital. Yes, I said, I should like. And in the
finish they patched me up and sent me home. And a damn
good job I did come. See the state things were in." And
he lay thinking of it, the thought of it bringing back the
bitter stink of his wound, all the rotten impotency of his
lot, the bed damp with the sweat of his suffering.

Until finally Collins came up and into the bedroom:
a thin moustached man, middle-aged, with vague grey
eyes, his cap cocked to one side, like a miller's.

"Want me?"

"Yes. Git off up to Top Land and git me ear or two
o' that wheat!"

"Anything wrong?"

"Anything wrong! Christ Almighty. You stan' there
knowing that wheat won't give above a quarter to th'
acre and then ask me if anything's wrong. The whole
bloody farm's wrong." He was shouting. "And you an' all!"

"I can't be everything," Collins said. "Horsekeeper and
manage the place and everything. Farm this size wants
half a dozen men."

"Oh! Funny thing as we did it wi' two, afore the war,
ain't it?"

"Times are changed."

"I think they bloody well have an' all, see the way Top
Land looks."

"We want a tractor," Collins said.

"Tractor? Then why the hell couldn't you say so? Get
a tractor. Get anything. Anything so's we get a crop worth
looking at."

He lay silent, near to exhaustion. Until another thought
occurred:

"How much them pigs fetch yesterday?"

"About ten pound."

"What were you doing?"

"Me? I was here, working that binder."

"She go by herself to market?"

"Far as I know."

"Far as you know, eh? Dressed up to the bloody nines, I expect!"

"Oh! didn't you? Another week you go with her, and keep y' eyes on her."

Collins said nothing. Weak, Tom lay quiet himself. From below hen-sounds came up as somebody disturbed or fed the fowls in the orchard shade, the sounds clear, summer-like. And from farther off still the meadow scents came up, meadowsweet and clover and the carried hay itself : sweet smells gone bitter.

And smelling them Tom aroused again, to say :

"Well, wha'd'y' starin' there for?"

"Thought you wanted me."

"Want you? Git off and git that wheat. And bring it straight up here. And tell the missus I want her."

Collins went, and soon, after Tom had played a kind of game with the sounds of the day and the farm, shuffling them over and over in his mind like a pack of bright cards, Rosie came up. And again she stood at the foot of the bed, tight-faced, a little weary, sleeves rolled up to her leather elbows, her voice flat.

"Collins said you wanted me."

"Yes." He spoke dangerously. "What game d'ye think you were up to at market yesterday?"

"What game?"

"Collins see you. All dolled up. Funny way to go and sell pigs ain't it?"

"Collins was here. He never set eyes on me."

"Ah ! What else you do, 'sides sell them pigs?"

"I got that cattle-cake order in. And the binder-twine. And –" Suddenly she was incensed against him herself – "Must I damn well give an account of everything I did an' see?"

"That's it," he said jealously. "That's it, y'see. Summat y' don't want me to know."

"So you got me up here to say that? Is that all?"

She turned for the door.

"You may well slink off !" he taunted.

"Who's slinking off?" She came back quickly, furious, checking herself at the bed-foot. "My God, what's come over you, since you come back?"

"Come over me?"

"You ain't the same man. Everybody says so. Even Maudie says so."

Her voice whipped her with bitterness.

"'Course I didn't git my damn guts shot out, did I?"

She could not speak.

"That don't make no difference, does it?" he said. "I ain't penned in this bloody bed, am I?"

"Folks might think," she said, "we never did nothing for you, the way you talk."

He was sullen, touched.

"If I traipsed up these stairs once today, I traipsed up 'em fifty times. And Maudie too. And that's all the thanks we get."

"Keep on."

"Yes, and keep on I will. If it wasn't for me and Maudie you'd have bin finished long enough ago."

"And a damn good job too !" he flashed.

Even though she had heard the words so often that

209

they lacked all meaning for her, the bitter syllables crackling in the air like empty egg-shells, she had not the heart to reply. She stood and stared out of the window, at the torn blue sky above the chestnuts, not thinking, as if waiting for something without knowing what it was.

And suddenly there was a change in him, almost a collapse, the fire of bitterness against both her and himself extinguished by physical need.

"Git mum," he said. "Quick. I want the bed-pan."

"I could do it."

"No. I want mum. I don't want no one else but mum."

And without speaking again she hurried down, glad to be out of it, calling the old woman across the orchard, her voice harsh from long practice in checking emotion.

And the old woman came from the garden, vague, on slow feet, lifting her anonymous face to listen as she came near.

"Tom wants you !"

"Eh? Ain't he up yit?"

"Quick. He wants you. The bed-pan."

"Time he was up."

And she shuffled into the house and upstairs, one foot, one step, painfully, muttering to herself, not understanding.

II

All through that summer, the first after the war, and on into the next winter, and the next spring, the old lady lived her anonymous life of futility : shuffling almost mindlessly through the days, standing in lost meditation to rub her bloodless hands together for warmth or comfort as though she were rubbing at everlasting ears of corn, feebly spreading corn in actuality on the orchard-grass for the chicken at all hours of the day, not knowing what she did. Forgetful, and very often, since between Tom and the land neither Rosie nor Maudie had time for her, forgotten, she lived one life with her body and another, the past, with her mind.

"Ain't Dad in yit? He's bin gone a 'nation of a time down at the mill. Tea'll be stewed to death afore he gits back. I aint' seen Frankie neither. Where's Frankie?"

Or the past would become in some way distorted, entangled with a fantastic present, making a rigmarole of pain:

"Can't understand our Tom, a-laying there. Frankie don't do it. That boy's up and out afore it's light. Tom's lazy. That's what 'tis. Lazy. Eh?"

So that in time, for sheer self-protection, Maudie and Rosie were driven to live apart from her, in a separate life. And driven apart from her, they were driven closer to each other. The life of the farm drew all its energy from them. They were like the twin pistons of its mechanism, tirelessly driving backwards and forwards in the socket of the day's making a bitter heat of friction that only the oil of sheer necessity could cool. And now Maudie, deprived of all outlet for passion, Ella dead, Turk vanished, the old lady too far gone for gossip, could only hoard her jealousies and fears and hatreds with parsimonious secrecy, miser-fashion, as against a day of evil necessity. There were days when they worked side by side, hoeing, hay-raking, potato-picking, and yet hardly spoke; and when the meal-table might have been some occasion of sombre feminine mourning, the old lady eating toothlessly at one end, Lily with half-ladylike milkiness at the other, Maudie and Rosie in grim opposition, not speaking. Fixed in the

steel sockets of their own ways, they suffered for Tom,
Maudie's lips unconsciously knotted and unknotted with
pain and relief, Rosie's eyes still and stoical as they
watched the changing of the dressing, all their acts and
emotions and impressions governed and shaped by a
common thought : the thought, in reality the knowledge,
that he would never get up again.

It was a thought they did anything and everything to
lessen and suppress. All through the war the farm and
Tom had been one. They were still one. To them it could
never be otherwise. They knew, at heart, that if Tom
should go the farm would go too. So, only half knowing
why they did it, they strove unrestingly and even against
each other to keep Tom going, labouring even harder
over his wounds and paralysis than they did over the
farm's furrows and its fertility. And always, though they
knew that his chances of survival were no more than a
fly's, they cheated themselves into the old belief that he
was inviolable, enduring as the land.

"Git another summer here," Maudie would say, "and I
shouldn't wonder if we got him downstairs. He could
lay out in th' orchard."

"I was thinking the same sort o' thing myself, yesterday."

"He's better in himself. You can see that. Mr. Franklin
said he could see a change in him. He's better in himself."

Franklin, entering up his last year of the circuit, still
came up to the farm. The war-time day visits had ended,
but he would come up in the evenings, big, pugilistic as
ever, and sit with Tom in the bedroom, to thrash out the
day's problems, to pour parsonic oil on the cancerous
bitterness brought on by solitude, and to help if he
could.

"Don't be afraid," he said, "to tell me if there's anything I can do to help."

"The bloke who could help me ain't born."

"Well, you know what I mean."

"All right, chum. No offence."

"So that in the autumn Tom said :

"You're allus talking about help. Want summat to do one night, help me git th'accounts straight. Depend they're in a bloody mess. Like me."

"All right. But swearing won't help."

"Ask the missus for the books. Two on 'em. In the bureau in the front room."

"Any bills? You want to check things?"

"Ah, bring the bills ! I don't trust nobody."

When Franklin came back upstairs with the old worn red leather accounts books, begun in the writing of Tom's grandfather, carried on by Alf Jeffery himself, and continued at last by Tom, Tom said :

"My father, and his father afore that, allus made books up after Michaelmas. Then they knowed where they stood for the winter."

Franklin laid the books on the bed, and Tom looked at his empty hands.

"Where are the bills?"

"She's finding them. Rosie. Mrs. Jeffery."

"You know what that means? She's lost 'em – never had 'em, some damn thing or other. That's women." He took up the big account book, savagely, propping it on his chest. It was mid-autumn, a dark evening, and Franklin moved the lamp farther across the bed-table, so that the light fell whitish-orange on the book. Tom was looking at the figures for the war years : the painful board-school hand of Rosie and Maudie, intermingled

with the new script of Lily and odd scrawls of his own
hastily scratched in on week-ends of leave, and finally
at the entries for 1918, the black year, the year of
hospital.

"Whose bloody writing's this?"

"Mine."

"Who asked y'to do that?"

"They did. The women. It got beyond them."

Tom made a sound in his throat in answer, a grunt of
doubt, jealousy, suspicion. Then he flicked over the leaves,
still in doubt, all his family pride on guard.

"You make up this profit?"

"Yes."

"How d'ye know it's right? Check it with the
Bank?"

"Mrs. Jeffery did. It was all right." He spoke softly. "No
need to get suspicious, Jeffery. It's all right. You can count
on me."

"Who's suspicious? I ain't suspicious." And then : "Two
new chicken houses. Forty quid odd. That's a hell of a
tall order, ain't it?"

"The eggs and the chickens have been paying pretty
well. I know that. Shall we get started?"

Franklin writing, they began on the accounts, checking
the rough entries from the small book, carrying on the
seventy-years old record of Jeffery profit unpunctuated by
a single dot or comma of a farthing's loss, Tom querying
each entry, turning it over and over, letting the figures
run through his hands like doubtful grain. Twice Franklin
went downstairs, once to fetch the cheque books, once
the pass book. Towards nine – they had been working
for more than two hours then – Franklin had the figures
almost straight.

"Tot it up as soon as you can. I'll check the stubs."

"I'll give you a rough idea in a minute," Franklin said. "It seems all right."

But when, five minutes later he had made the final run-over, there was something wrong. He checked the bank figures again, then the books, the figures still running against him.

"Summat up?" Tom said. "We ain't down the course, are we?"

"Forty odd pounds I can't account for." He ran over the subtraction again. "See if there's a counterfoil for forty-three fifteen six."

"How far back?"

"Might be anywhere. Or a blank counterfoil."

During the war Tom had left signed cheque books for Rosie's convenience, not transferring any account from his name to hers, Rosie paying all large bills by cheque, all smaller by cash drawn out by cheque on the first of the month. And as Franklin and Tom checked back the counterfoils all the amounts were in Rosie's hand, and Franklin said:

"That's a mystery. Every entry's been made with such care."

"Git her up! Call her!" Tom said. "If anybody knows, she does."

Franklin went to the stairs and called Rosie, and in a minute she came up, Franklin asking Tom in a lowered voice not to upset her, Tom's answer snapping out just before she reached the landing: "I don't trust nobody! Women least of all. If the war never learnt me nothing else it learnt me that."

"Steady," Franklin said.

Rosie came in. "Want me?"

215

"Yes! What the 'ell you spend forty-three quid on?" Tom raved.

"Steady, Jeffery, steady."

"She knows about it! Look at her."

"One moment, one moment."

"What's up?" Rosie said, quietly.

"We can't trace a counterfoil for forty-three pound fifteen six, and we wondered if you remembered it. That's all."

"That's all!" Tom roared. "Christ!"

"Let me look at the cheque books," Rosie said. "If there's anything I forgot to put in, there'll be a bill for it. Sure to be."

"We got every damn bill they is!"

"All right."

Sitting on the bed, she ran through the stubs of the three cheque books, working backwards, into the war years.

Suddenly, half way through the second cheque book, she got up and showed the book to Franklin.

"Looks as if it's been cut out with scissors."

Franklin, amazed, could only rub his fingers along the sharp hardly visible paper edge without speaking, while Tom raved from the bed:

"Gi' me that bloody cheque book!"

And with the book in his hands Tom lay furious, burning with suspicion, sickness magnifying the moment, charging it with hatred of them both.

"You know something about this!" he shouted. "Both of you."

"Don't be so damn silly," Rosie said.

"By God if I could git up!"

Then Franklin said: "What would be the date of the

cheque? You would know that by the date of the nearest entries."

And Rosie looked it up. "1917," she said. "Either September or October."

"I'd never been in this house then."

"No! But she had!" Tom raved. "Where'd you keep that damn cheque book?"

"In the bureau. You know that."

"Anybody else know that?"

"Everybody knew I did."

"Everybody? Maudie?"

"Yes."

"Git Maudie up!" he raved.

And again Franklin went to the stairs and called for Maudie as he had called for Rosie, and again, as her feet sounded on the stairs, he entreated Tom to be steady, Tom answering by raging at Maudie the second her figure was framed in the doorway:

"You know anything about this cheque?"

"What cheque?"

Maudie stood grim, and frightened.

"We're trying to trace a cheque," Franklin said, "for forty-three pounds odd. Taken out in latter part of 1917."

"I never had no cheque."

"It's been cut out," Tom said. "Show her, show her where it's been cut out."

Rosie took the cheque book from Tom and gave it to Franklin and Franklin in turn gave it to Maudie.

She stood white.

"Forty-three quid!" Tom raved. "What'd you do with it?"

"Don't accuse her," Franklin said. "Don't accuse her."

"I never had no cheque," Maudie said.

She stood stubborn and white, and Tom, almost exhausted, could not speak, so that for a moment it was deadlock, nothing happening again till Rosie spoke.

"1917. That was the year we had the gramophone."

"What's that got to do with it?" Maudie said.

"You ought to know. You bought it."

"Gramophone?" Tom roused again. "Gramophone? How much that cost?"

Maudie and Rosie were silent, but Franklin said : "No doubt it'll come right another night. Let me come up again to-morrow night." But Tom raved on :

"How much that gramophone cost? Maudie !"

"Twenty pound odd. It's a good one. I could git –"

"And you had that cheque to buy it with. And twenty over yourself. That the drift on't, aint it?"

"I never had no cheque."

"You got money of your own, ain't you? And Ella's money. You had that?"

"Yes."

"And then had this cheque too?"

"I never had no cheque."

It was the old answer, but she was crying now, the stupid stubbornness collapsing quite suddenly, the tears running down her cheeks in confession, her handkerchief screwed into damp knots of pain. And as she stood there, her iron lips hopelessly softened, her big wooden body quite broken up, Tom drove the last of his attacks at her :

"Allus so damn prim and straight ! Never do nothing wrong. Brought up chapel. And then do a bloody bit like this !" Until Franklin quietened him, and he could only shout with bitter impotency :

"Get out ! All on y'. For Christ's sake. Git out ! Git out afore I go mad !"

THE winter almost smashed him. Like a trap, confinement lacerated him to raw shreds. By a great effort of will he kept the farm at his fiingers' end, running it and planning it from where he lay. With the bed moved, set cross-wise, he could see from both windows, north-eastwards to Top Land and the fringe of larch fox-coverts beyond, south and south-eastwards across the river and the acreage of flooded winter meadows and the ridge of ironstone beyond. And with windows open he could hear the day going its course : cows up before the first daylight and in the darkening winter afternoons, the boom and rumble of the thresher, the milk buckets clanked down on the floors of cow-houses, the clack of muck-cart wheels, the wrangling of dogs and the wind-torn voices of the women calling themselves and the cattle, and over all the bass stutter of the tractor. And he would feel the day, taste its air instinctively : how fine it was, or how damp, and what was the promise of moons and sunsets. So that when Collins appeared for orders after first breakfast, Tom had mapped out the day by intuition, beyond argument. "Needn't git that tractor out. Ain't gonna to be fine above five minutes. Git the big wagon out and git down to the station and fetch that basic slag for Dark Closes. Advice note's here s'morning. And if it lets up git on Top Land to-morrow. That won' hurt. Dad used to say Top Land let it through like a sieve. But don' git on it if it don't leave off afore breakfast. Do, you'll have it dry and steely as hell. Anything you wanna know?"

"No. Wheat's through in that field this side o' Top Land."

"I know. I seen it yesterday. Through nice. And see it's kep' nice ! Bloody crop like we had last year."

"Anything you want in Orlingford?"

"No. Ask the missus to come up, that's all."

Collins would go, and Rosie would come. Gaunt, physically sulky, almost sour sometimes in the very early winter mornings, she would stand at the bedfoot and listen to what he had to say, or rather, more often, she listened and did not understand, her ears alone active, her mind still sleep-clogged, without response. She stood as if nothing mattered. And he would talk to her as if she were nothing but the bedboard itself, in the new army-fashioned voice, coarse with aggression, all its old drawling and almost stupid neutrality gone, all the old implied tenderness for her corroded out of existence. Hearing it, she felt no pain. She stood stoical, almost invulnerably insulated now against all shocks. The war had severed whatever it was that had joined them, a perpetual barrier cutting them off, he on the family side, she more than ever the outsider, the usurper, still after nearly twenty years a stranger beyond the pale of family jealousy and family spite and even family suffering. And after he had said what he wanted to say, catechised her, ordered her, even blasphemed at her, she would go downstairs and begin what was for her the pointless ritual of another day.

But on market days and on Saturdays it was different. She was dressed up then : rather fine, with her still good figure, and the big hats she always wore so well, and the splashes of colour, scarves of crimson and bright green, the rather haughty hat feathers. It was her one chance of escape, to dress up, to go to market, to have her glass of stout in The Bell or The Griffin, to shop a little and then return.

And he envied her even that.

"Why th'ell you hadda doll up for like that I don' know ! Why th'ell don't y' try an' look decent?"

"Decent ! Decent !"

"Look like some bloody tart ! My God, if I can't have nothing, you ain't goin' short, arc y'?"

"That's what you think of me."

"Think ! I don't think, I know."

"Mr. Know-all. Who tells you? Maudie?"

"Never you mind !"

"I'm not minding. I'm not minding. It's you who's changed, not me."

"Changed ! By God I am. And a dam' sight you care !"

In that way he hammered out the last of her feeling for him. His jealousies smashed even her decency of feeling. He brooded on her savagely, sickly, and sickness magnified her, painted the colour of her hats a brighter scarlet, multiplied her comings and goings, filled in the gaps that reality could not, started the wildest imaginings.

Until one afternoon, remembering her jibe of "Who tells you? Maudie?" he yelled for Maudie to come up.

"She ain't back yit?"

"Who? Rosie?"

It was February : a dry, savage day of iron cloud, an east wind flecking bullets of snow.

"Ah, Rosie. Why'd she go out on a day like this? Funny, aint it?"

"She's gone shopping."

"Shopping? Who's she see down there? Who's she got down there? Sees some blasted man, don't she? You know !"

"Tom !"

"You know, don't you?"

"I never seen her, Tom. I never heard nothing."

Her mind revolved swiftly, bringing up like a water-wheel its scoopings of past jealousy and anger and the festering of old hatreds. And as she stood there, trying also to think of what Rosie did and where she went on market days, she recalled how Rosie had, not long since, given her away to Tom – "as if the cheque wasn't every bit as much mine as hers, as if the money ain't ourn!" – and the new hatred whipped the old into fury.

Before she could speak, Tom said :

"She's had a man, ain't she, ever since I bin gone?"

"I don't know."

"I tell y' she's had one! She's got one now! Else I'm a damn fool!"

Maudie stood silent, stiffening herself for courage. Her heart pounded with malice that had in it an odd mixture of joy and fear.

"Why don't y' say nothing?" Tom said. "Ain't I right? Ain't she got somebody? Ain't she got a man down there?"

"I don't know. But –"

"But what? What?"

"She had one."

Tom lay stiff, upraised, on one elbow. He was abnormally thin, his face an odd straw-colour, his eyes very nearly fanatical in their yellowish weakness, his baldness dead white.

"Had one? When? Who?"

"Afore you went."

"*Afore* I went?"

He lay silent, his mind revolving backward, thinking, his recollections desperate. And Maudie stood outwardly quiet, too, charged with the powerful current of a new excitement, the blood tearing through her body with a malicious and almost lovely excitement, the moment almost too much to bear.

"Who was it?" Tom said. "By God, who was it?"

"You don't know?" Maudie prolonged the joy, put off as it were the flicking on of the switch of sensation for another moment.

"How the hell could I know? Who was it?"

And in answer Maudie almost shouted, her voice on the verge of hysteria, her control unequal at last, even after years of anticipation, to the magnitude of the moment. "Frankie! It was Frankie!" she shouted. "Our Frankie! It was our Frankie!"

I V

WHEN Rosie cycled home in the late afternoon of the same day, hands almost frozen on the handle-bars, the wind of darkness and ice cutting straight at her out of the east, the thin snow driving like frozen flint over the tree-less verges, she almost ran into a figure, staggering vaguely down the road to meet her: the old woman, helplessly driven about by the gusting of wind and snow, a mere huddled bag of fabric and complaint, piteously muttering to herself and the wild air and finally to Rosie that Tom was very bad and that she must get the doctor. Not stopping to think whether it were right or wrong, her mind frozen almost dead, Rosie turned her and led her back, pushing the bicycle with one hand and leading the old woman so slow on her feet that Rosie could have cried with the sheer pain of cold and wind and the bitter pellet-ing of snow. Then, half-way to the house, Maudie came crying along the road, hatless, waving gaunt arms of distress.

"Is that her? You got her? Oh, my gracious! Where was she? How far? Oh, Mother, Mother!"

"What's the matter? Why'd she come? She keeps talking about Tom."

"Tom's bad. Took worse since you bin gone. He's funny. I can't make it out. I can't make it out."

"I'll get back for the doctor."

And while the old woman and Maudie staggered back along the road Rosie struck many matches and at last lighted her bike lamp and then cycled dumbly back down the road.

It was dark, almost seven o'clock, when she got home again. The snow was still thin but fiercer, the dark wind a blast of pain itself. Her body had gone beyond feeling. At the farm the doctor was already there, Maudie running up and downstairs in hopeless distress, the old woman in bed. And while Rosie was still pressing the pain of coldness out of her hands and before she could go upstairs the doctor came down.

A young man, with gold-rimmed glasses, he stood in the kitchen and pulled on the big motoring gloves of sheepskin, and then for some reason, pulled them off again.

"It's the old lady I'm a little anxious about," he said. "How old is she?"

"Mother?" Maudie said. "Mother's nearly eighty."

"Well, that's a great age for shock of that kind. Let her sleep. Don't let her get up."

"Yes, doctor," Maudie said.

"And now what about your brother? He's had a shock too. What happened?"

"Nothing. He just went like that. Collapsed."

"Like what? He's had a shock of some kind. Did you say anything to him?"

"No, doctor."

"Nothing? He didn't get excited?"

"No, doctor."

"He didn't get out of bed? Try to get out of bed?"

"No, doctor."

"And you can't remember having said anything to him to upset him? – excite him at all?"

"No, doctor."

He drew on his gloves for the last time.

"Well, we shall see, to-morrow. I'll leave you sleeping draughts for them both. And, as I say, it's the old lady I'm a little anxious about. Not your brother so much. With him it's temporary. With people of his kind" – he turned for the first time to Rosie – "it's the will that keeps them going. Break the will and –"

"Shall I go up or not?" Rosie said.

"Keep away, if you can."

All evening Maudie scarcely spoke. At the back of her mind the links of old and new malice against Rosie coupled themselves into new chains of hatred, forged by the fresh heat of distress, hammered out by anger.

Rosie, in turn, scarcely spoke either. She thought less. Feeling and thought and the desire for talking had been frozen down into a solid core of resignation that was very near to hopelessness. What now? What was coming? What if Tom should go? The winter, if it had almost smashed Tom, had almost torn her to pieces. Anxiety and uncertainty had lacerated the skin of her endurance unmercifully. Her whole being was sore and tired out. She felt, now, that the farm had her imprisoned, the very solidity and the unchanging shape of its land standing like a blockade between her and whatever had gone before, the old life annihilated, the pub forgotten. Yet she clung, always, to the thought of the farm, to the hope of possessing it. She had grown harder, closer, almost desperate about it. After the farm – what? Without the farm – nothing. She was forty now. She stood, as it were, in the centre of life. She felt that the point of change had come, the crest, the moment of turning over, the descent, the beginning of whatever end there would be.

In the morning the old lady was worse. But Tom, miraculously, was much better. Then, when she went up to take his breakfast, she knew that something must have happened. He looked at her, without speaking, with a pitilessly hateful look, in silent malevolence.

"How do you feel?" she said. "Any better?"

No answer : only a continuance of the look of hatred. She spoke again, saying : "Did you know you had a sleeping draught?" but there was still no answer, only the relentless silence and the gaze of hatred. And finally, bewildered, not understanding, and very near to tears, she went out.

From that moment a new phase began : a phase when he would not speak to her. When Maudie came up to clean his room he asked after his mother, and then said :

"Tell her I don't want her up here."

"Not mother? Mother's in bed."

"No, her. Rosie. I don't want her up here. No more."

"What shall I tell her?"

"Tell her to go to hell ! I don't care. Tell her to go to hell."

All that day he lay very quiet, the draught bringing on periods of stupor and half-sleep. His mother lay in the room next to him, just beyond the wall. Whenever he roused up he would tap the wall very gently and call her: "How you feel, Mum? More yourself?" not knowing by the faint mumblings and creakings of her bed if she heard or not, until she answered once, unexpectedly, in a voice of surprising strength:

"I ain't for long, Tom. I don't feel I'm for very long."

The tears came out on his cheeks. To lie there, next to her, the wall between, and know that she was dying and not be able to help or see her was so bitter that he lay in a state of distress that was altogether new for him a state in which self-pity had no place, in which his heart was turned to water by the misery of thinking of her.

"Mother!" he would call. "Mum! Call if you feel amiss. Mother. Knock the wall."

Then in the middle afternoon she was silent. She would hear nothing at all. Alarmed, he would tap and call for her constantly, listening in the intervals for her breath, for a long time hearing not a whisper, until at last she did move. The bed creaked, the springs speaking rustily, and he called. There was no answer. He called again: "Mother! Mum! Are y'in pain or anything? Are y'all-right?" but she did not answer. The only sounds were the bed creaks and after them the stumbling sound of what seemed like her feet on the floor.

Another minute, and he heard the door of her bedroom open, and he knew that she was coming in to him. Check-ed by the paralysis of his legs, he could not stir. He lay taut, distressed, crying out:

"Mother! Mother! Go back. Mum! Go back!"

But she came on, and in a moment in spite of all his entreaties, his own door opened and she came in: small, white-nightgowned, colourless, her movements silly with

227

age and weakness, her hands groping before her as though for objects she could not see.

"Mother, Mother ! You must git back."

She did not speak, made no effort, but simply came straight on, feebly, foolishly, quite lost, until she half-fell, half-knelt by the bed. "Mother, Mother !" he kept saying. He ripped the coverlet off the bed and threw it round her. She said nothing, did not move : as though to be there were her ultimate object and she wanted nothing more. Then he put his hand on her head and made instictive motions of distress and comfort, stroking her head. Her hair was like old grey cotton, thin and tough. He could feel the skin old and scaly beneath it, his hands going on with their motions of comfort until he knew by her odd dead quietness that there was no need to go any longer.

Soon after the death of the old lady Collins left. "Think I'm goin' slave my guts out twenty-four hours a day, and then be swore at on top?" The women felt at once helpless. But Tom was indifferent, then furious. "Git somebody else! Plenty folks be glad o' the chance. Git somebody else!" Deep down, still, lay the untouched and unshaken notion that the Jefferys were big, that it was an honour to work for the Jefferys. It was the unspoken family creed. Maudie yelled it after Collins as he departed : "Think yourself lucky we stood you as long as we did!"

But the new man was a long time coming. A month passed, spring came, but no man. In the bedroom Tom interviewed applicants, catechized them savagely, put them through a kind of third degree, hurled insults at them and finally told them to get out. "Whitehouse, eh? I knowed your father! Never knowed which was th'arse end of a bullock. Git out!" And so, though Tom did not know it and though Maudie and Rosie only half-suspected it, the tale went round that Tom Jeffery was harder to please than a woman. Applicants thinned, then stopped. The women, with no help but Amos and a boy, stood on the verge of helplessness : a leaderless army against stupendous odds : their world, the spring world of thickening grass and birthing lambs and rising thistle and dock, turned suddenly upside down; the farm, though they did not see it, beginning to look ramshackle, forgotten, neglected, and almost, but not quite, poor. Somehow the air of prosperity, however thin, hung on, like good paint. Spring, the thickening orchard grass, the great chestnut leaves, the gold-spattered meadows, the feeling of midsummer rising in the land like cream, all helped keep the illusion, the illusion that the Jefferys were still big, the farm still as inviolable and imperishable as the land of which it was part. And somehow the women mucked along, slaving, noses close to the summer grindstone, waiting for the new man, hoping, cheating themselves that it was all right. They were saved, at least, the pain of seeing things in a new, a right perspective. Working close to the place, their eyes half-blinded by custom and association, they never really saw the shabbiness of the wagons that had once been as bright as caravans, the storm-smashed roofs of the barns, the shrinking of the ricks, the anyhow muddle of yards and stables and the half-groomed horses coming and going between what were now piles of half-derelict implements, of binders and hay-cutters nettle-grown and winter-rusted, of harrows broken and up-ended, of potatoes chimbled and rotting in forgotten corners. They believed in it all as firmly as ever, more firmly than ever. It was theirs; therefore it was all right. It was all right; therefore nothing could change it. If they had illusions they never spoke of them. They might have secrets from each other, but none to tell each other.

And then, just before midsummer, with hay-time coming, they had a new, a different shock.

"Aunt Maudie," Lily said. "I'm going to get married."

They were at dinner, the three women, Rosie and Maudie in muck-stained skirts and hair done up working-fashion, Lily in a white print frock, as milky and clean and virgin as ever, her nails half-mooned and pink as baby skin.

"Blimey," Rosie said quietly. "If you ain't the giddy limit."

"Well !" Maudie said. "Who to? Who is it?"

"Damned if you quiet 'uns don't beat the band," Rosie said. "Who is it?"

"The Rev. Franklin," Lily said.

"Blimey, a parson's wife !"

Big tears came into the girl's eyes at once.

"Oh, Rosie, you ain't good enough !" Maudie said, stretching out arms for comfort. "Making the gal cry."

"Oh, I'm sorry ! I never meant it," Rosie said. "I'm glad. It's a good thing for you. I'm glad. You'll be shut of it all then."

"Shut of it? Shut of what?" Maudie said.

"Us and the damn farm and everything ! I'm glad she's doing it. When's it going to be?"

"It'll have to be before he leaves the circuit in September."

"That's good. The sooner the better. I hope you'll be happy."

And that summer, for a little while, Lily saved them. She came between them and the farm, even between them and Tom. Most of all, she came between themselves. They magnified her wedding into all the importance it did not possess. Maudie, crying in secret, turned out her drawers of linen and calico, crammed now to overflowing by Ella's legacy, and gave Lily the best of things. Rosie gave her ten pounds. Jealous, Maudie gave her ten guineas. Lily was going to Torquay, where Franklin would have a circuit. It was a great way off, an incalculable distance, a new world. "We shall come and see you," Maudie said, almost gaily. "We shall come seaside. You see. One day when you least expect us, we shall come."

By the end of July Lily was married – "Get it over, for God's sake," Rosie said, "afore we begin harvest" – and by the beginning of August gone.

That year, the hottest for ten years, it was a better harvest than they had hoped. Corn ripened swiftly. Barley was white before the rustle of oat-heads had quietened in the rick-yard, beans were scorched from sun-split pods like coffee-berries, the crop spilling under the hook. Luck was with them : day after day followed each other without rain like the clear pages of a book, the heat white as paper. They worked on into moonlight, the peace of ghostly August stubbles shattered by the tractor, made more ghostly by the clack of cartwheels and the rustle of feet and forks on the sun-scorched straw. A new man came : an old soldier, who could stand, miraculously, the blasphemed orders of Tom, and with him a couple of shoemakers up from the town, old sweats, mowers out of another century, men ousted by the machine. And with the boy, fag-end in oil-darkened lips, driving the tractor, they managed to get through, to clear the big acreage of the fields of the last shocks, even of the last gleanings. Until in September Maudie could write to Lily : "Harvest is done and over. And seems good. It'll be Orlingford feast in three weeks. And after that we can shut the back door and claim winter."

It was the claiming of winter that they dreaded. If one winter had hammered Tom, what of another? The summer for him had been cruel : a physical cruelty of hot days without rain or release, very nearly without hope. Wasted

very thin, bed-sore, he brooded on Rosie more still on'
Maudie's shattering declaration about Frankie. Yet, as
though there were diabolical pleasure in the secrecy and
silence, he said nothing. Only, as she came into the bedroom to dust or bring his meals or his few letters or the
paper, ho would look at her: queerly, with eyes milked
dry of decency and tenderness. "The more I look at our
Tom," Maudie would say, "the more I see our Dad in
him." And Rosie, looking at the portrait of Alf Jeffery,
stiff-collared, bald, protruding-eyed, regarding the world
with disapprobation and cunning from behind iron-rim-
med spectacles, would see it too. There was something
cunning, now, about Tom: the same cunning surveillance
and jealousy of a world doing what he could no longer do
and what he would never do again. And Rosie was still,
for him, the centre of that world: but now with a difference that was almost catastrophic. She was the plague-
spot; all his envy and hatred were focused with the white
heat of a burning-glass on her. He raged with an almost
insane desire for retribution. Since the war had smashed
him it seemed a natural law that he in turn should smash
someone also. And why not Rosie?

In turn she tried to read it all as indifference. She was
troubled, but not frightened. He was physically less
dangerous than a canker. It was only the cankerous
silence of his looks and broodings that troubled her and,
though she would not say it, hurt her beyond belief. As
she looked back, the old days seemed very good: the pub,
the river, the first hot Sundays of the farm, even the days
when she had been bored and maddened beyond endur-
anc. The bread of existence, in those days, had seemed
very stale, saltless. Now it was bitterly salt.

Trying to read it all indifference, she would go into the

bedroom rather haughtily, silent, head up. She would not speak, and Tom would not speak. She would do what she had to do, depart, not come back until necessity forced her, and do her best not to make much of it. She was still proud, bitterly proud. Who the hell were the Jefferys?

She went in regularly, to fetch the dirtied crocks after meals. And one day, as she went in after dinner, the fork was on Tom's plate but not the knife.

"Eaten your knife too?" she said, in grim humour.

"It's on the floor. I dropped it," he said. "Under the bed."

She bent down, dropping on her knees. All at once he slashed at her, like lightning, savagely, the knife slicing the flesh of her shoulders.

It was all over, done in silence, in a moment. He slashed once and in a second the knife was gone, under the clothes, the bed-clothes blooded. She sprang up at once, scared, furious, and went for him. Scared also, anger bubbling out of him with little cries, he clutched the knife under the bed and swore at her, whimpering. She got him by the neck, with one hand, tearing the clothes off him with the other. Under the clothes he was making vain mad attempts to slash himself, his hands demoniacally twisted.

"Give me that knife ! Give me that knife !"

"I'll stab you, I'll stab you !" he whispered.

"Don't be so damn silly ! Give me it ! Give me it !"

"I'll git you ! I'll git you ! I'll do – "

She smashed the words out of his mouth, her hand coming down to his face in a frantic half-circle of rage. The shock staggered him. The knife dribbled out of his hands like a pebble. Little cuts and stabs were showing on his nightshirt and on the bed clothes, and a hot line of blood was running down her arm.

"I'll kill you!" he shouted. He was crying, out of rage, madly and stupidly. "I'll kill you!"

"Don't be so damn silly! Lie back! Lie down! Lie back!" He struggled feebly and vainly with his arms, trying to get at her. She threw the knife on the floor and went for him again, her anger and terror against his, her hands powerful on his weak shoulders. Blood was running and dripping everywhere in splashes of bright scarlet that opened wide on the bedclothes like flowers. Until at last she triumphed, had him flat on the pillows, pinioned back like a defeated wrestler, his cries and struggles useless.

"Let me go! You got me. Let me be!"

"What made you do it?" She still held him, hard, relentlessly. "What made you do that to me?"

He almost lifted himself and shrieked at her: "Frankie! I know all about it! Frankie! Frankie!"

"Who told you that damn tale?" She felt, in that moment, murderous herself. "Who told you? Who told you?"

"You killed Frankie!" he said. "If it hadn't been – "

"Shut up!"

Her hand smashed over his mouth again. It was her last effort. It silenced not only him but herself. The strength went out of her. Weakness shot up her arm like an arrow. The pain made her faint, the sight of blood suddenly sick. She could do nothing but stagger to the door, open it, and call faintly for help into what was really the empty house below.

"Maudie! Maudie!"

They were words into which, knowing what Maudie

done, she meant to put outrage and anger. They came, in reality, feebly. Then, when there was no answer, she went feebly downstairs still calling, dripping blood everywhere. It was the stairs, the descent, which finished her. She staggered feebly about at the foot of them until she fell down.

I I

THEY hushed it up, and after it was quieter. It was like a release of bad blood; he was weaker, but better. She in turn no longer went up to the bedroom. They were enstranged, irrevocably. The knife had cut the tendons of decency.

The drought went on until November. When it broke at it seemed as if their luck broke with it. The farm seemed suddenly to give up the ghost. Things went wrong, pointlessly, without warning, for no reason. Two heifers died, then a third, and it seemed that the whole herd might go. Until the vet came and had the meadows searched and the hot summer's harvest of nightshade cut out. So in several ways, little ways, slight but significant, they began to pay the price of neglect. The fences were bad, mere skeletons of stakes not repaired since the war, and a mare impaled herself in the meadows, the spike in her belly. Afraid, Maudie could say nothing to Tom. Always, when she spoke to him, things were going well, in the same old Jeffery way, on a course of cocksure prosperity. Rather tell a thousand lies than say that one heifer had been lost, or that the root-crop was bad, or that the bank balance was thin.

It was the bank balance which troubled them most. The pass-book, coming in at the end of January, gave them their first real shock, their first terrorized suspicion that things were not right. Heifers might die, chickens mope, the land itself turn sulky, but they were natural things, inevitable, understandable. Not so the balance. They could not grasp it. It was like the going wrong of a watch : something mysterious, beyond them. Heifers could be buried, forgotten. But the bank figures were there in pen and ink, with a naked imperishability that was tragic for them.

For Maudie most of all. "Less than seventy pound !" It was like a stone smashed down on the eggs of pride and security and tradition and life itself. "One time Dad had a thousand, nearly two thousand in the bank." Unbelieving, she wept.

Afraid, they kept the pass-book secret. "We ain't sold a grain of wheat yit," Maudie said. "After threshing it'll be different. Threshing'll alter the look of things."

And threshing, for a time, did alter the look of things. Threshed, the wheat was unexpectedly good, sun-hardened, beautiful grain. Sacks fat with a pregnancy of corn stood piled against the yard fences on threshing day, a prosperous monument to mark the year. As the thresher moaned and rattled, straw torn from stacks was upcast by the winter wind into the yellow flock of chaff clouding above the drum, until the forlornness of the place was beaten out, the farm made turbulent with life, the day like old times, Jeffery grain pouring into Jeffery sacks as though by the hand of a providence functioning for them alone. All day Tom was in a fever : tossing, anguished by corn-smells and thresher noises, his windows giving him no view except the sight of torn smoke and chaff clouds. And bitterest agony of all, though he tossed and swore and called all morning, no one heard him. The thresher

killed all noise, even his. Only at the dinner hour could he
make himself heard, rage for Maudie, and get the sample
of grain he wanted.

"Bring me that bloody wheat! Didn't I ask you? Blast
you, didn't I tell you yesterday to bring me handful out o'
the fust sack? God!"

And Maudie brought the wheat in a saucepan, on the
tray with his dinner. He took the wheat like a child taking
a toy, running the grain through his hands, smelling the
corn-sweetness, chewing it, quiet at once, his meal forgotten. Good wheat, lovely wheat. Hard as pebbles, some
sense. His meal cold, he chewed grain until it revolved in
his mouth like sweet elastic. And all the time he ran it
through his hands, in little golden cascades, shining and
soft as sand.

Until Maudie came up and was horrified to see the
dinner plate with its could and still uneaten meal.

"You ain't eat nothing!"

"I don't want nothing. Git me some frummenty. Take a
saucepan and git it on afore you forgit. Like Mum used to
make – plenty of raisins, and don't hurry it."

"I –"

"Don't stutter at me! Git on! How's that wheat pannin'
out? About six quarter?"

"I don't know."

"Then find out. Ask Meadows. Ask the foreman. You git
like some damned old yoe puddlin' about!"

"I ain't so young as I was."

"What if you ain't? You ain't old none the more, are
ye?"

"I ain't the right side o' forty by a long way." She raised
her voice at him. "Come Easter I shall be fifty!" Weeping,
she went out.

So if the wheat eased things in one way it tightened and worsened them in another. For Maudie, no longer young, harassed by Tom, worried by bills and bank balances, life was bondage. She began to feel, that winter, every one of her fifty years : her hair mouse-coloured now, her lips chiselled into the thinnest of lines by the time and bitterness and circumstances. And since the day of Tom's attacking of Rosie – "not as I take every word *she* says as gospel" – she was frightened at heart. Brought up under the creed that whatever the Jefferys did was right, she had sense to see that Tom was not right. Her heart turned over at his queerness and strangeness. She dreamed of him : odd dreams where Tom was her father and was beating her, terrible dreams in which Tom, walking again, patrolled the house with a billhook. In fear she saw catastrophe. Lying awake at night, she prayed for a miracle to change it all.

And at the back of it, deep down, in spite of everything, she still nursed her deadly grievance against Rosie. In the machine of life Rosie was the mainspring. She saw Rosie as the cause of all things : Frankie, Turk, Ella, Lily and now, last of all and most terrible of all, Tom. All the long racket of misfortune sprang from Rosie. "That's what she done for us !" And even, stupidly, foolishly, she blamed her for the sourest of all misfortunes, age and spinsterhood. "Hadn't been for her I might have felt ten years younger. That's what she done for me."

So, when necessity demanded at least a mutual respect, they had none. They were like mule and horse together in one pair of traces. They lacked trust, harmony, even the will for co-operation. They pulled their own ways, fiercely and independently, all summer. Maudie began to meet the postman in the mornings, hiding important letters. "Ain't no business of hers ! Not as I know." She kept the pass-book, hiding it for days on end, taking it back to the bank in secret.

The summer was wet, desolate. In June the lower meadows were flooded and in the big meadow, so long the pride of all Jefferys, hay swam about in squelching marshes, was never carried, and was hidden at last by the lush crop of July. And in August something happened that Maudie had not seen before : the soft emerald green shoots of new corn sprouting with the white silk of corn-roots from the ruined wheat shocks, the stubble half under water. To Land was a desolation, the straw mud-spattered, the shocks abandoned tents, the imprint of the tractor wheels like the chaotic tracks of a retreated army. Roots were good, clover rich. But it was the failure of hay and corn, the long established symbols of Jeffery prosperity, that shattered security and pride.

Then, in the autumn, Rosie chanced to find the pass-book. Maudie had hidden it between Bible and hymn-book, on the wool-tasselled bookshelves in the parlour. There were figures in red.

III

Alarmed, not thinking, Rosie began to go straight upstairs to Tom. The bank-figures chilled her. She felt helpless. Then at the head of the stairs, she had another thought. If it should come to a point, to a question of Maudie's word against her own? She turned and went downstairs. How long had the book been there? What letters with it? What did it mean? She put on her hat and coat, harnessed the trap, and almost savage with determination, drove down to the bank, calling angry excuses to Maudie, who fluttered out of the dairy as she drove away.

The bank manager, a local preacher, fat, singing-voiced, sat and looked at her out of a face of pink dough, kneading soft dough fingers together at the same time.

"You talk as if you thought the farm was going to rack and ruin."

"So it is!" she flashed.

"But not because of this." He played with the pass-book. "Not because of an overdraft of thirty-five" – he paused, put on his spectacles – "fifty-three pounds. Why do you say it's going downhill?"

"I know it. I feel it."

"But the facts."

"Damn the facts! I tell you something's gone wrong. Somewhere. I haven't lived on the place for twenty years for nothing! Another thing, it's too big for us. Over two hundred acres. It's too big."

"Plenty of farms bigger than that."

"But not with the farmer lying on his back. And never going to get up again. That's where we're done. It's like you trying to run this damn back lying in hospital."

"Well, it's simple. You could secure an overdraft. You could sell."

"Sell? Would you like to go and tell him that yourself? Try it."

"Well, I'd see him, if you liked. It might be necessary to have to arrange something about this overdraft. Some security. That's if you wanted more money."

"Money! Nothing but money, money, money. I'm sick of it. What we want is less land. If you could talk him into selling some land, by God you'd be doing some good!"

"It isn't my business to persuade him to sell land. Though –" he ceased kneading his doughy fingers and leaned forward across his desk, fat arms flattened – "I don't mind telling you this."

"What?"

"That I think farming's in for a rough ride. That's how I see it. Things have touched top. Land's as high as ever it will be in the next twenty years. If you're going to sell, sell now."

"It sounds nice. But you tell him."

"I will. I've said I will. I don't like to see him in difficulties. The Jefferys and my family have been to the same chapel for forty years at least. We should stand together."

"All right." She got up and put on her gloves. "Try it. I haven't an atom of faith."

The next afternoon he drove up to the farm, and Rosie took him up to Tom. Half way upstairs she heard voices from the bedroom : Tom's voice, and Maudie's lifted in reply. The bank manager hung back, hat in hand, almost ecclesiastical, while Rosie opened the bedroom door.

"What's up?"

"No damn business o' yours !" Tom shouted.

"He's for everlastin' wantin' a gun. A gun up here. What he wants a gun up here for I can't think."

"To shoot you, y'old bitch !"

"Tom !"

"The bank manager's here," Rosie said. "Just quieten down for five minutes."

"Bank manager ! What th'ell's he want?"

"Good afternoon, Mr. Jeffery. It's all right. I can come in I suppose?"

"Aft-noon. What's up wi' you?"

Rosie and Maudie stood waiting, Rosie quiet, almost grim, Maudie white-faced, almost afraid.

"You damn women git out !"

"I'm staying," Rosie said, quietly. "It's my business."

"How the hell do *you* know?"

"I'm staying."

"She stays," Maudie said, "so do I."

"Christ, if I had that gun !" He glared at the three of them for a moment, and suddenly, lying back, quietened. "Well, what's up? Summat you been hatching up together? Some damn jiggery-pokery?"

"It's about the overdraft," Rosie said.

"Overdraft !" The word and the effect of it was like a shot. "By God you –"

"Steady, steady." The bank manager raised helpless doughy hands.

"Why didn't I know? Why didn't nobody tell me? Who the 'ell kept it back?"

"I didn't," Maudie said.

"It was a mistake," Rosie said. "A clerk made a mistake. Forgot to send the statement."

"Mistake? Bloody likely."

"Steady now, steady. It was a mistake all right. It's nothing."

"Then what the 'ell y'up here for?"

"Your account's down, that's all. You can't come to see me, so I've come to see you. Banks don't arrange for overdrafts without security. Collateral. That's all. You know that."

"Want me to mortgage, don't you? I know !"

"Mortgage, no. Security. That's all. Your deeds or insurance policy. Anything that has a redeemable value. Just to tide you over."

"Pawnshop, eh?"

"Or you could sell some land."

"Who said there was any land to sell on this farm?" Tom shouted madly. "Th' ain't a bloody acre for sale and never will be !"

"Land's high. Higher than it ever will be again – in our lifetime."

"What'd' *you* know about land?"

"Well, perhaps I'm wrong, but –"

"We got too much land by half," Rosie said.

"You shut your mouth."

"If you want to have the land we must have more men. And you know what that means," Rosie said. "More money."

"The issue's quite simple," the manager said.

"Simple? You got a fat lot to lose, ain't y' !"

"Nobody's going to lose anything. You're short of money, that's all. Either you can get it by selling land or by securing an overdraft. That's all."

"We got money !" Tom shouted. "Money enough in the family. Ella had money. Maudie's got money. We can make shift w'that !"

Maudie stood white, ghastly, not speaking or even attempting to speak.

"You got money, ain't y' Maudie? How much Dad leave you?"

"Two – two hundred."

"Well, you got that. And Ella's money."

"I –"

She could not speak. She simply stood with open mouth, whiter than ever, her lips almost insanely apart, her eyes stupid with tears. Only her hands were not motionless. She began to flutter and wring them, like a

244

child, helpless, beside itself with pain, and in great trouble.

"By God, what d' y' bawling for?"

"He took it! He had it!" She was speaking at last, torrentially, foolishly, repeating the one thing over and over again in her anguish. "He took it! He took it!" Her tears began to flow as freely as her words, salting them with agony. "He took it! He took it!"

"Damn fool, who took it?"

"He did!" She turned on Rosie with a new ferocity, all the bitterness and jealousy of years in her distraction. "Your father! I lent him it! I lent him it."

"Christ Jesus."

They were Rosie's words, quiet with shock. In another second Maudie was flying at her face as though to smash the mouth that had spoken them out of existence. Rosie held up wild hands. Maudie tore at her hair, bringing down her hands to make great nail scratches, her voice crying distractedly: "That's all the good we ever got from you! That's you! That's you! That's what you done for us!"

Until at last, Chapman, the manager, could hold her, pin her arms with the strength of his own fear, and Rosie could stand away, dazed, bloody-faced, her breath short and dry as chaff, her hair wild.

And Tom could say from the bed, half-moaning the words, eyes on Maudie's stupid, weeping face:

"My God, you fool, you blasted fool. You damn fool." And lastly, defeated, speaking to Chapman and Rosie alone: "Git rid o' Top Land. Git rid o' Top Land afore we lose that too." He could scarcely speak. "The meadows'll keep us."

CHAPTER III

I

BEFORE the spring Top Land had gone, and with it the fifty-acres fringing the cart-track and fronting the road : the richest limb of the place. And since it was so rich and precious, for so long the family pride, Maudie depreciated it, cheated herself into making little of it going. "Tell the truth, I ain't sorry it's gone. Dragging up there, all hours, harvest and gleaning. It's a long drag for anybody. Another thing, I ain't so set on crossing the road nowadays, motors tearing by. 'Sides, we got plenty o' land. That meadow land'll keep us. Grazing's the best round here for a good bit. And they say it's going to be all milk now. That's where the money is. Milk. We can keep more cows, same as everybody else. No ! I ain't sorry we got rid o' Top Land if anybody else is."

But when, in the autumn, the thin finger of Dark Closes followed it she was almost beside herself. "What'd our Tom want to get rid o' Dark Closes for ? That's where we used to play tea-party as kids, me and Ella. And git th' harebells." The field was like the womb of the farm : shallow outcrops of stone had been dug long since, for the building of the house and barns, leaving little hills and hollows thistle-starred and hung with harebells in late summer, the grass fine and sheep-cropped between the hawthorns. For Maudie all the catastrophe of the failing farm was in the selling of Dark Closes. "And let it go to Will Middleton, of all ! Our Dad'd rather *shot* 'isself than let anything go to Will Middleton. *That* man !"

246

Rosie too was upset, but in silence, by the loss of it. She remembered, so long ago that it seemed like the event of another life, lying in the far hollows with Frankie, hidden, in summer darknesses.

Only Tom was resigned, a fatalist with reason. "What the 'nation good's it keeping Dark Closes, if we gonna give the sheep up? Might as well keep a stable without a horse." And always, at the last, most bitterly : "And what th'ell good in keeping a damn field as I shall never see again?"

That summer, wet again, with summer floods in the meadows, the doctor allowed him the gun : a light air-rifle. He could hold it as he lay in bed, close to the open window, and pop at odd sparrows or early black-birds on the cherry trees, the sharp spit of the pellets often waking the women in early mornings. The gun consoled him, eased him in some way. The ragings against the two women quietened, grew rarer, almost ceased. If he nursed any bitterness against Rosie for Frankie or against Maudie for Turk he never showed it. It was as though he worked off his hatred and madness through the gun.

Then, in the autumn, when pheasants began to plane across the orchard or the paddock, coming to roost sometimes with squawking clatter in the chestnuts or the fruit-trees, and were still boldly there in the early daylight, he longed for a bigger gun. "My God there's a dinner sits on this fust Blenheim every morning. Give me that single barrel. Maudie, it's a dinner for you. Just the single barrel and half a dozen cartridges. Go on. Maudie. Maudie. The cartridges are in a box in the bureau well. Go on Maudie. It's a dinner for you."

"Whittling about that gun. You could never hold it."

"Don't think I'm safe, you stop here while I shoot."

"I'll ask the doctor what he thinks."

"Damn the doctor."

Later, early one morning, he called her in petulant and excited whispers until she woke. Thinking he might be in pain or trouble, she went into his bedroom. "By God, Maudie, look ! Look at him ! In that fust Blenheim. Big as a duck. Look at him. Run and git that gun for God's sake. It's a dinner."

And not really thinking, still in her nightgown, Maudie went downstairs and found that gun. When she got back upstairs Tom was in a state of strange excitement, almost fever. His hands were shaking so that the nose of the cartridge chattered like teeth with cold on the gun-breach. Then, when he took aim, with Maudie standing by, clutching the breast of her nightgown, he seemed to make an immense effort, stilling himself with an almost ferocious will, until the barrel was steady and he could shoot.

The shot and his almost mad cry of joy as the pheasant came down woke Rosie. Running into the room, scared, in her nightgown too, she was angered by his instant shout at her :

"Run down and git it. By God. Run down and git it !"

"Git what? Bawling about. You'll make yourself bad. Git what?"

"The pheasant, y'damn fool, the pheasant !"

"Nice thing, I should think." And to Maudie : "And *you* ought to be ashamed o' yourself."

"Git the pheasant, Maudie. Take no notice. Take no notice. Git it ! Git it !"

And for one minute, standing there in their nightgowns, sleep-tousled, Maudie's hair ragged and screwed up into knots of iron, Rosie heavy-eyed, they looked at each other

with a contempt skinned of all respect, until suddenly
Rosie flounced out to dress, calling as she went :

"If you've no more damn sense you must take the
consequences ! Giving him a gun. I should like !"

In retaliation, almost in revenge, Maudie let Tom keep
the gun. "Just like her. Interfering. What business is it of
hers? What harm's it do?" In a way it was a little triumph
for her. It reinstated her with Tom. It cancelled out some
of the memory of her colossal folly. They were brother
and sister again, Jefferys close together, in clannish dis-
like of an outsider.

"Good old Maudie. I'll git y'another. A brace. You could
hang 'em till Sunday."

"I'll leave the cartridges. She says anything you tell her
off. Don't stand it."

"Nip up if the doctor comes."

At breakfast Rosie said, calmer :

"You never left him that gun?"

"Think I got no sense?"

"All right, only I don't want trouble."

Coming across the orchard at noon on the same day
Rosie heard a shot, the smashing crack of the bigger gun.
Furious and afraid, she rushed indoors and upstairs, fling-
ing the bedroom door to find Tom loading a second shot,
his face livid with delight. "Put that gun down !" she
said. He looked up, fierce, but quite silent : a strange gaze
of unfaltering malevolence and joy. Before she could
speak again, she felt a change in him. He was not looking
at her, but past her : at the door, the wall behind. All the
time he was putting in the cartridge, pressing it smoothly
in, almost absently. She watched him closely, fearfully.
"Put that gun down !" she said again. "For God's sake !"

In answer he lifted it. She went stiff. He pointed it

at her, insanely, shaking. She turned and almost threw herself at the door-gap in terror, smashing the door shut a second before the shot itself smashed out, the sound vibrating the house, the door splintered and shattered.

Sick, terrified, her legs strengthless as wool, she hung for a minute on the door-knob, eyes shut. She half lay on the floor. Nothing happened. No sound at all from the bedroom. Then, getting up, pulling herself weakly upright, she caught the buttons of her sleeve against the door-knob, bone against metal, and the sound was like the signal for the second shot. It crashed wildly above her, ripping the deal panels like reeds, shaking the house like a wild burst of thunder.

It staggered her also into activity. She tore downstairs. "Maudie! Amos! Maudie! Maudie!"

The third shot tore out of the window as she herself tore across the orchard, the spraying shot shattering the window glass. Wondering, the men ran out of the barns, Maudie with them, in guilty terror. Dazed, Rosie ran among the trees, helplessly. There was no need to call now. The men began to run towards the house, shots smashing out again as they reached it.

"How'd he git that gun?" Meadows shouted.

"God knows, God knows!" said Maudie.

"Stan' back, all on y'." They were gathered in the kitchen, Maudie and Rosie, Amos, the boy, the old soldier. "Git back. Don't speak. I'll go up. We had a bloke went like this in Singapore once."

Upstairs, on his belly, the old soldier crawled along the landing. Nothing happened. He could hear nothing. At the top of the stairs he had taken off his boots. He moved like a caterpillar, up and on, on and up again, until he was lying by the door.

The room was dead quiet. Then in a minute he spoke. "Tom." At first very softly, a mere whisper, then louder. "Tom, Tom boy." No answer. Then still louder : "Tom ! Tom, my boy. It's Joe." The room seemed quieter than ever. "Tom." He tapped on the door panel with his knuckles. "Tom. It's Joe. It's Joe Meadows. It's all right. Tom boy."

The shot smashed out as he raised his knuckles to tap the door again. It hit the door lower down, at breast height, as though the aim had been taken with deliberation. The panels were splintered now, open, the stink of powder thick. The old soldier lay for an instant in silence, listening and deliberating, and then crawled back and downstairs.

"What cartridges he got? How many?"

"God knows?" Rosie said.

"A boxful." Maudie said. Distracted, she spoke without thinking, not lying this time, her voice hysterical. "He wanted – he wanted –"

"A boxful? Twenty-five? Christ."

Maudie did not speak, and before Meadows could say anything another shot smashed out, a wild aimless crack that splintered the remaining glass in the orchard window.

"My God, he'll kill hisself."

"Better git the police?"

"What can the police do? How many shots he fired? That's what. Did anybody count them shots?"

And distractedly, between them, one against another, they counted and miscounted the shots, listening for another, bewildered, not knowing what to do. Until Meadows, calmer had plans.

"I bin thinking. I was to git up there and let him shoot

251

once I could be in and on top of him afore he could load again."

"He's quick as lightning."

"I could do. Anybody come? Two on us and he'd be done."

"I'll come," Rosie said.

"No. Let Amos come."

"No, I'll come. I want to come."

She took off her shoes and went upstairs after Meadows, keeping a distance, not coming within two yards of the door until Meadows lay flat beside it. After that they did not move. She stood pressed against the wall, stiff, listening. Then, in a minute, Meadows tapped the door, low down, and called again as before, soft at first, then louder, and at last:

"Tom boy. Tom ! It's dinner time. We wanna go dinner. Tom boy ! Tom –"

The shot tore at the door low down, a foot above Meadows' head. For a moment it knocked him silly. He leapt up, dazed and went for the door, opening it just in time to see the barrel levelled again, straight at him, with insane deliberation. He slammed the door shut with a sound like a shot itself. "He's mad ! Git down. Git down." Grim in terror, Rosie ran downstairs. She could not speak. Maudie stood in terror too, but differently, wild, rather guilty, her tongue frantically chattering.

"He's bin wanting it weeks. Worried the life out of me. Worried – bin wanting it weeks. Wouldn't let me rest."

"He's mad. He's sitting up," Meadows said. "He'd got me set."

"Sitting up?" Rosie said. "He's never sat up, properly, since he was wounded."

"Sitting up, I tell y' ! Stark as a ghost."

They stood in the kitchen and held frightened counsel, one against another, Maudie crying, until Rosie said at last:

"Stop grizzling and get a drink."

"A drink? What?"

"Anything. Whisky. And then get your bike and go along to Gus Warren's and fetch Ginger. He's a fireman. He may do something."

"He's mad," Meadows kept saying. "He's mad. I seen 'em before."

"Drink some whisky, Maudie, for God's sake, and then be off."

"Goodness knows how I s'll ride."

"Ride like hell!"

After the whisky Rosie said:

"If Ginger comes and would go up a ladder, outside the window, and let him fire, we might do it from the door."

"He's mad. I ain't on it. He's mad."

"We'll try it. See what Ginger says."

Until Maudie came back with Gus Warren's son there were no more shots. Then, as Ginger, a big red-haired man with a pancake cap, walked round the orchard, and reconnoitred, a crack that ripped off the yellowed apple-leaves tore out of the window like a warning.

"He's mad," Meadows said.

"If Ginger'll hold a cap or something at the window and make him shoot," Rosie said, "we could go in from the door."

"I'll try it," Ginger said.

Already, on the roadside, the crowd had begun to gather, a clot of men and women and vehicles congealed by the orchard-gate, men leaning on bicycles, horses restive in carts, motor cars, women with tousled hair and folded arms. Between them and the house the figures of the farm and the family went on crazy purposes, running and walking, to fetch ropes and ladders and the pole for the decoying hat, Maudie crying in little bursts of terror and anguish whenever she saw a new acquaintance, Rosie more silent than the men themselves. Until in the early afternoon, when a policeman cycled up, the crowd had oozed through the gate and into the orchard itself, men offering advice, the close blobs of women broke up by the coming and going of people. And when the whole crowd was suddenly shattered by the crack of gunshot smashing through the orchard boughs above their heads, bringing down a yellow terrifying rain of leaves, the women drew back then beyond the hedge, shoulders up, with scared faces, to give their verdict :

"Ain't been right for long enough."

An espalier pear-tree went up the side of the house by Tom's room, still thick-leaved, and finally when Ginger set the ladder against it, the crowd was hushed. Inside, on the landing, Meadows and a policeman lay on the floor in stocking-feet, a chain of men behind them, on the landing and downstairs. Up the side of the house ran the ladder. Ginger raised an old bowler-hat of Tom's own, men relaying in hushed whispers the points of his progress to the men on the stairs, the word running up the stairs and along the landing like a fuse of quiet fire, until they were ready at last.

The hat went over the window-sill with a kind of cautious respect. The crowd was dead quiet. The men on the landing did not breathe. In thirty seconds the hat was over the sill, a black target, swaying slightly. Nothing happened. The hat moved along, horizontally under the cracked and smashed square of glass. The crowd was silent, with uplifted fascinated faces. Nothing happened. "Oh! they're cunning, they're cunning," a woman whispered, and the words were more startling in effect than even the gunshot could have been.

And the gunshot never came. The hat went through its crude movements again, then again, going over the sill, too far, almost into the window. But nothing happened. On the landing the men breathed again.

And then, after ten minutes, Meadows spoke. The old words :

"Tom. Tom boy. It's Joe. We wanna go dinner, Tom. Tom, old boy. Tom?"

But there was no answer. Meadows stood upright, flat against the wall, and touched the door-knob. Nothing happened. He rattled it, the loose rattle of brass, but the bedroom gave up nothing but the echo.

"Open it," the policeman said. "I take responsibility for opening it. Open it."

Ten seconds later they opened it, inch by inch at first, until the gap was wide enough for the policeman's helmet and then the heads of the policeman and Meadows and the first men of the chain behind.

"No wonder's he never shot," Meadows said.

They were the only words that any one spoke before Rosie herself came up, pushing through the men and standing by the bed at last.

"He's gone," Meadows said. "The shock would kill him."

"Get out," she said. "All of you. Get out."

"I must –" the policeman began.

"Get out," she said. "All of you." She spoke quietly, bravely. "I can do what must be done."

CHAPTER IV

I

SHOCKED, the women lived in a kind of chastened peace with one another, almost in mutual esteem. They went about quietly and warily, as though the ice of life were very thin. Somehow, at least until they were forced into another decision, the place had to be kept going. It was their life. They were desperate to keep it.

And for a time things went well. They worked hard, with the relentless animal hardness of long habit. Up at daybreak, dragging out the day till past sunset, they worked almost without rest, never giving in. They worked in obedience not only to habit but to a new desire, a desire to show each other how hard they could work, how little rest they could take. It was in reality a new form of antagonism. They never spoke of it, very often did not think of it. But it was there: a kind of hidden motive force, compelling them in all they did.

It kept them going, in a subdued fashion, into another harvest and another sowing, almost into another summer. Then they began to be aware, quietly at first, casually, by bits of market gossip picked up, by the newspapers, by mere feeling, of a new element: something concerning them and yet beyond them, out of range of their responsibility.

A kind of blight seemed to be settling on the land, a reaction from prosperity. At first they thought of it as concerning only themselves. Wheat prices were bad. Barley was worse. Perhaps they were bad bargainers?

Then they began to see that it was something outside themselves, a common affliction, that the land was sick, caught up in the crisis of depression. And they saw not only a change in the feeling of things but a change in actuality. Not only was wheat fetching nothing at all, but less wheat was being sown. They saw land about them, turned up for fallow, go far beyond fallow into weed-sown sickness, a derelict misery of neglect and decay. Less wheat, more cattle. For a summer the valley was thick with cattle. But, the papers said, and soon men were saying it after them, times were bad and beef was no longer eaten as it used to be eaten. And since times were bad, therefore beef was bad; and since beef was bad, therefore cattle was one with wheat. So there was a vicious circle of corn and cattle, sheep and grass, high costs and low prices, a paradox of pinching and plenty.

At first the women only saw it, were simply aware of it going on about them. It did not touch them. They clung to the old idea that they were immune, inviolable. Even Rosie had an idea that, since the land was theirs, nothing could touch it; that since it had endured for so long, there was no reason why it should not endure for longer, perhaps for ever. It would last, at least, as long as they themselves would last. And if they worked, as they did work, what was to stop their reaping a reward? "Folks'd work a bit harder," Maudie would say, "the bread wouldn't be so dry." And since they themselves had always worked hard and had plenty to eat, what was to stop them from going on working hard and having plenty still? Illogically they reasoned it out, comforting themselves that it was right.

And as though to confirm that it was right they kept the place going. "Good land, good folks on it," Maudie

257

would say in echo of her father. "You can't git over that."
And again, coming home from market with the news, "I
hear Sam Holland's about broke," or "Maskells o' Dean
are in a poor way I hear," she would cap it with : "It's
these jumped-up 'uns as can't stan' it. Take folks like
Gus Warren and Jack Spong and us ... you don't see
folks like that going under. Folks like that 'ave got
foundation." Yet sometimes they had surprises, even
shocks; as when Gus Warren failed. Warren had farmed
the land next to their own for more than forty years,
following his father. "Remember the days he took on,"
Maudie said. "I was a little gal. And now ... that's good
land. Like our'n. The same land runs right through.
That's land enough for anybody." And for a time the
failure of Warren brought the sense of crisis nearer; yet
still only the sense of it, and not the crisis. "Gus Warren's
seventy if he's a day," Maudie said. "You couldn't expect
him to go on."

And all the time, thin though the year's profits were,
Maudie behaved as though they had money : with the
old family arrogance, boastful but pinching, pinching but
wasteful. She went on, as always, throwing milk to the
pigs, breaking half-loaves to the hens, scolding the baker
for forgotten farthings. "Think I am? A farden's a farden.
We don't make money so easy if he does !" She still gave
way to life-long weaknesses : hucksters and travelling
drapers and tin-pot men who had called ever since her
mother's day. And now there were new car-driving trav-
ellers with soaps and face-powders and patent devices :
hair-curlers, clocks and patent stoves and carpets and
carpet-sweepers.

"Let me sweep the parlour carpet for you, madam.
Let me try it."

"It's oil-cloth."

"Well, some other carpet. The oldest carpet you've got."

"No, no. I don't think so."

"No obligation. No charge. Just a free demonstration."

"No."

"You needn't buy."

"Oh ! well. Go on – you might as well sweep the floor as me, for what I see."

And so the young man would sweep the carpet and cajole and flatter her and break down her resistance : "And if you'll say you'll have it I'll tell you what I'll do. I'll give you a discount of ten per cent. That's over thirty shillings."

"It sounds nice, but I don't think so."

"That would buy you a new dress."

"Tell you the honest, I can't afford it."

"Can't afford it? Pay each week. Each month. Pay a little at a time."

"What? On the never-never? Me?"

"Last week," he would say, "I sold two sweepers – different model – to Lady St. Just over at Sheltoe. And she's paying – perhaps you won't believe it, but it's God's truth – she's paying by the month."

"Folks like that?"

"My dear madam, why not? It's secret. Nobody knows."

"But I –"

"And if you had this model all you need pay is – every ha'penny – five and six each week, and I'll give you the thirty shillings discount now. In cash. Right here. Before I move an inch. If that isn't a fair offer I don't know what is."

And finally she would succumb and sign the paper and

then, as she had done before with bills and pass-books, lock them in the bureau and forget all about it. So that in time, the young man would turn up again, in complaint, to ask for an explanation or threaten reprisals. If Maudie were there she would apologize and pay and the thing would be ended. But sometimes Maudie would be out, down in the fields or at market, and Rosie would go to the door to find the young man there.

"What purchase? She's never said anything to me."

"For the sweeper. She's undertaken to pay per week, by instalments, and she hasn't paid. No doubt –"

"No doubt what?"

"No doubt it's slipped her memory."

"No doubt it has. But I got enough things to worry my head about without worrying it over you !"

"I'm afraid, if she doesn't pay, we shall have to remove the sweeper."

"Oh, remove the damn thing ! It's falling to bits anyway."

"I couldn't do that without the lady's understanding."

"Oh ! couldn't you? Well, how much is this weekly dole-out?" And then, suddenly, with the old fury, but now in a kind of defence against Maudie : "How much is the damn lot? Taking advantage of helpless women. I got something else to do besides fiddling here with you on a cold doorstep."

He would look it up. "Nine pounds fifteen still to pay."

"Blimey, you ought to be shot ! Nine pounds for that thing? Here, you get off while your shoes are good, young man."

And she would pay him, doling the pound notes with bitterness, standing over him while he made the receipt, and then terrifying him into retreat at last :

"And now get off. And don't you let me see you this side o' that damn gate again ! Getting round women !"

Then, when Maudie came home :

"I had your fancy dealer here today. Paid him the nine pounds odd you owed him."

Foolish, found out, Maudie would say like a child : "Oh ! I was going to pay it. I meant to of paid it."

"Well, it's paid. Paid and done with."

"I'll give you the money."

Sometimes Maudie would remember the money; more often not. But whether she paid or whether Rosie paid, the money came out of the farm. At the time they did not notice it. Hadn't they always lived on the farm? Hadn't everything always come out of the farm? Then the rates would fall due, or the insurance, or the threshing bill, and for a time they would be pinched, pinched hard, almost impoverished, living on the hope of harvest or on some vague general hope that things would be better. "I never known things like this," Maudie would say. "Never." All the time they took comfort, almost cheating themselves, from the plight of others. "Same everywhere. You can't talk to nobody. I see in the paper only yesterday – a man offering to give his land t'anybody as'll farm it. Giving land away. You fancy. You fancy giving *our* land away. That'll show you how bad things are." As though to say : "That'll show you how bad things are for other folks," Maudie's belief in their own immunity as strong as ever. Or : "Ask me, I think we do very well. At least we *pay* our way. And that's more'n some do or *could* do."

Until, at last, they muddled into their own crisis, victims of their own honesty : paying too well and too readily. The tractor of Tom's day was worn out, obsolete. Mesmerized by a young salesman who called for three autumn afternoons in succession, they bought another, Rosie signing the cheque for it on the day of delivery. That payment carved their resources down to the bare bone. It cut off the little fatness of that year's harvest in a single swoop. Long before Christmas they were faced with an overdraft that made them sick.

"Overdraft!" Rosie said, she alone stoical or capable now of anything like clear decisions. "Enough overdrafts in this damn valley to build Jerusalem with. What's an overdraft? I gone past being frightened by overdrafts. We must do the same as other folks. Mortgage."

"Mortgage!" Maudie was horrified, the word poisonous. "Be no mortgaging on this farm, not if I know it. That wasn't Tom's idea, be a long way, either. That wasn't his way."

"If we got to mortgage we got to mortgage, and that's all there is about it! What's Tom got to do with it now?"

"Tom –"

"It ain't what Tom thinks now. It's what we think. What I think!"

"Mortgage. I could never –"

"You don't understand the first damn thing about it. It's either mortgage or we get out. Sell. Things get worse instead o' better."

"Sell? What you saying? Sell? You can't sell our farm."

"Who can't? Whose farm is it?"

"Things'll be better in the spring. The papers say so. Everybody says so. Sell? – you can't do –" And then the last burst of desperation, almost tearful : "What'll happen to me if we sell? Where'd I go? Where've I got to go?"

"Come to that," Rosie said bitterly grim again, "I got nowhere very fat to go myself."

"You're different!" Maudie burst out. "You're different. You ain't fifty and alone."

"Different," Rosie said. "I don't see no damn difference. We're all in the same boat as far as I can see."

And Maudie's antagonism, so long dormant, sprang up again: the old fester of bitterness and jealousy hot and black in her brain, her thoughts spasms of angriest hatred. "Tryin' to sell our farm. Trying to mortgage it! I should think so. Who's she think she is? If our Tom were alive he wouldn't stan' it. Our Tom wouldn't stan' it. And where's she think I'll go? What's she think I'd do?" All her instinctive love and jealousy for the place sprang up. It was her home. She had been born there, had grown up there, wanted to die there. "What right's she got? She ain't one of us. Never was. Never would be. Ever since she came up here that day, barmaiding, after our Tom, there's bin trouble. What good's she ever done to us? Never went chapel. Never behaved decent like other folks. Killed our Frankie! And now wanting to sell the place! Wants to git me out! That's all she done for me!"

And, as of old, she lay in bed at night, tearful, her worn body thin and anguished against the worn sheets, and thought of it all, forging her words into clumsy symbols of prayer: "O Lord, let not thy servant go in want. Don't let her git me out. O Lord, thou knowest this is our house, always has bin our house. Thou knowest she ain't got no right. Guide her mind aright, O Lord, don't let her git in the way of transgression. O Lord, don't let her do it. Don't let her do it."

She went on until prayer and hatred and jealousy were once again an obsession, until she saw in every flick of Rosie's head and every uplifting of her finger a new gesture of duplicity; thinking: "She'd git me out tomorrow if she could. She always has wanted to git me out." She did not ever know that Rosie was so tired of it all that she could have relinquished anything without a word and without a condition, that virtually she kept the place going for Maudie's sake. She could only hammer out her hatred into a new creed:

"If I live to be a thousand I'll never forget what she done for us. I'll never forget. I'll never forget. Nothing'll make me forget."

But unexpectedly, in the third winter after Tom's death, something caused her to forget. A letter:

"Dear Miss Maudie: You must wonder where I got to. Well, I had a rough time and things is not right yet, no, by a long chalk. I didn't have no luck in London and nowhere else come to that. I'm getting so as I feel an old man now and the object of me writing this is to ask you old friend for a little help I got nothing but the things I stand up in. You don't want to see your old friend in trouble in the workhouse I do know so I write to ask you if you will meet me at Hitchford Bridge eight o'clock Sunday night and bring me a few shillings to help me last out my days. Perhaps a pound only don't tell her nothing please or else I'm done. Your truly, T. Perkins."

Perkins? She could not remember. T. Perkins? She looked at the postmark: Huntingdon. And then at the letter again.

Suddenly, with a shock of sickness, she remembered. Perkins. Rosie's name. Turk. Her heart stood still.

II

Turk stood against the stone parapet of the bridge, huddled up, back to the river. Maudie could not see his face. Rain had started to fall a little, icily, the wind vicious from over the dark water and the land.

"And then I got in wi' a rum lot. Card sharpers. I never bin much of a card-player. Never played much. And that done it. They skinned me. Every penny."

"All that money you took?"

"All on it. They sharped me. And I got windy. Daren't come back or write or do nothing. I was broke to bits." He was talking easily, lying, his voice mournful, his words softened by self-pity. And standing there, in the pitch winter darkness, huddled, his face blotted out, his voice alone tangible, he seemed to Maudie very desperate. He touched her easily. She had come against her will, uneasily, almost frightened, after her first anger had passed. Now she stood quite still, almost but not quite glad she had come, her mind empty of grievance and of anger. She was simply bewildered and touched and, at heart, still a little afraid.

"Why didn't you come home?"

"Rosie. You know her? You know how it would of been?"

"We could have gone on keeping it to ourselves. We'd kept it long enough."

"I was broke to bits. Smashed up. Oh! Moses, I went through something. I went through something."

He looked up and down the dark river, forlorn, a lost soul, fetching up at last a raking hard-thickened cough that was a lie in itself.

"That cough ain't no good to you," Maudie said.

"I know. I'm done. I bin going rough. Workhouses. Ain't had a penny." The words were like mournful easy sparks, running and firing each other and breaking into flame at last. A flame of humblest anguish :

"You ain't – you ain't brought nothing? No? – you know."

"Money?"

"Yes," she said quietly. "I brought it."

It was on the tip of his tongue to ask how much when he heard the click of her purse-clasp and the rustle of paper as she unfolded the notes. Now, in turn, he could not see her. He could only hear the crisp unfolding of paper and her occasionally withdrawn, as though tired, breath. Then she said :

"I don't know as I'm doing right. Where are you going? Where'll you go if I give you this money?"

"Nottingham. I forgot to tell you. Nottingham." He was lying quickly, glibly, his mouth plausible and mournful. "They's a chance of a job there. Billiard marker. A man I knowed years ago at The Angel keeps a big pub there. Twelve billiard tables. Moses, I –"

"Pub," she said. "Don't you think you ought to keep away from pubs?"

"I ain't touched a drop," he said, "not since that day. Not since they skinned me."

She was silent a moment holding the notes, relieved but still uncertain. "I'm glad," she said at last. "That was something I was going to ask you. To leave the drink alone. I was going to ask you to promise me."

"Promise? Moses, ain't no need to promise. I bin on the wagon for so long I hate the sight of anything. Can't look at it. Can't stan' it."

"I'm glad."

She held out the notes. They remained in her fingers, folded up, two of them, somewhere in the darkness between Turk and herself. Then, in a moment, as Turk reached out and took the notes she felt at once foolish and strangely exultant. It was like being the Good Samaritan. It was a thing He would have done. It was forgiveness of sins, what Mr. Franklin used to call a living act of Christian faith. She wanted to cry. But it was so cold now, the rain so bitterly cold from over the river, that the tears felt frozen and her lips were like stone. If there were any tears at all they were in Turk's voice :

"Y'ain't hard on me, Maudie? Y'aint got nothing agin me?"

"If there was anything," she said, "it's forgive. I forgive it long ago."

"How about her?"

"Her?" Her voice was stony now, hard bitter. "You might know she don't forgive – nobody, nothing."

He was silent for a moment, indrawing breath in a sigh of resignation; and then : "Moses, it's hard to believe she's me own daughter."

"For me," she said, "you could come back tomorrow. Tonight."

"But not her? She wouldn't?"

"No. She talks of selling the place now. Selling it. Our farm. She ain't got no right !"

"Don't you let her. Don't you let her do it. That's like her. That's Rosie all over."

"I've lived there all my life," she said stoutly, "and I'll die there. I'll die there !" Then suddenly she felt so cold, her bones stiff and heavy as iron, that she remembered he must be cold too, that it must be time to be going.

"You better get on !" she said.

"If I walk to the cross-roads," he said, "as far as The Unicorn, can I catch a bus there?"

"I think so," she said. And within a minute he had gone and she walking away in the opposite direction, parallel with the river and the icy darkness, the rain flicking her like lead, her heart, all the time in spite of the rain and darkness, filled with exultation.

It seemed to increase as she went on. It warmed her, kept away some of the coldness of wind and rain. She had done something; she was like the Good Samaritan. She felt extraordinarily glad, excited. Hurrying, shivering, she looked back on the years of Turk's absence. Deep down, always, she had felt that it was all right, that, like a miracle, it would be made clear. It never did to judge folks too quick. She saw that now. It never did to be too hard on folks before you knew. What was it in the Bible? What did it say? Judge not that ye be not judged. That was it. Judge not – supposing she'd judged? Supposing she hadn't of gone? He might have ended up in the work-house, in gaol, anywhere. That's why – she saw it clearly now – it never did to judge nobody.

Except folks like her ! She didn't forgive nobody, nothing ! How could she expect to be forgiven? She hurried along the dark roads, against the wind, with a shivering exaltation that had in it also the leaven of fresh hatred. If it wasn't for her Turk could come back ! He could of come back. She might of had him again. She wasn't too old for that. She wasn't too old for nothing. It was only her that stopped it. Only her !

And caught up in the force of rage and sorrow she wept at last as she half ran, half walked along, the tears bitter on her frozen hands.

III

"No," Rosie said. "You don't get up. You lay there. A day in bed and you'll feel better again."

"I'm all right. I –"

"You lay there. I'll get onion gruel for you. I don't like that look round your eyes. That yellow look."

Later she came up with the gruel: "You get that across your chest. Quick, while it's hot. How d'ye feel? Better?"

"A bit thick, that's all."

"Well, if that's chapel on winter Sunday nights I'd give it best if I were you. At your age."

Flushed, strangely tired, Maudie lay quiet, saying nothing. Perhaps she'd been silly? Perhaps – exultancy had turned to fear now, the fear increasing as the gruel-sweat broke out on her body like warm oil, the constriction of her breath not eased. And her fear sometimes was shot with suspicion. Perhaps she'd got her here for something? Made her stop in bed while she – She remembered Turk's words. They seemed significant now. "That's like her. That's her all over." And a kind of sick strength would possess her, a fierce determination not to give in, to go under, to be a victim of any secret scheme.

"Rosie! Rosie!" she called once. "Rosie? You there?"

And Rosie came up. "Well?"

"You ain't going out nowhere? I thought if you wanted to go out I could get up."

"No. I'm not going out. And you're not getting up."

"Who's that downstairs?"

"Nobody."

"Not the doctor? You ain't sent for the doctor?"

"No, but I damn soon will if you don't git down now and git some sleep. It's sleep you want."

Rosie smoothed the bed-clothes, tucking Maudie up. A warm sweet vapour of sickness hung about the bed. Maudie seemed, in bed, strangely small, unexpectedly bony and thin, her face moist with sweat.

"You're hot."

"It's the gruel. It's only the gruel."

"That's good. That's doing you good. You'll feel better."

But, as the day went on, she seemed to feel no better. She fretted and tossed, slept a little, and waking, she called Rosie, suspicion prompting her. "You aint been out? I thought I heard you go out." And later, when Rosie brought her tea; "I ain't heard you go round for th' eggs. Ain't you bin? Ain't you going?"

"I got no time for eggs. What with you and everything. Eggs must go for a day. There won't be a sight, anyway. The hens on this place beat me lately. We don't get half a score a day. They seem to be like the rest o' things here – gone over."

"The place is all right? You –"

"You drink your tea and don't talk so much. And get some sleep again."

In the evening Maudie felt strange : her body light and uplifted, the bed like air, a swooning unworldly feeling. Thinking, she would be borne away into vaporous confusions, of mere feeling, into fainting darknesses. Coming back, she tried to place it all, to place herself. It was all strange and yet familiar. Then she remembered : the gas, the dentist's. It was like the swooning sick blackness of the in-breathed gas when she had had her teeth out. Nothing more than that. Then she seemed to be carried away on immense labouring wings of blackness, her own great breaths uplifting the wings, so that she was no longer on earth.

"How do you feel?" Rosie said, coming in finally, with her candle.

"I feel funny. Light somehow."

She wanted to say something about the farm, to protest, to underline as it were all her grievances and fears about the place. But the words were lost.

"You get to sleep," Rosie said. "And if you want anything call me."

And in the night Maudie called, like a child, whimpering, in pure fear.,

"I feel so strange, so funny. What time is it? I'm so hot."

Rosie held her candle in one hand, flattening the fingers of her other hand on Maudie's forehead, caressingly, almost in fear herself, Maudie yellow and frightened and small in the candle rays.

"It's three o'clock – just after. Soon's it's light I'll bike for the doctor."

"I feel so funny. Stop in the room. Stop with me."

Rosie stayed in the room, until at six o'clock, stiff, eyes clogged with sleepiness, she could see just enough to stumble across the yard and get her bicycle and ride down to Orlingford in the miserable steel-coloured light of winter daybreak.

When she came back, about eight o'clock, hands and face stiffened and half-skinned by wind, she put her bicycle against the yard-fence and went straight through the kitchen and upstairs, the feeling of her hands and feet muffled, her eyes watering with wind-tears of pain.

Maudie's bedroom was empty. Scared, a little angry, Rosie called and went from bedroom to bedroom raising her voice from bedroom windows, "Maudie, Maudie!

Maudie !" going downstairs at last to her, in the passage, the quiet noise of movements in the parlour.

And in the parlour Maudie, in nothing but night-gown, a sick figure of shivering flesh and almost as white, as the flannelette of the nightgown itself, was searching the drawers of the bureau for something, her hands slow and dazed, the floor littered with papers.

"My God ! Can't I leave you a minute?"

"Leave me be, leave me alone." Kneeling on the floor, Maudie raised her hand to her head like a child expecting a blow, her body almost too weak to sustain the movement. She swayed and moaned a little, moaning still as Rosie dragged her to her feet, her voice losing strength, ceasing altogether, as Rosie reached the stairs with her and dragged her up.

It was a voice that was never the same again. For years so acid and biting, everlastingly upraised in bitterness or protest, it was now strangely quiet. Pneumonia changed it into the voice of another woman. It had not even the strength of petulance. When it uplifted itself a little on the evening of the same day and in the very early morning of the next it was not even coherent. It broke and faded and stammered like the voice of some ancient wireless speaker. It seemed to have come from a long way off, the sick, almost the real voice of a woman who was struggling to be heard and not to die.

"You ain't – you ain't bin and? I –" The thought never resolved itself. It faded and trailed off into others, in turn never finished either.

"You ain't goin' – you – the farm – you –"

Once only, just before the end, she made a supreme effort to conquer incoherency, to say clearly and swiftly what she had been trying to say. She tossed from side to side and raised her head the merest fraction from the pillow and framed a thought that had a flicker of passion in it, her eyes in the candlelight strange and burning with the brief heat of dying bitterness.

"I see him ! I forgive him ! I forgive him !"

It was the last cry of antagonism, almost of triumph. The voice burned for a moment like a paper-flame and then went out. Rosie stood by the bed, waited, stiffened unconsciously with the iron antagonism that had held them apart and yet together for twenty years, and then ran forward with outstretched hands.

In another moment Maudie had gone.

CHAPTER V

"A WHISKY," Rosie said.

She felt that she needed something, after the sale, and everything. Then looking up, she saw the price list. It hung on the wall, behind the bar, above the permed head of the barmaid. Whisky had gone up a bit since the old days. Blimey. "Here. Make that a stout," she said.

"Quite sure?"

"Yes! Stout! And don't you be so snotty."

Haughty, the barmaid turned down the whisky glass and poured a bottle-stout. Rosie paid. The barmaid handled money and stout as though it were poison. "Jesus," Rosie thought, "the way some folks fancy their chances. The way things change. I don't know." She took her stout and sat down in the corner of the bar, at a table, tired out. Drinking, wiping the stout-froth off her lips with a sort of flashy elegance on the back of her hand, she looked round the bar. "Blimey," she thought, "you wouldn't know the place. Ain't a pub no longer. More a hotel." It was early evening, nobody in much yet, nothing doing, and the electric chandelier blazed on an almost empty bar, the gloss-painted walls shining like enamel. Drinking again, her eye caught something hanging above the bar, against the ceiling: the old pub sign, the angel, a girl with wings. And underneath a notice: "This sign is all that survives of the original inn The Angel, destroyed by fire on 9th September, 1909."

9th September – that was the night she had come down with Frankie. Then she remembered another thing – that

274

sign was really her. It had really been copied from her when she was eighteen. She looked at it again. The chap had copied her one summer afternoon; she remembered sitting on a boat, on the old landing stage, back to the river. He had painted her on a large square of wood and then had given her wings. Blimey, did she look like that?

Looking at the sign between the drinks, watching people come in and go out, she drank her stout slowly. No hurry. What'd she got to hurry for? Now? She had nothing; nowhere to go, nothing to do. No hurry. The farm had gone; the old resolution had been made a reality at last. And why not? What good was the farm to her? What could she do, alone, on a place like that? After Maudie's death she had seen the Jefferys' solicitor. There was nothing left. Then, because of the mortgage, the bank had chimed in. And the thing had dragged on, eating out her patience, a miserable confusion of letters and deeds and overdrafts that only accentuated the loneliness and misery of the empty farm, with the forlorn bellowing of cattle waking her on winter nights, so that she felt like a lost soul in an empty world. Until now, with the sale over, the last heifer knocked down, the kitchen fender and Frankie's telescope bundled together in one cheap lot, the rooms empty and quiet, the windows dark, the whole place derelict, it was almost spring.

After spring, summer. And after summer -- what? Where was she going? What was she going to do? She hadn't even a place to sleep. Until last night she had slept at the farm, in a bed already lot-numbered for sale. To-night she could book a room at The Angel – funny to sleep in the old place again. After that? Stoically she drank her stout. She couldn't go on booking rooms at The

Angel for ever and Amen. What little money she had she wanted. A case of turning every penny over and spitting on it for luck.

Another thing – and she felt it worst and sometimes only when she sat down, as now, after the racket of a long day – she wasn't so young as she had been. She was over fifty : rather florid still, but hard, her eyes tired, even the shadow of her flashiness gone. And now she wanted to sit still, not worry, not think any more; let things go their own way. The farm had gone. Well, let it go. What good was the past to her any longer? Let it go where the rest had gone.

And for a time she sat thoughtless, drinking her stout, staring. The bar filled up a little. The barmaid's sharp voice scissored the air in snipped repetitions of orders. The talk of the men was low, unexcited.

A man was looking at her. Nothing in that. She returned the stare boldly, head up and a little sideways, not quite haughty but distant, aware of him but indifferent. No one she knew, anyway. How many years since she was in The Angel? She tried to remember, was too tired, and elegantly drank her stout again.

The man was standing at the bar, leaning back, waistcoat medals showing in a silver crescent : a man of middle height, almost fifty, genial, with small light eyes. Drinking his bitter, he seemed troubled, almost nervous. His eyes were fixed on Rosie. His mouth made motions of indecision, twitching, as though he wanted to speak or smile.

Rosie was wooden. Getting off, at her age ! What next? Who'd he think he was? What the pipe? Distant, head up, she drank her stout.

She was setting down her glass when he walked across

the bar. He came straight for her. She paused in the act of wiping her lips.

"Beg pardon," he said, "but don't I know you?"

She did not speak, did not move at all except to lick a bead of stout off her lips.

"Sorry if I made a mistake," he said, "but ain't you Rosie Perkins?"

She changed at once, almost softened.

"I was," she said. "Who the pipe are you? I don't know you."

"I know y'do. Charley. Charley Turner. You know me. Charley? Old Charley?"

"No."

"That you do." He sat down. "You know me as well as you do yourself. Charley Turner. Old Charley. I used to come in to Th' Angel every day. Twenty year ago. You remember. I used to lodge with –"

"Half a minute. Didn't they used to call you something. Something else? Something funny?"

"Yeh! Pincushion. On account o'me hair. It ain't no better now." He took off his soft hat. "See. It ain't no better. Sticks up like a lot o' pins in a cushion."

Rosie was laughing. "Pincushion! Soon's you said that I *did* remember. I remember plain enough now. Of course I remember. Well! old Charley. Pincushion." She surveyed him, ironically, grinning. "Your mother know you're out?"

"Ha! Just like old Rosie. Rosie all over. Ha!" He put his hat on the table then on the floor. "Have something? Something to drink?"

"I got something."

"Ah! but drink up. Drink it up. Let me get you another. Have a whisky?"

"Give me elbow room !"

"Ha ! Well. Just fancy. Fancy lighting on you. I'd have known you anywhere."

Rosie, a little excited also, drank her stout, emptied the glass.

"Now have something else? Go on. Let me get you a whisky? Another stout? A gin?"

"Half time !"

"I tell you what. Have a gin-and-it. That's nice. I'll have one if you do."

"All right. You talk as if you were selling things."

"So I am." He began to make off for the bar. "Tell you about it in a minute."

When he came back with the glasses he said : "I been selling loud-speakers. It's a good game too. I made money. But it's hard work. Too hard." He looked at her, grinned genially. "Ain't so young as we used to be."

"You speak for yourself !"

"Ha ! Anyway I'm dropping the loud-speakers. Looking round for something else. Quieter."

"Just like you," she said. "Off one horse and on another. That's you all over. Remember that time you tried to make mustard?"

"Ha !"

"You said if you made mustard and took it round in pots to all the pubs in England you'd make a fortune –"

"Out of what people left on their plates ! That's it ! Ha ! I had some schemes. I made unsinkable boat once. I was going to advertise it – Unsinkable boat for lovers. Remember that?"

She was quiet, not speaking.

"Quiet all of a sudden," he said.

"Well, I must breathe."

"It's a licker," he said, "seeing you. Where've you been hiding? It's a wonder I didn't run again' you, out and about like I am. I got a car, y'know. Outside now."

"The way some folks get on."

"Now then, Rosie, now then."

"What's up?"

"Same as ever. Ain't changed a bit. Sharp as two pins." He drank, urging her to drink too. "But where've you bin hiding yourself?"

"Oh ! I got married. You know that?"

"I *heard* things, rumours. But you know –" He shook his head, generous, warm-hearted. "I don't believe nothing till I hear it from the horse's mouth."

"Ah ! Well," she said, "it's all over now."

They were silent a minute, drinking, staring at the passage of drinkers in the bar, until Charley spoke again.

"I'm sorry, Rosie, if things have been rough."

"Rough?" She flared up, proud. "Who said they was rough? You can't expect a farm to be all honey."

"A farm? Farming? Is that what you're doing now?"

She shook her head. "It's finished. I sold up. It's finished."

"What now, then? What're you going to do now? Where you going?"

"Nothing. Nowhere."

"Dead end?"

"An end all right." She grinned, took up her glass. "But blimey, I ain't dead yet."

"Good old Rosie. Have something else to drink? Another gin? Finish that up and have another? Feeling all right?"

"Grand."

She spoke the word generously, meaning it. She felt

stirred, warm-hearted, the effect of the farm receding, loneliness and the terror of loneliness melting like ice. After every drink her heart seemed to swell up against her breasts, her head singing with elation.

"Made the old place different, haven't they?" she said.

"A lot," Charley said. "I don't say as I like it though. Give me the old place. Now that *was* some sense. That *was* a pub. But this thing – it might be a vestry hall or something. Anyway I'll see my old pub ain't like it."

"Your pub?"

"Didn't I tell you?" Charley said. "Did I? I'm after a pub. I'll tell you all about it. No, half a minute. Have something else to drink? Go on, have another gin? A sherry? One more and then we'll go for a ride round in my old car and I'll tell you all about it."

"Well – got nowhere to doss. Nowhere at all. I ought to look for something."

"It's early," Charley said. "Have another gin, then come?"

"All right. Anything for a quiet life. Only don't drive fast. It gives me – makes me – well, *you* know !"

"Ha ! I know."

They had another drink and then, outside Charley backed the car out of the pub yard and Rosie got into the front seat beside him. The stars were shining beautifully, the air cold, wind-sharpened. Charley leaned across Rosie, pressed against her and banged the door. "Now you hold it," he said. "It flies open if you don't hold it."

So she held the door and they drove off. In the cold air she felt stirred, reckless, her head spinning at corners.

"It's an old pub out in Huntingdonshire," Charley said. He slowed the car down. "Where shall we go, anyway?"

"Anywhere. I can't see. Just where are we?"

"Just come over the bridge."

"Oh ! anywhere."

Charley drove on. And then, in a moment or two, she saw where they were; she began to see the familiar winter-stark trees, the field-gates, the odd lights in the farmsteads. They were driving up the valley, towards the farm.

"Once we started," Charley said, "we got to keep on. I can't back her properly yet. Well, I was telling you about the pub."

"Keep on. Anywhere."

"It's a good pub. I ain't certain what the takings are, but I believe I could develop it. I know I could. There's money in it."

"Always money where Charley is."

"Well," Charley said, "here I am with my own car, and money in the bank, and free to do as I like. What more d'ye want?"

"Nothing."

"Feel all right? I mean – you ain't – you know?"

"I feel just right. I never felt so right for years."

And, almost before she was aware of it, they were level with the Middleton land, and then with the Jefferys'. An odd sensation came over her : a strange apprehension, something very near to unhappiness. Through the windscreen, in the starlight, she could see the chestnut trees, drooping, the wood silver in the car-lights. And beyond them the barns, the few remaining ricks, the house itself. It was quiet all about the place, nothing moving or crying, the cattle gone.

"Stop a minute, Charley."

"Here?" Charley slowed the car down, stopped by the verge, put her in neutral.

"Feel dicky?"

"No, I'm all right. This is my old place, Charley. The old farm."

"Is it?" Charley peered out of the window. "Don't look very lively. Looks like a barracks or something."

"Barracks!" she flared up, fired by pride again. "That's a good farm. The best farm for miles round. The best land in this county, or the next. Don't you say anything against it."

"How long'd you live there?"

"Thirty years."

For some reason she could not speak or go on. She sat tight, stoical, silenced by feelings too complicated for her own analysis. She felt very near to tears : inexplicable tears, not of grief, but regret. She felt that if she cried she would be chastened. She would feel better. Underneath it all, behind it, she was quite happy; stirred to a kind of silly joy by the drinks and the friendly patter of Charley's voice.

"It's at a place called Staughton," Charley said. "Nice place. I only got to say the word and it's done. I reckon I could make a go of it. I know I could."

Talking, Charley grew lugubrious, his voice shot with a kind of friendly passion, so that in a moment or two his hand was on Rosie's shoulder, in a half-embrace, and she let him keep it there and nothing mattered. Then he talked a little more : about the pub, the old life, Rosie herself. "I was married myself," he said. "You knew that? But – " After that he was silent. Then suddenly he put his free hand across Rosie's breast. She did not stop him, did not move at all, and he began to make clumsy, friendly efforts to caress her, the movement of his hands not moving her at all at first. Then, when his hand was quiet again, she wanted him to go on again : the lack of friendly contact suddenly unbearable. Then when he went on again she was moved, almost excited. She could feel too his own excitement rising, generating into passion. She was not thinking at all. She was borne off into spaces of feeling, away from herself, trusting to her feelings as she might have trusted, to wings. Then finally Charley said at last. "Why don't you come – why don't you – we could make a go of it at the pub."

"Oh ! I don't know."

"Where you going tonight?"

"I don't know. I thought of going back to The Angel. Booking a room there."

"Come to my lodgings," Charley said. "There's a spare room, or – "

"I could sleep with you if I liked?"

"Well, I wouldn't say no to that."

"Let's go back," she said.

Charley turned the car in the road, bravely, striving to impress her. The car circled across and over the verge, straightened, and moved away. As they drove along Rosie looked out of the windows. The fields receded, were lost in blackness. The familiarity of the land was made strange by the car lights shining into the outer darkness. Beyond the light she could see nothing. It was as though there was nothing there : as though all she had ever known meant nothing and had been annihilated.

"Say you'll come," Charley said, "I got money. We could make a go of it."

For a moment she could not speak. She sat quiet, bewildered, struggling against her feelings. She could smell the land through the open windows : the familiar spring smell of wind and dried earth, exhilarating, almost bitter.

"Say you will," Charley said.

She was crying quietly, without a sound. Now at last she was broken up.

"All right, I'll try anything once," she said.